INFINITE
HOME

ALSO BY KATHLEEN ALCOTT

The Dangers of Proximal Alphabets

INFINITE

HOME

KATHLEEN ALCOTT

RIVERHEAD BOOKS
New York
2015

RIVERHEAD BOOKS
An imprint of Penguin Random House LLC
375 Hudson Street
New York, New York 10014

Grateful acknowledgment is made to reprint lyrics from "Chattanooga Choo Choo."
Music by Harry Warren, lyrics by Mack Gordon. Copyright © 1941 (renewed)
Twentieth Century Music Corporation. All rights controlled by EMI Feist
Catalog Inc. (publishing) and Alfred Music (print). All rights reserved.

Library of Congress Cataloging-in-Publication Data

Alcott, Kathleen.
Infinite home / Kathleen Alcott.
p.   cm.
ISBN 978-1-59463-363-8
I. Title.
PS3601.L344154   2015   2015013742
813'.6—dc23

Printed in the United States of America
1   3   5   7   9   10   8   6   4   2

Book design by Gretchen Achilles

For the writers who brought me here:

David Alcott, 1941–2004

Carolyn Power Alcott, 1953–2013

No man has ever died beside a sleeping dog.

—JOY WILLIAMS

INFINITE
HOME

T HE NEIGHBORS HADN'T NOTICED the building's slow emptying, didn't register the change until autumn's lavish colors
arrived and leaves sailed through the windows the man hadn't
bothered to shut. The wind captured various vestiges—a sun-
bleached postcard covered in outmoded cursive and a chipped
plastic refrigerator magnet shaped like a P and a curling photo of
a red-haired woman asleep on a couch—and flew the tenants'
things before relinquishing them to the sidewalk.

He was often visible in the evenings, backlit by a feeble table
lamp, immobile in a plastic school chair placed against a top-
floor sill, and he seemed untouched by any changes in sound or
light or weather, an ambulance's amplifying moan or the snap of
a storm on parked cars or the inked saturation of the sky at dusk.
Some nights his seat remained empty, and yellows and whites
and golds briefly filled each room before darkening and appearing in the next, the lights traveling from the first floor to the
third, and the movement of electricity was a quiet spectacle, like
the reappearance of hunger after a long illness.

When the cold knock of air came and New York turned white,
he closed the windows.

One Year Earlier

ASIDE FROM THE GIRL on the top floor, they all came out to watch the fire, and most saw the woman walk into it: Thomas still wearing his disability like a new shirt, unsure of how it fit his body; Edward in the baseball cap pulled low that had been his uniform all summer; Claudia and Paulie, she begging that he not ask the firefighters any questions about their outfits; Edith repeating the name of the neighbor trapped inside, a woman she'd known for forty years. Three stories above them, Adeleine came and went, a face in a window, her hands often tugging at the curtains.

"It must have been candles," Edith said from the lowest stair of the stoop, as if naming the ingredient at fault in a lackluster meal. "She does love those, the tall kind with the saints." She was the only one who did not appear panicked, who did not worry that tragedy might prove contagious. Sitting beside her, Thomas held the wilted side of his torso with his right arm and stared at the idling ambulance, trying to divest himself of personal associations with it. He didn't ask Edith where she was going as she rose, slowly as a diminished balloon, didn't watch as she moved towards the throbbing orange light.

Paulie, as excited as he'd been to comment on the show of red hats moving through the dark, had soon settled all his six feet and two inches onto his sister's frame, his chin sharp in her collarbone, and closed his eyes. Just beyond them, taut hoses crossed from their hydrants to firemen who stood with their feet planted on concrete, who gripped ladders that emerged from the trucks at a lean.

It moved from the first story to the third in a matter of minutes.

Standing with a hand still on their gate, Edward looked down the slight slant of the street. All the buildings had emptied of people, some already dressed in pajamas and nightshirts, and they moved together in the dynamic flicker, passing sweating bottles of water, readjusting the children on their hips. The low thrum of air conditioners and the silver-blue glow of devices in the apartments they'd come from were briefly forgotten as they speculated on the fates of their neighbors, four of whom had already departed in speeding, flashing fanfare.

"Nothing brings a community together like a good old fire," Edward said. "'And how'd you meet your wife?' 'Fire!' 'Where'd you get this wings recipe?' *'Great guy I met at a fire!'*" Claudia permitted herself a restrained snort against the tightness of Paulie's body, which pressed against her like a vigorous current. Through the curls of her brother's hair, she saw Edith's slight shape moving and raised her hand to point.

"Hey," she said, trying to reach Edward through his cynical haze. "Hey, that's your *landlord*." His face slackened from its smug expression and assumed a limp astonishment as he watched Edith step beneath the angle of a ladder, her wizened body newly divided into frames by the steel rungs. He gestured to Thomas, a low, brief fold of the hand, as if indicating the fleeting presence of a grazing deer or a rare bird. In one square, they saw the veins of her upper legs, the cotton of her shorts tucked higher by sweat on the left side; in the next, her torso, the arms reaching away.

Edward and Thomas abandoned their disbelief almost immediately, and soon they were crossing through, placing their hands on anonymous shoulders, kicking their knees up to step over rubble, holding their shirts over their mouths, working towards the glow.

A fireman had reached her before they could, had shoved her from risk, and as they approached, he looked down at Edith as though she were a total impossibility. She opened and closed her mouth but it was apparent, without being able to hear over the roar, that it produced no words, did nothing, a door blown unlocked by bad weather. When they got to her, when they each took a flaccid elbow, he had brought a small black box to his mouth and was speaking into it. "Yeah, I need an escort for a possibly disoriented older woman. That's correct. She almost walked right into a fire here."

"There's no need for that," Thomas said in the brawny man's general direction, determining his confidence in the statement as he went. "We're her neighbors. We can take her home."

"Just across the street," Edward said, motioning with a quick shrug, as though denying his involvement in a crime. The man raised his hat a little to look at them, the odd slump of the taller one's body, the established sweat and food stains on the shorter one's shirt, and pressed a button on the device, preparing to issue some further instruction.

A sound filled the next moment, something like the forcing

of an object into a space much too small for it, and the man in the heavy black cloth was gone. The two neighbors, briefly meeting eyes over the meager fluff of their landlord's hair, began to advance, their fingers still fixed to the crooks of her arms. Thomas took naturally to small reassurances, the restrained lilt of them, and with each step he offered another. "We're just going to head home. We're just going to get you out of this heat. It's only a little farther now." Twice Edith looked up at them, examining their faces, giving off benign blinks. The crowd parted like water around a rock, and they watched her shuffling in the same way they'd watched the windows of the ignited building buckle.

Outside their home Thomas and Edward waited, their backs turned to the heat, for her to speak. When she couldn't, they began the work of filling the air. "Here we are," Thomas said. "There's your kitchen window, Edith, with the spider plant and the rosemary soap you like and the tall blue kettle." Rattled by the pressure to comfort her, Edward spoke too loudly. "And there's the front door, and just inside the brass mailboxes and that ridiculous sign that says No Flyers What-So-Never." As Paulie untucked himself from his sister, he seemed to spring into his full height, the jungly curls of his hair moving half a second behind the momentum of his body. Confused by the nature of the game, he mentioned objects as though they were questions. "A bucket full of umbrellas no one uses? All the doors painted differently?" Edith's stare remained fixed on something they couldn't see, and her mottled arms hung limp as dishrags.

Claudia, behind Paulie, made faces at Edward and Thomas, raked her teeth over her lips. The men looked at each other, mouthing words: *Well? What now?* The night had become, after the swiftness of the lights and sirens and the unremitting whip of the heat, very long.

After a minute Edith moved, her shoulder blades working, her feet flexing tentatively against cushioned sandals. "Oh, forgive me," she said, picking up some unknown conversation where it had left off. "It's gotten late." As she climbed up the stairs, both hands on the left railing, her torso contorting to meet its line, she murmured, "Good night, good night," and the sound of it paralyzed them, her inflection like that of a young woman turning in after a long, amorous outing in a car.

DECADES OF NEGLECT had left the property an elaborate obstacle course, and navigating it depended on delicacy and memory. Of the sixteen interior steps from top to bottom, two were unwise to use and rotted quietly. The tenants left these stairs to the wear inflicted by former occupants, as they did much of the leaning banister, which from any given angle revealed at least four layers of dark red paint. The wallpaper that ran along the stairs had not seen a change since the late sixties, when Edith had requested Declan install a pattern she'd fallen in love with: gold leaf details of trees, the background beige but made rich by the gaudy foliage, all of it smeared with a sluggish gleam. It hadn't detached or discolored except at the base, where the sun reached it, and served as one last tribute to Declan's craftsmanship, the forest he had pasted there to stand forever. The peeling door of each apartment was a different color, some by most definitions ugly and others slightly more palatable. Declan had insisted on this from the beginning, thought it a unique touch that spoke to his role as an eccentric. Edith's was a deep royal blue the color of the Atlantic at a certain time of summer, Paulie's a pastel pink nearing heartburn antidote that he called "The Terrific Tongue," Edward's a lavish purple he forever hated and for whose retirement he campaigned, Thomas's a kitsch butter yellow he secretly found quite pleasant, and Adeleine's a bath-tile green that suited her no matter what because after all it was a door she could close.

HAD SHE NOT BEGUN mentally confusing the words for appliances with those for breakfast items, had she continued as the attentive and reliable and well-liked landlord she once had been, Edith would have noticed. The turnover in the building had always been high; she had always kept around the ad she placed when an apartment opened, pulled it from the same bulging, marbled green file that held decades of obsolete lease agreements. She had liked this coming and going, especially the moment when she opened the door into the newly empty space, walked around it remembering her own first tour of the building. Had she not begun discovering her purse lodged in the freezer, her keys hidden in the forest of her potted plants, she would have understood that her current tenants were terribly intent on staying, that each of them had seemed to grow roots in an urban area known for a perennial turnover of wealth and identity, for changing impossibly around any fixed point. She might have observed that Edward retained a garish and incongruous set of silk curtains for most of a decade, and surmised he was waiting for the redheaded woman who'd lived with him to come back and take them down. Certainly, she would have recognized that Paulie's sister, Claudia, had barely looked around the place before she signed the lease, most likely because there was no one else in the city who would rent to a strangely loquacious man of six-two with an eight-year-old's disposition. She knew Thomas better than the rest of them, and she would have continued to visit him, seen the frames and canvases bulging from closets and cabinets, from under his couch and bed, and sensed the irrational belief he lived daily: that he had to stay in the place where the stroke had found him, where his gift had left him, in case it returned. She would have knocked on Adeleine's door for never seeing her and concluded that the stockpiled cans of nonperishables, the desperate collection of coin banks and postcards, indicated a woman who kept her entire world close at hand.

But Edith didn't and couldn't—her incapacities growing each year—and still the tenants avoided the fourth and ninth steps, knew intimately the three important milestones in unlocking the front door, forgave the brokenness of their pre-war windows, placed pots under leaks and called the sounds of the water coming in familiar.

SINCE THE DAYS when Myrtle Avenue around the corner was nicknamed Murder for cautionary reasons, the days before crews from the city came to dismantle the yellow cane seats and leather hand straps of the elevated train, the days when men who built ships at the Navy Yard used to travel in packs with their cigarettes rolled up in their sleeves and curtsy at women and hoot, the days when several generations of family overflowed onto their stoops in the summer: sixty-six years she had spent at the same window. Of course there was much that remained: the magisterial art students from the nearby institute, their fashions shifting but their insolence and unwieldy bags of supplies the same; the steady pour, between six and seven o'clock, of those with jobs in Manhattan, the grunting up their stairs nearly collective.

At her core, Edith believed herself to be the same person she'd been at five, twelve, twenty-three, and so aging was mostly a point of interest, almost an entertainment were it not for its increasingly tangible interceptions in her daily life. Were these really her veins, a purple so bright as to seem inorganic? Her hair, thin and staticky, so reluctant to cooperate? She forgot sometimes: that these were hers, and more recently other things, gaps she found amusing or depressing, depending. Using a can opener became a deliberate, thought-through act; while reading, she had to concentrate, or else she was likely to follow some memory around a low-lit corner. Her daughter Jenny's first birthday, the living room vibrant then and filled to the ceiling with balloons the baby didn't know whether to carouse with or to fear. She and Declan, just married and new owners of the building, naked and sweating out August in one of the apartments yet to be rented, her linen dress balled under her head as a buffer between her tawny waves and the hardwood floor, his expression so different than when he'd courted her with flowers and offered handkerchiefs. How feverish her sister June's eyes had gotten when she'd visited Brooklyn and then the city, how she'd marveled at Edith for going without hose and hailing black taxis. Owen, born second, surrounded by primary-colored blocks, content to play alone. The taxi he insisted on taking to college with money he'd saved.

Declan, an Irish drinker with a nervous heart besides, buried twelve years now, and Jenny gone or dead more years than Edith had actually known and held her. The same building, their apartment unchanged, though the spring before Declan died he'd had the whole thing repainted the color of milky coffee, had enjoyed sitting on the scaffolds with the men, yelling things down to her and passing emptied glasses of lemonade back through the windows. Theirs had been a protected love, this fact reliable to her since the Navy Yard produced vessels as tall as seventy men, and even after he collapsed, finally, while applying lather to his face with the wide-bristled brush. It was another object she kept in a box full of things that told her the story of her life, and she fingered it some afternoons and felt wildly envious or obsessively tender, it being the last item that had touched the perfect line of his jaw.

The tenants over the years had followed a cycle nearly generational, seeming to arrive and leave in demographic groups, their incomes growing and manner refining as the years went by. The couples who showed up with hands clasped, the women peering into the closets as if they might find another room or some other unexpected benefit, the men checking the locks on all the windows: few, in the decades of suburbia's blossoming, lasting more than a year after the appearance of children. When they knocked to return their keys, the towheads balanced on their hips and reaching for their mothers' earrings, Edith always wished them well in their new lives.

The present mix of renters was somewhat unlikely; that is, Edith might have thought so had she possessed the curiosity and energy to find anything at all very strange. She drank them in like tap water, unconcerned about their original source and the details of their travels to her, though she welcomed them in for coffee or tea and always waved when they passed on the street.

The young-seeming man in 2A, right above her, was certainly the kindest. He called her "darling Edith" and "Rose garden" and smiled at her so broadly that she never minded the music he made, which filtered through his floor down to hers, a muddle of cymbals and electronic keyboard and fractured song. There was something wrong with him, she'd noted when he first moved in: a slant to his eyes and point to his ears and thud to his step. His sister, a tired woman in business attire, stopped by daily, her arms often full with groceries.

Across the hall from Paul—who preferred "Paulie," or "just 'pal,'" he joked—was another man, and he didn't look or behave young at all. He'd been there the longest, fifteen years or twenty, and had changed as much as the neighborhood. A stand-up comic, or he had been, in the beginning, and doing well—gigs at all the best clubs in the city at a time when New Yorkers lined up around the block for the chance to laugh and drink beer in those crowded, sub-street spaces—though things had slowed down for him and he didn't seem all that funny anymore. Edward used to have people over, loud ones who seemed to be competing with one another for the sonic space until the outbursts of synchronized laughter came, amplified by liquor. When Edith saw him now, he always seemed to be burdened, ascending the stairs slowly, sometimes sitting on the stoop for hours at a time with a pen and a small black notebook, rooted and still. She had once spotted him at the corner bodega, standing in front of the glass doors by the six-packs of imported lagers, and nearly approached but retreated when she noticed the shaking of his shoulders and shining of his cheeks.

On the third floor, sweet Thomas. He reminded Edith of a professor, the way he thought so visibly, part of his forehead often wrinkled. A few weeks after it happened, he had recounted his stroke to her over tea with such grace that she had reached for his hand—the one he could feel—and squeezed. Struck with an urge to give him something, she hurried down to the long-untouched portion of her closet, withdrew Declan's favorite sweater, wheat with leather elbow patches. He had not recoiled at the dead man's cardigan, had instead pressed the wool to his face and breathed in, and after that he wore it regularly and always attached small notes or pressed flowers with his rent checks. When they appeared a few months later, Edith did not ask about the scars on his lifeless arm, the lines straight as the grids of maps. His thirty-four years had done almost nothing to dull the glowing skin of boyhood, which made the slack left arm, the unmoving side of his face, even harder to witness.

The girl across from Thomas, in the last years of her twenties, acted like something hunted: Edith doubted she'd seen Adeleine four times in the past year. She dressed much like Edith had when she'd first arrived in New York: tailored wool skirts and silk gloves, hats with netted veils, leather clutches. Her hair crafted with the care that had disappeared from fashion long ago, her lips colored but not glossy as was typical of young women now. Either she came and went in the middle of the night or she came and went very little, and her hands shook like underthings on a clothesline. The few times Edith had been up to the top floor recently, she had lingered outside Adeleine's door, drawn by the sounds: warm, crackling music, low but still audible, songs Edith had spent time with decades before. From the street, one could see the browned lace curtains that hid the girl, and the lights, always on, attending to her as she fought off sleep.

Thomas had been an artist, had made things that explained systems: the way in which a cloud processed water; a methodical rendering of the evolution of architecture, from the woven shelter to the skyscraper; the journey from zygote to infant to octogenarian. These processes were expressed in captions and careful colors and an arrangement of space that suggested plans drawn in pencil, calculations and rulers. He had started to show in galleries that used light with the precision of scientists and hawked absurdities for too much money; to sell his wall-sized pieces to people who invited him to their opulent homes and stared at him, waiting to understand his composition, loosening him with bitter beers and aged Scotches. He had begun to think this was his life, days of work chased by dinners with patrons, restaurants in lower Manhattan that served ludicrous small plates, seaweed foam and hay reductions.

His friends had told him to think of the stroke as offering a new set of parameters to work within, but he could tell by the protracted way they looked at the old pieces that they didn't believe it. He had never been one to enjoy rolling around in the abstract, and so the thought of using the partial death of his body as an excuse for paintings that merely *suggested* depressed him so much that he set about eliminating the possibility, putting his paints and graphite pencils and fine and broad brushes and scissors away without knowing if he'd take them out again. With the apartment suddenly bare, he understood that he had been living life as completely as he'd meant to—an idea he meant to follow pinned to every surface—and from then on, he kept it clean and stark as a reminder of how much there was to fill.

He began to see the friends who stopped by as silly, vapid vessels, containers of undercooked opinion and little feeling. His congenital kindness remained, but he couldn't bring himself to dance in their conversational circles anymore, could not bear to discuss whether some video artist had effectively captured the spirit of the working class through the documentation of silent after-hours factory break rooms, could not say with confidence that he saw one creative life as worthless and another as formidable. They sensed his discomfort and shifted the conversation to gossip. A woman he had dated, a beauty but something of a drunk, had lit a bathroom trash can on fire at a recent party and stayed on the toilet laughing for a full ten minutes until the flames reached the curtains and someone came in with an extinguisher. Could he believe it?

Yes, he said. He could. What was there to doubt? Nothing of their lives—the gathering of warm bodies to trade catty comments, the rush to make a late-night train, the unlikely success or failure of an acquaintance—felt remarkable to him. He began to find other things amusing. Washing machines, for instance; that self-important buck when they started. The tendency of rats eating their breakfasts on the rails of the subway to sit up on their haunches and sniff arrogantly, and all the people above waiting, refusing to touch each other. If grief was finding laundry comical, and the thought of picking up phone calls from family members and friends peculiar, and newspaper headlines or pedestrians on the street below more and more foreign, then so be it. He still found plenty of reasons to get up in the morning. Edith, for one.

He made a mental list of things he liked about Edith; it made him happy to put names to them. He enjoyed the way Edith disliked openly. She didn't feel the need to offer complex criticisms or to imply that her preference came from superiority. Tomatoes? "Hate 'em!" she'd said. Also: sweaters that pilled, the man at the corner store who always said, "You look tired," the smell of unwashed art students in the summer. She threw these off her back with efficiency and purpose, as though beating standing water from an awning, and it made Thomas feel more at home with his own distastes. But he adored Edith for plenty of other reasons: She understood slowness. She knew how to wait for the kettle to warm, how to move across a room and appreciate each photograph and plant within it. She was careful about laughter, went to it only when it truly called her. The anecdotes she offered were always well-formed, compact things he felt he could keep and carry with him. "Edith," Thomas had said on several occasions, in moments drunk on self-pity. "Sometimes I just don't know! What recommends the rest of my life?" She was the only one he exclaimed around. When he said such things, she made a crumpled face, waved her hand through the air to banish his wallowing as it bounced off the high ceilings. "Dear heart," she said. "Of course you don't know. How could you? But have you ever been astounded by what you knew was coming?"

EDWARD USED TO BRING WOMEN home only to make them laugh, to watch as the different points of their naked bodies rippled with a punch line in the half-dark, as their ringed hands playfully slapped him to stop. He would calm enough finally to do what they expected, to cup their breasts with hunger and move and keen until they were still. Sometimes he even managed the tenderness afterward, the holding and sighing and postcoital half-sentences, the wiping of sweat and come, the leaving for two glasses of water with the promise to be right back. But then he was onstage again, there in his own bedroom, doing his best to make the girls cackle and stay awake on a mattress growing lumped, and he would remember how it began.

He'd never been able to sleep; neither had his brother. Their parents were not alcoholics or child abusers, nothing so directly antagonistic, but they cultivated in their children a mounting fear of the universe, a suspicion of evil in the familiar that transcended caution and became paranoia. They spent breakfast stabbing at the pages of the newspaper, challenging each other to produce the more horrific news story. *A father, somewhere in Kansas, who killed his wife and children before cutting his own feet off! Drug lords in faraway cities keeping prostitutes in cages and feeding them only dog food or Styrofoam packing peanuts!* Three and four decades later, Edward had a hard time deciphering which of these had been exaggerations; the text of those headlines seemed to pulse at the periphery of his thoughts the moment he walked a darkened street alone, approached a window at home he didn't recall opening.

They had brought their horrors in closer circles, too, warning Edward and Zachary about the gas station attendants three blocks down—hoodlums, criminals—and the single man up the street with the many cats: *There is something about him I just don't trust*, his mother had said.

At night, instead of letting all these things sift and combine into a web of nightmares, Edward had crept into his younger brother's room and lain on the floor, kneaded his fingers into the carpet kept so clean, and invented a place for himself and Zachary to hide. Edward made shadow puppets on the wall: talking heads of their parents bickering about the exact ingredients of the pastry they'd shared; the older girl down the street with the huge breasts and the way she tottered forward. He impersonated their grade school principal, who Edward thought spoke as if concealing a vat of cream cheese at the back of his throat, embellishing the nasal insistence, the sounds of the fat cheeks' suction on squat teeth while he delivered the overused catchphrase. *Dish-ipline will be dish-tributed*, Edward would say. *Now build me a schity of bagels!*

His inability to play the somber lover aside, some of the women returned, insisted on it even, pushed him up against the sandstone of Greenwich Village and offered to hail a taxi. He always had trouble, though, giving them a humor they could confidently claim was inspired by their bond, personal between the two of them. Or not saying anything when they farted in a particularly musical way, even if their eyes said, *Not now, not today.* The ones he didn't abandon out of sheer negligence, failing to call for days, left him violently, always using terrible names like *bastard* and *narcissist* and making dramatic accusations about the poverty of his heart.

This was the period after the glow of quitting his day job had worn. He'd begun appearing on nighttime television, sitting with an ankle on a knee in one of those interchangeable plush chairs and gesturing with the provided coffee mug actually filled with water. He still preferred the tiny, sweaty crowds, the possible explosions given the night's chemistry. He brought other comedians and audience members alike back to his apartment in Brooklyn, always paying for cab fares and drugs and drink, thrilled each time by the continuation of the night. Wary of his success, he kept his cheap apartment.

A woman who could spit back and thrive in the unsavory back rooms and at the mostly male after-parties, Helena became a fixture by the mid-nineties. She wore high-waisted linen trousers and pale silk shirts that buttoned up the back in the fall, oversized maroon faux-fur coats in the winter, and her bones formed a collection of angles he grew to need. She worked for little pay as a social worker, touring the homes of destitute families, and talked about them over dinner, their names and misfortunes floating over the candles on the cramped restaurant patios where she and Edward ate.

The night she moved in, she hung small globes of light, placed red porcelain mugs in the cupboards, swept corners it had never

occurred to him were dirty. Even when they fought, she exer-
cised perfect timing, and after, while they made up, she held his
arms against the sturdy wood bed frame she'd also brought with
her, and insisted that the lights stay on.

He liked to maintain that she'd left when his success dwindled, despite so much proof of the contrary, and clutched this in
his mind with all other things growing old and ossifying. But
then he remembered her soft murmurs on waking at four a.m. to
an empty bed, her coming to him on the couch and curling up
and expressing fond interest in the decades-old movie keeping
him company. The moment when she got up to put the kettle on,
the sound of the old drawer unsticking so that she could retrieve
a spoon for his sugar. How many times she had fallen back asleep
there, in his lap, though the bedroom was a mere ten feet away.
The way she accepted his deepening morbidity, listened intently
to the story of his mom forbidding him to leave the house for two
weeks at the rumor of a nasty flu, of the cleaning tasks she'd
assigned her son during the quarantine. How Helena had insisted
on washing the sweatpants he'd begun resigning himself to, how
the use of fabric softener was evident. How he had cried when
she cut off her hair the month before she left him, a child who
couldn't recognize his mother, and how she had held him, even
then.

As a child, Paulie had liked to wake his parents with song and, once his hands were able to manipulate the large carton, glasses of orange juice. He called his mother Lovebird and his father Mr. Sheep, after his other favorite soft but crusty-looking thing. They had adored the intensity of his glances and taken to calling him The King for the way he trounced around the house, assigning all objects an enthusiastic nomenclature. His teeth, so pointed, so white, always showing. And the singing: a song for the dishwasher, the morning, the cat, the routine appearance of the mail through the metal slot in the living room, the shifting colors of a laundry cycle.

Of course there were signs, of course there were, but Lydia and Seymour rarely had time to finish their conversation in the mornings, she brushing her teeth while sitting on the master bathroom toilet with her nightie bunched around her hips, preparing herself for the task of waking and guiding two children in picking clothing and eating breakfast, and Seymour at the sink splashing cold water in his eyes and clearing his throat. He was a good husband, that evident always, and he kissed her good-bye no matter what, and sometimes arrived to the office ten minutes late on account of hearing her troubling or wonder-filled dream. In any case: they loved Paulie, loved the dramatic curvature in his chest, loved his upturned eyes. They loved his inability to grasp the ambitions of villains in the films that flickered across his tiny body where he lay on the carpet.

With the beginning of school, it changed, and they could no longer misbrand his behavior as idiosyncratic. Lydia remembered it sharply for the rest of her life: How well it began, how she exhaled with relief when Paulie ran up to his kindergarten teacher—a woman who must have been trying to look like Ms. Santa Claus, a rope of white hair down her thick torso and wire glasses that clung to the tip of a diminutive nose—and introduced himself. How impressed the woman had been when Paulie spoke: "Hello there, I'm here to learn and laugh, if you don't mind, my darling!" But within two weeks the phone call. Paulie had come out of the bathroom with his pants down several times and politely requested the teacher's help; he could not participate in an activity wherein she asked the students to draw simple shapes. Lydia had begun to protest, but Ms. Susanne had interrupted gently: "I'm not saying he refused to, Ms. Fontaine, or that he tried but his coordination was below average. I'm saying that he looked at his pen and paper and he looked at the blocks in front of him and he looked at the other children and he plainly *could not*."

Lydia did not tell Seymour for a full two days. When he came home from work, he was tired and slow, and quite often the only thing that visibly cheered him was Paulie. Paulie balancing on his leg; Paulie offering impersonations of a humpback whale, a jet plane, a Christmas tree. So when she finally did it was unplanned, it just came out, while she was sitting on the closed toilet watching him shave, in sobs that attempted words and reverted to sounds. Once he'd comforted her enough to understand what she was saying, he called in sick and tucked Lydia into bed; he promised that when he returned, they would figure it out, and he took Claudia to school.

He let Lydia sleep most of the day, and in all the time she was out she hardly changed positions under the great white comforter. Through the morning and afternoon he watched Paulie, held his hands and then his feet, listened as his son told him a story about an elephant searching for a tree large enough to shade his mother during the summer. "Where did you hear that story," Seymour asked, though he already suspected the answer. "From my daydreams, of course!"

L

EDITH AND DECLAN had always prided themselves on their taste in people. Their renters, mostly blue-collar and from somewhere else originally, paid on time and stopped to say hello to each other in the hall; they held doors, gave away laughter freely and sat out in the overgrown back garden in the summer together, sharing sun tea and simple sandwiches. For a full decade, theirs was the most-attended Fourth of July party in the surrounding blocks. Declan would weave among the tenants and their friends, a lit sparkler attached to his thin silk tie, spilling whiskey into glasses without asking, butchering patriotic adages with his thick Irish accent in a way that left his guests cackling.

Declan made himself available to his tenants, and so did Edith, although after he died she began widening the scope of her generosity, drawing leases to those she found unusual, or hurt, or in visible need of asylum. She knew what he would have said, how he would have bit down on his smoke and brought a palm over his cheek—that it wasn't her job to mother the world, no matter what regrets she had about their own children. But he was gone and that was his fault, she reminded herself frequently, for living hard on his body like he had. He could have quit the cigarettes, could have downed a few more vegetables, could have ended a few nights without landing in the bed like a felled pine.

For a year she rented to an out-of-work opera singer with

hollowed-out cheeks who was always late with the rent but put on a suit every morning and practiced his scales. A single mother of twins famed for her colossal Afro and her abilities as a wrist wrestler, who often accepted Edith's offer to babysit while in her apartment she held raucous tournaments attended by bearded men in loud prints. A substitute teacher with a quivering Adam's apple and a stutter and a little beagle that forever ran ahead of him. A balding snake collector always clad in Hawaiian shirts, who claimed no one else would rent to him, and who cooed into his many cages like a proud father. An Ecuadorean widower who worked construction and came home almost unrecognizably dusty and who nervously patted the front pocket where he kept his wife's photo. A retired Barnum and Bailey performer who had asked Edith if, for the sake of old times, he could hang a tightwire across the backyard. She had obliged him, and spent a number of spring evenings with a shadow plaid blanket around her shoulders, clapping as his toes gripped the line and he blushed with remembering, as he brought one gnarled foot in front of the other and hovered four inches above the long untended flower beds, perfectly still, waiting for a strong breeze to pass.

H AD SHE FELT ANGRY about how far removed she'd grown from the world as everyone else knew it, Adeleine might have placed the fault on the ages of her parents when they conceived her (forty-two and fifty-three) and the cultural diet they'd fed her, a closed world of musty books and antiquities; but, like most people growing ill in mind, she did not feel in any way ashamed of what she deemed preference. Her rejection of modern society and her collection of previous eras' talismans thrived like weeds, without any cultivation, at a rate she couldn't control.

Edith advertised only through physical postings in a five-block radius of the building, and Adeleine had detached the unevenly perforated slip with great anticipation, happy for what she could touch and hold. Finding an apartment without consulting the many efficient tentacles of the Internet had grown next to impossible, and she signed the lease without looking anywhere else.

Over time, her apartment came to appear smaller than the others in the building—so overcrowded did it become with adopted velvet ottomans and other people's photo albums and a variety of barely functional mechanical devices—though it was actually the largest. She had adored it straightaway, the crown-molded archway between the kitchen and living room, the claws of the forever slightly dirty bathtub, the scratched hardwood floor, the rusted fire escape available through the window in her bedroom. Bit by bit, she filled the space with bygone decades, even the most utilitarian items—the fans and egg whisks and combs—older than her father or mother. She collected until the point when she couldn't make it more than a block before turning around, her gaze fixed on her windows, and trotting back towards their promise. It was as though she knew she would soon be without any external entertainment: she attended every stoop and estate sale, showed up early and bent her body towards the boxes others ignored, took buses to time-stopped reaches of Queens and then trains upstate, under each arm an empty, beaten duffel bag.

A shelf displaying twenty century-old glass soda bottles, a jar holding a massive tangle of skeleton keys, a box of discarded photos detailing a 1967 vacation to Hawaii, a radio whose speakers had broadcast World Wars I and II: she told herself she was honoring the lives of the people who had touched and loved these objects, remembering them in a way that their death had otherwise precluded. What had begun as a collection of oddities had eventually crowded out reason, and soon required two walls of sagging floor-to-ceiling shelving.

Adeleine's parents loved to tell her what a *happy* child she'd been, loved to present this and let the questions that followed arise tacitly. She resented the presupposing. She pointed out that while they may have found endearing the energy their six-year-old daughter had spent writing and illustrating a book about jellyfish who felt invisible against the dark of the ocean, the pages probably pointed to something larger.

Adeleine received her diagnosis, after a period of five days' virtually uninterrupted sleep, from a sweatered psychiatrist in a small corner office at the college health center. She accepted it without surprise. She agreed to try the pills, to consider depression as a disease. She opted to keep all this from her parents. She assented to the distraction of a double major in music and literature, to the praise from professors who were quick to label her essays "multilayered" and "blooming." She began to drink an awful lot, despite this course of action coming not exactly recommended as company to the orange bottles she got filled and refilled under fluorescent lights.

Why was she so sad? The unspoken question had dangled over the beige couch and the framed degrees and the economy Kleenex. He commanded a cache of *Ohs* and *I sees* in varying grades of volume and texture, knew when to prod and when to sink with her. Why was she so sad?

Adeleine was sad because she was sad because she was sad. She experienced extreme difficulty in reaching past the tautological. Sick of being asked, after six weeks of treatment, she slipped a brief and incomplete laundry list under her psychiatrist's door. It read:

Because how are you supposed to draw a map for the future and believe it will apply at all

Because my father corrects my mother's speech until she stops speaking

Because there are lives more or less completely forgotten with every minute

Because I'm supposed to think it's normal and comfortable to learn, through a lit-up screen and a cheery blue website, how every person I ever knew is failing or fulfilling their potential

Because we value things we can touch less and less every day

Because it gets dark every single night

After that, she never went to the little office anymore and avoided passing it, though she could always sense it from across the trimmed lawn, the concrete staircase that descended from the bright world of couples splayed on the grassy grounds to the subterranean entrance.

E DITH SAW IT EARLY ON, the way her children curved out to such opposite ends, far from most and still further from each other. Even when Jenny was a child, her imagination, the point from which she saw the world, seemed too remote. She once gathered up a basket of flowers in Fort Greene Park and, while Edith wasn't looking, ingested all of them. Edith turned and saw the last of the stems peeking out the sides of her eight-year-old's mouth, the peach-soft skin already turning drab with nausea. Jenny had vomited for hours, and Declan, leaning on the bathroom door, shifting between worried and amused, repeated to himself, "Loved the flowers so much she had to eat 'em!" But Edith saw nothing funny about it. You weren't supposed to swallow up beauty whole, weren't supposed to rip it from its nest and insist it was yours alone.

Owen, on the other hand, was sovereign from the first. When he was a baby, Edith would sometimes rock him and get the feeling it was more for her peace of mind than his. He had learned to use the telephone in a single afternoon—Edith watched as his fingers spun the rotary with efficacy—and had called the bank and asked about opening an account. Edith, listening from the kitchen, could tell that the person on the line had asked his age from his answer. "Six," he said. "But I have twice as many dollars as years." Since asking for and receiving them for Christmas that year, he had carried a wallet and a comb, had taken to sweeping his room and whistling.

These were the stories she had told her friends, though she framed them as entertainments and withheld the starved feeling they gave her. Of course she loved her children—this was never in doubt—but when they became, more and more, the people they were, Edith felt as though nothing she could have done would have made any difference. She prayed for them in ways she knew were ridiculous: *Dear God in Heaven, it's fine if they both have to be alone*, she bargained, *but could they at least be alone together? Could you send down some shared interest?* Once she whispered to Declan, "I could hang a thousand Christmas ornaments from the ceiling and these kids still wouldn't look up."

The summer Owen turned a confident nine and Jenny remained a childish twelve, he had assembled a Popsicle stand from cardboard, painted it carefully to resemble a storefront, and made his first sale minutes after opening. Edith, watching from the window, had called to Jenny in the living room behind her. "Why don't you go join your brother," she'd said, painting cheer onto her voice. "I bet if you offered help refilling the cooler with ice, or making change, he'd cut you a bit of the profit." Instead, Edith had observed as Jenny slumped out, barefoot, squinting, and crumpled on the concrete some ten feet from Owen. From the pocket of her cutoffs she had removed a number of stones—treasures, Edith knew, from a creek they'd walked along on a rare trip upstate—and set them in a ragged line, occasionally pushed at one with a big toe. When a neighbor, Popsicle in hand, drifted with pity to Jenny's odd station and asked how much, Edith had strained to hear her daughter's faint reply. "Free," she had said, barely moving her head from its place between her raised knees. "Came from water." The man nodded and moved on empty-handed, and Owen had laughed like he did at the stupidity of half-wit cartoon characters, the ragged coyote who looked down his fate only after passing the end of the cliff.

Jenny spent the next six years growing more inscrutable, drawing vast spirals in her school notebooks and keeping odd pets, toads and then millipedes that Edith and Declan had paid for as though they were lottery tickets, chances to make their daughter's life rich. She left for San Francisco the day she turned eighteen. Declan, who liked to believe himself wild, the kind of person who could appreciate the untamed in others, told Edith not to worry, but she already knew: she had already spent more time losing her daughter than she had having her. Jenny bought a rose suitcase and painted it with words from a song she liked; Jenny brushed out her always-tangled just-brown hair in their bathroom one last time; Jenny put on teal eye shadow that looked to Edith like the color of an empty hospital room; Jenny took the bag of fruit Edith had prepared; Jenny hugged each of them, and then Jenny was gone. She sent three progressively more disturbing postcards that said things like *Really letting my body return to the earth* and *I speak a new language every day*, and then one day they saw her on television. The news special about Haight Street and all the young people and all the sex and all the drugs, and then, for an excruciating twenty seconds, Jenny, writhing. She wasn't wearing enough, a paisley handkerchief stretched taut across her chest, jeans mutilated and discolored. Sitting in the lap of a bearded man in a crocheted vest who held her by the waist, she chewed on a piece of her own hair as though hoping to extract something vital, and her eyes with their enormous pupils lolled. She kept moving her hands up and out, rhythmically, as if trying to keep some wall from caving in. "Aren't you concerned about her?" asked the reporter. And the man shrugged: "She's not mine, man."

Owen had earned good grades and befriended beady-eyed little boys who turned into greedy, scheming young men. Edith made them after-school sandwiches and listened through the door: they afforded no one mercy, not the shy bucktoothed girl with long braids or the young teacher with the stammer. Once he got to high school, Owen, already tall and fine-fingered, developed a reputation as a salesman. He sold pencils and toffees at half the store cost at first, then expanded his enterprise through the hire and development of a ring of bookish types who wrote term papers feverishly in the library. Edith learned about it only when a concerned mother did Owen the favor of calling his parents rather than the principal. Afterward, he made atonal apologies and pursued his studies with new conviction, often tacking up and checking off neat to-do lists in capital letters, and ultimately landed at Duke on a full scholarship. Following one sixteen-hour return for Thanksgiving, during which he spoke only to ask after salt and pepper, he expressed implicitly that his need for family—had it ever been there—was no longer extant. Edith and Declan were to him like a house he had once rented.

Declan took pains to keep up with Owen's professional pursuits, but Edith stopped sending birthday cards after five years without a thank-you note or a call, and often recalled breastfeeding her son, how much less urgently he had sucked than his sister, how infrequently he'd cried.

D IAGNOSES OF WILLIAMS SYNDROME were rare then— one in twenty thousand births, sources would note much later—and Lydia quickly lost the energy required to say, "There is something different about my son, yes, but he does not belong here." "Here" being among these other children labeled as impaired, sedate and taciturn compared with Paulie. *He is six years old and understands and uses words like magnetic and illuminate*, she always felt like asserting. *He remembers whole songs after hearing them just once.*

She began homeschooling him after the third failed experiment in an institution for "children like him," undertaking the mission as if it were as natural as breathing, forever designing lessons and searching for signs that he'd absorbed them. She tried and tried with numbers, with zippers and shoelaces, and later rewarded him (and herself, she admitted) with narrative and music, the environments in which he thrived. When Seymour returned home, she smiled up at him wearily as Paulie yelped and covered his father in kisses. Love grew a bigger mystery by the day.

It was only after a sudden and ambitious cancer finally nullified the electricity of Lydia's thoughts and the generosity of her limbs that the heartfelt profiles of others like Paulie appeared in the *Times*, on hour-long specials on NPR. That the experts marveled, as Lydia had, at the bubbling wit of those with Williams syndrome, the unflagging affection and trust, the proclivity towards music and song; at the inability to complete the simplest puzzle, to understand the way quarters became a dollar. That studies identified an array of likely comorbidities. More often than not, congenital heart disease. Anxiety. Hypothyroidism. A shortened life expectancy.

Seven years after Lydia's death, while sifting through staticky radio stations on an autumn drive home, Seymour stumbled across a program that came through the airwaves as clear and bright as a gong: it told the story he'd sat in the middle of without hope of understanding, and he pulled the car over to the shoulder and gripped the leather steering wheel, and was, for a full fifty-three minutes, still.

With the fading of the nineties, Edward had watched both himself and the crowds at the clubs changing. They were more tired and less willing to laugh, and he, equivalently, felt less and less like teasing their Coors-addled brains. His hair grew long from neglect, and he alienated most audiences, though he garnered a minuscule cult following of people who dubbed him "the lost comic" for the way he wandered across the stage, gaping at the spotlights as though they were cryptic signs in a foreign tongue. He couldn't explain it except to say that *it* had simply ceased, burned off like an atmospheric layer—"it" being whatever had lived in him that had drawn punch lines from human behavior, that had identified the rhythm stitched between silence and speech, between precipitation and execution. The clubs eventually withdrew their offers, at least those he hadn't severed ties with of his own profanity-strewn accord, and his friends took to rolling their eyes at his endless string of clichéd ontological concerns. They would come over and he would fix drinks and put on avant-garde albums—one favorite a meandering recording of airplane takeoffs and landings—and he would say absurd things like: *Do you feel that growing old is something we should all be doing a little more consciously?*

And: *Have you considered that probably each day of your life has changed you? If there was a way to track that, would you?*

And, of course: *Have you seen Helena? Has her hair grown out or has she kept it short? Does she still walk like that?*

THE FIRST WINTER WITHOUT HER, Edward read Kant and Wittgenstein with a sophomoric fervor and an oversized highlighter, dressed in grays and blacks like the rest of the city, and avoided a series of phone calls from Los Angeles. Thirteen months before, towards the beginning of the end, at the urging of his agent, he had written a screenplay during a five-day cocaine binge. It was an insipid script—write a Christmas movie, his agent had said, they want one from you, the "they" always changing, the interest always urgent—that concerned a down-on-his-luck mall Santa and a series of perfectly timed misunderstandings, plus a beauty far out of Santa's league and a greasy Italian shoe-store owner as the antagonist.

"The thing," as Edward called it, never referring to it by its ludicrous title, had now sprouted hideous blooms everywhere: billboards in subway stations, marquees downtown, print ads, echoes of punch lines in sports bars by men whose idea of humor was straight regurgitation. He would see a particularly beer-saturated group outside a pub, their breath visible in the fifteen-degree weather, their Neanderthal faces red and loosened, and sense it coming like an arthritic feels a storm. *Hey, Antonio, check out this North Pole!* And he would hurry around them, eaten with alarm.

He continued to accept payment for the thing, though even that filled him with pulsing dread: in every gourmet dinner he ate or cashmere sweater he purchased, he saw the look of panic in the main actor's face as frozen in the poster, the jumble of gift boxes at his feet, the beauty next to him with a shopping bag, the evil shoe proprietor leaning in with a textbook smirk on the other side. He had gone to see it the very first week, if only to grasp at some understanding of the man who had been capable of such asinine pursuits in the name of too much money. He left waitresses and cab drivers, especially those who seemed unhappy, extraordinary tips drawn from a great well of guilt. He tried to forgive his mother, which he found much easier since her death, and let his father talk to him about the monstrosity of the world for as long as the old man deigned. He cleaned the dishes until they were gleaming, the brilliant red pots Helena had left behind in her hurry to transform, and spent slow hours imagining an inviolate place where he wouldn't feel his past as if it were some punishing physical affliction.

Mostly, he thought of Helena, and sometimes his neural pathways brought her so close—her left index finger crooked from a childhood Ping-Pong accident; her long-limbed way of occupying and redefining physical space; the face she offered upon waking, both confused and grateful—that he felt like a magician.

E DITH AND DECLAN HAD LIVED a life together. She needed
to remember this, and she worried she could no longer do so
effectively. At times, she explored the possibility that all their
possessions, all this carbon proof, might have been placed strate-
gically throughout her living space as some elaborate ruse. Of
course this was not, could not, be true, but her brain stumbled
blithely over the sentiment that this would be an easier truth to
accept. Where *was* he, then? Why hadn't they spoken? What had
he forgotten to tell her?

At the funeral, dressed in an old black suit and pearls, she had
kissed everyone's cheek, had told the story of their first storm in
the house. How they had run around placing pots under every
leak, and how that evening they had sat on the floor with a blanket and felt like they'd been given, instead of a nuisance, a mel-
ody. How that had been what he'd given her all their fifty-six
years together, songs where they weren't expected. She had stood
at that carnation-wreathed podium and looked out at the rest of
her life blankly: there was a question, surely, but couldn't someone please repeat it?

In the first months without him, Edith had marveled at how
many different types of quiet there could be. What had been so
different about the levels of noise with him sitting in the chair,
reading for hours in his drugstore glasses? Why did every shower,

now, feel like such an exercise in fallacy, preparation for an event never coming, though this had always been a lone ritual?

She had been a stunning woman, a pronounced presence; Declan had been there to remind her of this, and now he was gone. She needed it to be communicated permanently in some way, so she could take full ownership of this new body, covered in layers of sweaters, these feet in their padded shoes.

"Aging gracefully" was a model much talked about, though Edith doubted anyone ever felt elegant or nimble amid the nearly inescapable fatigue, the persistent mutations of once-simple tasks and the shame thereafter. When the time came to collate all the rent checks and utility bills, she put the task off for hours, then days, dreading what an ordeal adding and dividing had become, the way she would sometimes face off with a column of numbers and realize they meant as much to her as someone else's mementos. She would wipe her face and begin again, reading each figure out loud, entreating it to stay in the room.

T HE KID ALWAYS SAID HELLO. Never just a cursory nod. Had insisted on learning Edward's name when he moved in, not to mention his favorite flower and fruit. "Is there a nickname you like?" Paulie had asked. He preferred those ending in y. "Eddy?" he suggested. Edward's head that day had been thick and jumbled: he couldn't summon the energy to reject the suggestion, and from then on it was always "Hiya, Eddy!"

For a while the kid was practically Edward's least favorite thing about living, and he timed his entrances and exits to avoid him. But even if he made his ascent during the kid's violent assault on his stand-up Casio, Paulie would hear him and be sure to pop his head out: "Hello, my friend! What does the weather say today?" Edward made eye contact when guilt tugged at him enough—who was he to crush such benevolence, he wondered— but mostly kept the shade of his hat on his face, and the line of his sight on the unclean carpet. He knew from his own nocturnal schedule that Paulie also kept late hours, though for the kid they were celebratory, active, while Edward just prayed for sleep. Music always: singing, sometimes words but just as often not, sounds like a gang of monkeys bickering. Edward stopped crossing the hall to ask that Paulie turn himself down in order to avoid his neighbor's repeated reflection that Edward looked sad. He bought noise-canceling headphones and played recordings of rainstorms across the world. Austin. Bangkok. The Amazon. Paulie was crazy for offering people tea; Edward had overheard him selling it to the other tenants. Chamomile Lemon English Breakfast Green Ginger! Always in the same order. The kid's brain was broken, but Edward couldn't of course recommend the health of his own. Paulie, it was clear, chased and cornered happiness daily.

Edward was asleep when it happened, and the cry came into his dreams as the voice of his brother. His unconscious re-created the familiar childhood scene of Zachary asleep and whimpering in the next room, victim to the awful stories their parents fed them, nightmaring of kidnapping plots and elaborate suicides. (He, too, had called him Eddy.) Edward, then, had felt useful and important when he went to him, as well-appointed and comforting as a chair by an open window. He would scoop up Zachary, who was always a little too thin, and speak with measured softness about the silly inventions of our brains while we sleep, then get right up to his ear and begin with the noises. The finest impressions of farts anyone in their neighborhood had ever heard, high trilly toots and trembling wet ones, plus a bassoon-like moan for good measure. It had never failed. In his dream Edward was brilliant and electric as he cradled his brother, who giggled and shook and held his little penis to keep from peeing.

Edward, turning against his flannel sheets, couldn't understand why the sounds continued, until finally the banging on his flimsy door wrestled him awake.

When he opened the door, Paulie was standing there gushing red, and it took a moment in the sudden and grainy light of the hallway to identify the source. The kid's hand was bleeding, saturating the fold of shirt he'd hid it in.

"Well for fuck all," said Edward. "Get in here already." Between cries and yelps he gathered that Paulie had somehow managed to drop his keyboard on his foot, which had set off a chain of events including a brush with the sharp edge of the kitchen counter, the swing of a cabinet door, and a cascade of glass. His face was contorting repeatedly, as though on a loop.

"I knew you were up!" Paulie spouted while Edward led him to the bathroom, and Edward understood the bumbled apology in the statement. He sat the kid on the toilet and calmly opened drawers, surprised at how easily he could assume the role of caretaker. Then he kneeled before Paulie and got his closest look yet at the upturned eyes, the undersized teeth, the signs of aging present on his forehead and around his mouth and in the sag of his ears: the kid was much older than Edward had assumed, maybe halfway into his thirties. Edward asked him to take deep breaths then showed him how—in for one, two, three, four, five, then out—while he examined the wound, applied antiseptic, wrapped gauze around it. Afterward, Paulie remained shocked by the sight of his blood's great escape, and Edward took the initiative.

"Come on," he said. "Let's watch some bad TV."

In the living room, Paulie revived and quickly grew curious as he moved from the couch to the stack of DVDs beneath the television. Edward held his breath while Paulie destroyed the alphabetization, formed leaning piles on the floor, ran his hands over every cover, mouthing titles with a blank face. Edward let his attention drift from Paulie back to the screen: a bus threatened by a ticking bomb couldn't stop, and a brunette actress he'd once insulted in a bar grew progressively more anxious.

Paulie squealed and Edward panicked, but the source of the cry was not the wound on the kid's palm. It was *the thing*, its DVD cover: the leading man in the Santa hat, the beauty struggling with her holiday accoutrements, the character actor with the busy eyebrows. Edward had been sure he'd hidden it.

"My *favorite*!" Paulie said, his whole face open with joy. Instead of taking the case from him, instead of suggesting another film, Edward admitted what he'd sworn never to again.

"*Santarella?*" he said. "I wrote that."

The bubbly pleasure drained from Paulie's face. He looked at Edward like tourists look at the *Mona Lisa*, searching and wary as they wait to be touched by glory.

"Eddy," he said. "*What?*"

THERE WEREN'T WORDS for it like there are now, weren't aisles in bookstores where people dog-eared pages that suggested the roots of their psychic pain, where they grubbily fingered titles offering recovery; there weren't these cloying instructions that led a person directly from guilt to forgiveness, as though taking one left, then a right. Edith simply saw what she saw, shortly before evening in October of 1960, and never forgot.

Jenny, on the bed, ten years old, her reddish hair gilded by the late afternoon. Her treasured gingham skirt—the one she had rushed to in the store, buried her face in and begged for—pushed up in the most hideous way, crumpled like dead things are. Owen's hand over hers, her freckled knuckles lacking their typical pink, his face dropping onto hers like a hammer onto a wall, the noises like kissing but also not, as though something were being excavated. Edith stood there absorbing the unclean smell, the color of Jenny's face made wild and blotched, the twitching mobile of cutout trees hanging above her for which she was already too old.

Edith had not yelled, or rushed over to the bed and lifted her son from his place on her daughter, or beat her fist on the door to protest the quiet in a room meant to be filled with the babble of children. She gave an insignificant sound, one as echoless and quickly spent as that of a bird leaving a fence. Year after year she would remember this, how opening the door had let in a crack of hall light that divided her vision of her children, its beam separating the boy from the girl; how Owen had simply slipped off the bed and past her where she stood in the doorway. Edith went to Jenny on the bed and pulled down the hem of her skirt, patted the pleats in place, and held her, determined, like algae clinging to a sea-beaten rock.

Back in the kitchen, there was a water-dappled bunch of spinach in the sink, and chicken defrosting on the counter, and breadcrumbs to coat it in, and cornbread batter to mix, but Edith couldn't bring herself to the task of preparation. Her attempts at the small and precise work of it failed, and that evening she and her family went out to eat. She slid into the diner's red vinyl booth after her daughter and gripped the overstuffed cushion under the table while Declan told a long and familiar story, pausing to laugh and stroke his son's hair. Appetizers in red-checked waxy sheets and Coca-Colas with paper straws and hamburgers and desserts appeared and vanished, and they all drove home in her husband's bouncy station wagon, and only after all this did she tell him.

He dismissed it outright, even laughed. "But Owen's *younger*," he said. He told her that children learn and play in all kinds of ways, and that possibly, probably, she had just stumbled in at the wrong minute. "What are you accusing him of, exactly? Kissing his sister? Aren't you always worried about them getting along? They're our children, honey," he said. "Remember? We made them. They can't be too bad." And he winked, and kissed her forehead. When she didn't loosen, stayed tense and wouldn't turn to him with her normal happy sigh after he snuffed the tobacco light of the standing lamp, he returned to her comfort. "Edith," Declan said, in his thick accent that seemed to brighten dark subject matter, "what was Jenny doing when you walked in? Didn't you say yourself she was still? Didn't you say she wasn't even crying?" In the dark, Edith nodded, rolled over to think under the scant light seeping in from the street. She reasoned herself away from worry and back to it, the flight of her thoughts as panicked as bugs moving towards brightness. It was true that Jenny hadn't been giving any of her brother's affection back, and also true that she was a child who lived most hours deep inside herself. Edith had visited her at school, watched her blinking on the periphery, untouched by offers of jump rope or jacks, content to balance on the beam that divided the playground's concrete and sand, one foot raised a few inches, her arms spread.

Edith spent the remaining years with Jenny in pursuit of understanding. She accompanied her on long walks, let her lead the way through industrial areas and under overpasses, stupefied by the hours her child could spend entertained in this way. She helped her build her collection of buttons, the vivid jars that spread on Jenny's windowsill and that she fixated on before falling asleep. She took her to films, felt no greater joy than when she heard Jenny gasp at the lush colors of Douglas Sirk. Though it gnawed at her, the question of what had happened in that room, that Jenny and Owen remained as distant as passengers on the same train, there were comforts, also: Jenny perched on the toilet, watching Declan as he shaved, transfixed. The sudden, unrelenting pressure of Jenny's sharp forehead on the small of her back while she stood on the subway or chopped vegetables, a way of saying hello. When these reassurances arrived, brief as they were, she leaned into them, rested there.

PAULIE'S SISTER, CLAUDIA, who cloaked her significant height in tailored beige pants and bland gold accessories, had found him the place just around the corner from hers. Her husband didn't think—*well, how could he put this*—that it would be best if they all lived together. The other tenants nodded at her on her daily visits, as she balanced bags of groceries on her hips and adjusted the leather bag that was permanently cutting into her left shoulder. Paulie was enthused to see her every time: he liked to clap his hands to his face, then to hers. She had to remind him to save the hugs for after she had brought the various bags and packages inside, and he'd recall that, yes, one time he had been so glad to see her that he'd accidentally sent a watermelon bouncing down the stairs. (He'd thought it looked lovely, he had told her, at home in flight, like the blimps that used to hover over the freeway when he and their father went on long drives just for the sake of the radio and the wind.)

Despite being exhausted from long hours in a corporate public relations job she had hid in for years, despite sometimes requesting that Paulie speak a little more softly, Claudia made sure her brother knew he was loved, knew he was seen. She listened to his new songs repeatedly and told him the parts she liked best, she took his dirty laundry from the sloping piles on his bedroom floor and brought him hand soaps that smelled, as per his preference, spectacularly of pomegranate. On the weekends, they took the subway—Paulie loved the hurtle, the bright orange seats, the light in the tunnel present long before the train itself was visible. It was everything she could do to keep him from striking up conversations with all the people clearly taking refuge in the urban privacy of the C or D train, but watching him ascend joyfully towards the skyscrapers of Manhattan was worth it. They went to the Bronx Zoo, where Paulie observed that the giraffes must have been made by someone talented but distracted. He delighted in the New Museum, the exhibits one could touch, and rushed to the flashing interactive electronics, the video art, the generous plush headphones. They lay in Central Park, exhausted, where he confessed to her that to him, horse poop smelled *friendly*, somehow. "Think about it. Is there any other poop that says hello like that?"

Sometimes they talked about their parents. Paulie said things to Claudia that stuck to her, and when she arrived home to her new husband, she lacked the ability to explain what had affected her so and why she couldn't turn over to him to listen to the story of his day.

"You know, Claude," said Paulie. "I think that probably Mom and Dad are holding each other under an apple tree, and the roots are all twisted in their bones, and they have these long conversations about us that travel up into the trunk and branches. And that tree makes the best apples anyone has ever had, and people come from miles to taste them. But we don't get to know exactly where it is or to take a nap under the leaves. Know why? 'Cause we grew up eating those apples." He could sound like some slightly warped and delirious Hallmark card, a nursery tale fed ayahuasca, but his insistence on determining a why, on explaining away sorrow, made her feel she was some inferior model of human, resourceless, easily jammed.

Paulie rarely seemed unhappy when she left, and liked to make little jokes about the luxuries of the bachelor lifestyle—"Don't worry about me, sis. Guys like me prefer it alone!"—but still she imagined him all the time, trying his best to navigate physical space, remembering to feed himself and flush the toilet, and she grew hamstrung with the thought of an obligation unfulfilled. She spent $2,400 a month on an aide who came once a day and helped Paulie with chores and escorted him on walks. When he called her at the office to talk about his dreams, Claudia put her work on hold, swiveled her chair away from the desk, and pressed her forehead to the window. She tried to associate him, in lasting ways, with energy, with optimism, with things clean and good. She tried to match every compliment he offered with one of her own. She kept a memo in her phone of all the strange or benevolent things he'd said that had touched her in a particular way and reviewed it on days particularly stressful, those when he called five times to report on the path of an ant or to cry about a smell. She put his music on her headphones at the gym as she increased the tension on the treadmill and opted to look past her reflection, through the windows, where New York changed incrementally, a Korean bodega emptying of its merchandise, a For Sale sign, leaves drifting down as slowly as sleep.

THOMAS'S FIRST IMPULSE to drag a blade across his skin had bubbled up from an overwhelming and noisy spell of boredom that had nagged at the edges of his thoughts until it resounded, inexorable: *This is fine, but does it make up a life?* His mood had been relatively even earlier in the day, almost pleasant; his anxieties had shifted from the fact of the stroke to how quickly he'd grown used to it, forgotten to miss his left hand. He'd sat at a café around the corner and admired the dogs and the babies sniffing at each other, felt grateful for the temperate fall weather and the breezes he could feel tugging at the warm air, read the last sixty-four pages of a multigenerational saga and felt his throat catch at the death of the stubborn matriarch. With the passing of mid-afternoon, he tightened with the familiar panic of *what next* and returned home to fix a meal from the varied excess of groceries—the impulsively plucked overpriced fruits and exotic grains—that he bought ritually to ease his feelings of aimlessness. He sautéed a chicken breast in white wine and assembled a salad of spinach and apple, lighting with pride at this small accomplishment as he ate and then feeling disgusted by how his worth was constituted. His heart withered, then, at the long task doing the dishes had become, the awkward manipulations necessary to clean all angles of an object, the plates, he knew, never truly clean. When it finally arrived, the thought came to him like a pleasant, ignorant suggestion from a well-meaning relative—*you could just*—and it was completely foreign, suddenly divested of associations with troubled teenagers and occurring to him as a compelling option.

That day, after raising a knife up from the sink of soapy water and sighing at a crumb still clinging to the serrated edge, he brought the blade across his left forearm, once so well used but now distinctly smaller than his right. He sliced just deep enough to bring out a steady pulsing of blood, impressed by how his right hand's fingers still grasped so well that they seemed almost a part of the object. The red traveled down his arm and into the sparkle of soap bubbles. As it reached the water and clung to the oily rainbowed trails, he stood there transfixed by the colors, remembering the joy in seeing one shade meet another, the clumsy affair of two things combining, which felt so slow until it revealed its enduring result.

ADELEINE TREMBLED UNDER THE TEST she had given herself: if she could blend in on the subway, she'd decided, she could forgive herself her retreat, believe that someday she might return to the world of intersections and green park benches and strangers' elbows. A man opened the door between cars, appeared with a waxen cup and delivered a mumbled speech about poverty and diabetes and spare change for food, and when he flourished it in her direction, she closed her eyes and thought of the clean white sheets on her bed, the red alarm clock that shook like a cartoon, her alphabetized records, the predictable drip of the cold water tap in the bathroom. When she opened her eyes to the world again, he had disappeared into the next car, and she looked around at the other passengers for clues on how to behave: they stared into nothing or electronic screens that cast icy glows upward, making small, swift gestures with their thumbs and forefingers. Five minutes of relative peace followed, but then a crowd of twelve- and thirteen-year-olds in windbreakers and sweatpants boarded, turned on music that screeched and throbbed. As the train tore into lower Manhattan, they defied space with backflips, they looped their knees around the metal rails and reached for one another through the air, they swam down the aisles requesting donations, they chanted in unison. Their energy felt to her like a practiced assault, a technique designed to extract a confession. Tightening her crossed arms, pressing her polished opal nails into her skin until the sensation blotted all else, she curled down into the softness of her knees and remained in that created dark until her stop arrived.

At the station, she made it a few feet into the light above and stopped at the head of the stairwell, where people diverged around her like cars avoiding a spill. At the tail of the rush, a man with a damp face and a burdened suitcase came upon her and stopped.

"Hey," he said. "Do you need help finding something?"

"I know where I'm supposed to go," she said, turning a severe bun in his direction. Three bobby pins had slipped halfway out of position, threatening to destroy the form, and the skin of her nape was patched red.

"I don't need any help getting home," she said.

I N THE DAYS AFTER THE STROKE, delirious and sleep-sodden as he was, Thomas hadn't always been sure that Edith's voice was actually there, outside his door, muttering in circles about her small offerings. Stacked on the worn sandy carpet that ran the length of the hall, the things she had left confirmed it: plates of cheddar mashed potatoes and roasted chicken and dark greens, just cooked, the steam finding a way through the tinfoil; recent *New Yorkers* and puckered crime novels taken from her own shelf; six-packs of soda water; his mail; a lily in a cracked ceramic mug; a scarf knit into a loop, the signature merchandise of a stormy-faced vendor who was always outside their subway station.

He would be on the couch, chasing a nap despite having been awake only two hours, and hear the clearing of her throat, the sound in two parts.

"Okay," she would say, with the voice of someone speaking to a colleague about a routine procedure, an issue with the copy machine or a slight change in schedule. "I'm leaving a few things here. Something for eating and something for reading and something else just because. They're just out the door to your left. I know you probably have silverware but I put some in there because what the hell. All these things are only if you want. The vegetables are a little swampy. Can't ever seem to avoid that hellish feature. It's food. It's definitely food. All right, I'm headed back to my pensioner's grotto now."

After a week of that, her odd discursions often the only points of amusement in his otherwise black days, he heard the shuffle of her approach and startled her by opening the door. It was he who should have been embarrassed, he thought, he who had not bothered to crawl even briefly from his depressive hole and leave a note of thanks, but as she entered, she kept her sight fixed on the tray she had brought, reddening like someone allergic.

"Well, I know I've been a busybody," she said, her eyes scanning the room for a place to set the platter down.

"Anywhere is fine. Here, on the counter. You haven't at all. You've been some kind of magic post-catastrophe elf. And *I* haven't paid rent." He gestured for her to sit at the bare kitchen table, and she gripped her hands on its edge to lower her stooped frame into a chair. Her hair was carefully curled, the stiff white reminiscent of a subaquatic reef formation, and her wedding ring sat bright but noticeably off-center on her diminished finger.

"Elves are meant to be a little quieter, probably."

"It's true I could hear you bustling out there."

He laughed for the first time since his injury, and it surprised his voice, which strained at the exertion. She had the kind of older face that hinted at its young features, as though it were a hologram that could be tilted, the murky slate of the eyes restored to their former inquiring blue, the wattle of the neck tightened to reveal the stark line of the jaw.

"Never my strong suit. Never a suit at all, in fact. Not even hanging in my closet."

He carried them over one by one, the teapot, the mugs, a jar of almonds, and Edith knew not to offer her help, not to watch as he arranged the things on the table. She drank the still-warm tea gratefully, as though she hadn't prepared it herself, thanking him, looking around and complimenting the large wooden blocks he used as coffee tables, the bright teal of the couch, a series of octagonal shelves he had mounted on the longest wall. She didn't mention the vestiges of his work, which infested the sizable corner of his space where a tarp lay to protect the floor.

And then she barked out the question, the one nobody else had posed alongside the stilted condolences they'd e-mailed. She offered it without the upward lilt at the end, like an appraisal of something obvious, a foul smell or a probable rain.

"And how are you."

"I'm shit," he said. It was a relief to say so.

"Can't say I expected anything else. You were handed some misadventure. Is this retribution for some former crime of yours? A nun you robbed?"

He smiled modestly, as though afforded a compliment, grateful under the generous cover of her humor.

"At nun-point," they said, nearly at the same time, their embarrassment about the weak pun turning to delight in the coincidence.

"About the rent," she said. "You shouldn't—"

He put his hand up, let the unkempt line of his amber hair fall over his eyes.

"I should," he said. "And I will. I'll get you a check—"

"But how are you going to—"

She stopped, immediately aware her brash tongue had taken her for the wrong turn, and communicated her apology by tapping a hand to her mouth and cringing.

"That's okay, Edith. It's a good question. I'm okay for a few months, and then I don't know. My gallerist wants to put together some . . . memorial show, it seems like to me, although of course no one will call it that. The things I had finished and a number I hadn't."

"Then I'll buy some. I don't have anything on my walls but twenty years ago."

"I hope that won't be necessary. Maybe I can give you one."

In the way that it sometimes does for people whose rapport has advanced very quickly, the open speech had dried up, as if to reflect on how recently theirs had been a cordial but transactional relationship. They assessed each other in the silence, making eye contact then letting it break.

"Well," she said. "I could bring you some lunch tomorrow. Will you be here?"

He was. She did. For weeks it became his only routine, and he had showered for it, cracked windows here and there, swept.

"WHY DON'T YOU CALL IT *A Living Question*," he'd said, over coffee with his gallerist, a woman whose hair was always mounted asymmetrically and who typed intermittently on her smartphone as she spoke to him, ostensibly taking notes.

"Oh, that's good," she'd answered, not detecting the dark humor in his voice, spitting a little through the signature gap in her front teeth.

"No, Ivy, it's—*I'm* the—"

"Of course this is all up to you. But I was thinking we could mount them from finished to un-, so we're sort of watching the progress in reversal, almost a record of decay." Her voice was rich with her own regard for it. Thomas tried to cover the disgust he felt appearing on his face with a hand over his mouth and a series of discerning nods.

Chased by absurd nightmares of poverty in which debt collectors followed him in Groucho Marx masks, Thomas had agreed to meet Ivy for the sake of his practical future, but the thought of his unfinished pieces on display, the naked lines in pencil, made all the pulse points in his body raise up and hammer.

In the weeks that followed he agreed to almost everything she suggested, curatorial statements and promotional photos and times and dates. He made clear that he would not be in attendance at the opening, and she didn't protest, his absence being something she believed might sell. Several anticipatory write-ups appeared, which she forwarded to him, and which remained unread.

The night that people in ironic jumpsuits and vintage fur coats gathered in oblique lighting before his paintings, he was perched on tiptoe in Edith's bathtub, making marks in pencil on the wall above it. Thomas had kept one for her: six by four feet, a pictorial rendering of continental drift. Over several years, in fertile browns and cold blues and sylvan greens, he had translated the formation of the Appalachians, the dwindling of seaways, the birth of glaciers, the rise of submerged islands. He had worked at it as though it were a marriage, fighting with it and watching it change, and he was glad to appoint it here, let it alone.

He felt the hum of his telephone in his pocket and silenced it without a look. It was Ivy, texting to say that some tech celebrity, the founder of a location-based dating app, had purchased a triptych of his paintings. The sale could support him for a year, two if he was careful.

When he had finished he called to Edith in the kitchen, where she was cursing to herself and filling the building with the smell of a roast, carrots in brown sugar and butter. In another life, one he had enjoyed until just recently, he would have refused to hang it there, would have warned her that the steam from her long baths would warp it. Instead, he offered her the strength of his forearm as she climbed over the porcelain lip, and they raised the wooden frame of the canvas together, making small adjustments as they searched for the nails he had driven, commenting on the angle, tugging at it until it was straight, and flush, and bright.

Later, he would come to wonder. As she lay in the bath, her mind going, did she consider what hung there? And was it the thing that called her back, to her cluttered papers, to her life's quiet routine; or was it the thing that lied to her, muddling chronology and nibbling at private truths, and led her, with a gentle hand, away?

PAULIE TRIED not to give in to the feeling but some facts rendered him melancholy no matter what kinds of songs he'd been playing or if the clouds were forming pointy faces or if he'd run into any ugly dogs that day.

For as long as his memory went, Paulie had loved children. When his mother's sister had a baby and brought it over and it started crying, Paulie was the only one who could get it to stop: he'd made up a song about the ocean, about how waves only leave so they can come back larger. The choking sobbing had stopped, the starfish hands reached up to grab Paulie's nose, the eyes formed invisible lines right to his, and he had known right away how much he wanted this, to be the center and the protection of another's life.

For his tenth birthday he asked for a baby doll, a blue-eyed boy in washable velour, and named it Oscar and tried to never lose sight of him. He slept with him in his bed and sometimes his breath grew constricted, so nervous did he feel that he might fall asleep and roll over onto him. He learned how to sleep like a pencil. He brought Oscar along on trips in the car and pointed out the trees whose names he knew, white pine and dogwood and redbud. He made sure his socks and soft blue cap and clean cotton pants went into the wash frequently. He stayed up in bed explaining the things that had puzzled him once, where all the household garbage went and who decided when to open the post office and what made heat lightning and how sex must feel.

Oscar's silence and slumped way of sitting grew tedious, but Paulie valued the feeling of worth that came from putting the world in order for someone else, from folding the tiny sweaters. When he was fourteen, his true capacity for love filled with the arrival of Eleanor, a neighborhood beauty imported from the mysterious wilds of North Carolina who spoke slowly, wore old-fashioned saddle shoes, and had a cocoa-colored birthmark shaped like a bow tie on her nose. After a long week spent skulking around the street they shared, singing the romantic songs he knew on the edge of her lawn, he confessed his affliction to Seymour, asked how one went about asking a girl to be the mother of his children.

"Do I go up to her and say, let's combine bodies forever?"

"I think that might scare her, Paul. People generally like to think of their bodies as just theirs."

"Okay, how about—"

He thought his father was joking when he told him. Seymour said the probability of passing it on was about fifty percent, that the limits of his condition made parenthood impossible. Paulie, stunned, protested. "But you've always said I was an exception to a lousy rule. But I can look at a person and know what kind of story they need, you said. But I can light a room like that's my job on the planet, you said!"

He had cried with dedication, the tears leaking down onto his teal hoodie and matching sweatpants. He saw in front of him the visions he'd always cherished—himself as father, tucking a lock of hair behind an ear at bedtime, teaching his son about which fish glow in the dark, sitting with him at the piano every day after school—and tried to reach them but couldn't. His gut felt like fire spreading through a forest. "It hurts me, and I'm so sorry to have to tell you this," Seymour kept saying. "Then don't," Paulie said. "Then why would you?"

Wants could remain possible, Paulie still believed, so long as you didn't speak them aloud.

He remembered, then, the synchronized sacrifice of all childhood things. How the boys and girls from his street suddenly sprouted longer limbs and adult shadows, how they dropped their baseball mitts and water balloons and Halloween masks and turned away. His father held him, and Paulie tightened his shoulders against the embrace as he saw the unbearable length of it, the life in which he would always be a child.

E DITH WAS IN GRAND CENTRAL STATION and did not know why or how or even when. She wished for hats, a sea of them, cashmere gloves and polite nods, leather suitcases of browns and greens with sturdy locks. Fine pocketbooks where the tickets paid for lived until you pulled them out to show the conductor proudly, there on the train, where everything fit into roomy compartments above and below, where the world was stacked neatly.

But where were they, the fine pressed brims and tie clips and stockings with the clean black line down the back of the leg? No matter how long she closed her eyes, each time she opened them the people did not belong. Little girls crossed the floor in baseball caps, and under scrolling electronic screens grown women in clingy whites bickered. They all carried beach bags and neon-colored towels and not one of them stood up straight, not one of them was someone she could imagine knowing.

Where was Declan? Had he gone to buy the tickets? Was it already the season for the cabin and the red-and-white-checked tablecloth and chicken salad and watermelon? Edith scanned the little vendor windows, their gratings' gilded curlicues familiar, the counters still marble. That, at least. But his shape was nowhere, and the shoes on her feet had two strange straps that did not buckle, that just stayed somehow. Her elbows had pasty folds and the skin on her hands looked as if it would tear. Not one of them was someone she could imagine knowing!

And then she was or had been yelling "Declan," but she had stopped because he always said if they lost each other in an urban sea to root herself just like a tree. She looked through the glass at the moving dark tunnel and knew many truths about her life at once: that Jenny practicing spelling on the kitchen table while she steamed spinach was what she liked best, that when she sat upright in her wooden school desk she could feel the sixteen-year-old boy behind her thinking of undoing the button at the back of her neck, that she liked math for its clear-cut authority and always found test days reassuring. That her father liked to braid her hair when the chores were done and the chairs were on the porch with their familiar groan and the smell of biscuits drifted outside. That when she was particularly well behaved her mother would place her on her lap, let Edith steer the big round leather wheel and look through the windshield at the people lining up for the matinee under the marquee the town got together to pay for.

But then there was a new set of competing facts: This train moving fast. The woman next to her, with a cloth over her breast, nursing a baby of indeterminable gender. And the sounds that must be coming from her body, words that didn't come together in the way she needed them to, *where* and *stop* and *Declan* and *Jenny* and *Declan* and *stop*. The mother of the baby had vanished and there were several faces around her asking, asking, asking, and Edith said, "You fucking people, I don't know any of you fucking people, not one." Later, in the back of a police car, made frightened by the cage that divided front and back, she practiced a small form of weeping, determined to keep any more of herself from them. When they pulled up at the brownstone she and Declan had bought to fill with their life and future, they insisted on walking her in. She flinched at the policeman's light touch on her elbow, thanked God and heaven none of her tenants were descending the stairs. When she went to retrieve her keys, she saw that the hands that couldn't be hers were reluctant as abused animals, and the broad-shouldered policeman moved to place the brass in the lock and she hissed, "I don't need your help." Finally in her chair, the scalloped velvet worn in the seat and arms, she rocked a little, but the motion didn't soothe. She waited to recognize the place around her, the room growing dark as a well, her life crouching somewhere nearby, hiding from her.

ADELEINE RARELY CONSIDERED the ventures at which she had failed in the days when she was able to leave the house, and instead threw herself into the task at hand every day, grateful for any paycheck.

She had met the woman by the 59th Street entrance to the park, by the swan pond and the stone bridge that arched over the passing reflections of families, the New York Adeleine felt she could still love. Settled on a bench in the fading autumn light, which appeared to stir its colors in protest of evening advancing, Adeleine had wished for the winter, which would forgive her, cradle all her could-nots. The woman at the other end of the painted green planks snuck glances periodically before finally remarking on the rarity of Adeleine's hat, dark blue felt with a netted veil that hung over her face and fluttered like a hesitant wing when she sighed.

"I used to have one just like that," said the woman. "In fact, my father was a milliner. One of the largest in New York."

"That must have been wonderful," said Adeleine, "watching someone you love make beautiful things with his hands. I often think if I'd had more of that, I'd be someone else."

The old woman spoke in sentences that seemed fixed, repeated and perfected over time, and said her name was Miriam and fussed often with the ring on her wedding finger. As their shadows grew longer, couples rose from the grass behind them and retreated to the nearby subway, and the birds in the chilled muck began to return to each other. Miriam seemed enlivened by what she saw as Adeleine's willingness to listen—a tendency to nod excessively that actually indicated social discomfort—and unfolded her personal history in various directions, unable to decide which aspect held the greatest importance: the friends she'd lost to swift diseases, how money had made her husband sad, why she had stayed when the New York she understood began shifting identities at an accelerated clip. Looking out at the man-made swamp and the geese idling there, Adeleine felt some maternal urge to place a warm hand on Miriam's neck, or just to call the old woman by her name.

By the end of an hour and a drop of three degrees, the arrangement was settled. Adeleine would receive a generous rate by the page, as well as an ample initial fee, to transcribe the journals Miriam had begun keeping at age ten, as well as the twenty-four shoe boxes of letters and postcards. They would speak on the telephone when necessary to discuss the project's evolution. Miriam told Adeleine her new job was to make sense of Miriam's life—she couldn't herself, not ever or anymore.

"Something to speak for me when I can't," she said.

And so it went that Adeleine spent her days even more consumed by old things and transferred memories. She would see later it was this chance proposition, this agreement formed in a park in autumn, that allowed her to fully retire into her third-floor island, the place she had built to ask very little of her.

THE FIRST TIME the doctor had informed him of the term for the precursors to his migraines, the prohibitive clouds of sound and color, Thomas couldn't help but sneer. "An aura?!" he'd said. "Think of it like a warning sign or a stoplight," the physician had said. "It's your cue to grab some aspirin and have a seat."

Eventually Thomas grew to like the auras, thought of them as a unique part of his life, a bittersweet drug his body sometimes produced. He had learned to enjoy the sensations that came before the pain: light stretched and brightened playfully as his hearing hummed and sharpened, and his body felt lifted, excused from duty. Then darkness crowded and bubbled at the edges of his vision, and he knew to lie back and let the monster have its way. Over time he came to recognize the signs so clearly that he would put down his paintbrush or stub of charcoal or pencil without frustration. He liked to move to a space that was free of clutter, shove open a window and lie flat, and enjoy the corporeal deviations, try to filter questions through them. Sometimes during the pre-migraine oddities he chanced on the direction he needed to finish a work, or saw a vivid smear of the precise color for which he'd been looking.

Because of the reverence he had cultivated for these shifts in perception, the afternoon that would leave him disabled for the rest of his life did not alarm him as it should have. The aura lasted longer than it typically did—hadn't the doctor said no more than twenty minutes? But having worked all morning, having endured a particularly soul-hollowing conversation with his mother, he took the excuse for incapacity gladly. When he'd felt it coming, he had managed to draw the linen curtains, stretch out on the couch, and place a pillow under his head. The March sky through the window, he would remember, was a covering of gray on a growing blue.

Later he couldn't remember: was it one hour or two before he'd succumbed to panic, began to miss the light as it would appear naturally, to fear that he would never see it again. How much time until he had tried to make a call but couldn't recognize the symbols on his touch screen, and curled his knees into his ribs and began praying for the migraine to hit. His pleas were absent of God; he was petitioning himself, scouring his mind for the corrective mechanism. But the headache didn't come until dark, and when it did it took hold with the swift efficiency of a team of movers: whole parts of his body emptied in minutes.

He had eventually managed the three emergency digits, had heard himself report that one side of his face and half his torso and left arm were not responsive, heard himself describe his symptoms with the clinical acuity he'd developed as a strange child studying the habits of backyard birds. While he waited, he looked around his apartment politely, like an uncomfortable guest early for dinner.

The medical term for the type of stroke he'd had, he'd learn later, was a migrainous infarction, something signaled by changes in sensorium that persisted too long. He arrived home from the hospital, bit off the patient bracelet with his canine teeth, and didn't speak for eight days.

GIVEN HIS INABILITY or unwillingness to work on anything new—the first being his own belief and the latter the suspicion of his crueler acquaintances—Thomas took to things he found beautiful in only the purest sense. For the first time in his life, he appreciated photographs of mountains, saturated paintings of cornfields. He liked to tell friends who called that he had misplaced his taste somewhere, that they could forward any and all snapshots of rainbows and glaciers his way. His growing fascination with Adeleine followed from this naturally.

She seemed made of words often paired together, and observing her helped Thomas to understand the hackneyed couplings: creamy skin, shining eyes, flowing hair. He hadn't truly noticed her in the year and a half she'd been across the hall; perhaps he had found her perfection boring. The women who had stomped across his life before had always been jagged in their appearance and furtive in their intent: a sculptor who wore gray exclusively and brought him back to a charcoal-painted apartment twice a week for silent, brutal sex; a jilted pregnant woman with coarse eyebrows who only wanted to be held and fed; several who drank too much and stood by his canvases nodding before becoming bellicose and picking circular fights.

Adeleine was different: symmetrical and soft and glossy to an extent that didn't seem naturally occurring, with cheeks that glowed like peaches in commercials and eyes as violet as industrial fireworks.

Even after he realized the extent of her beauty, Thomas had no interest in talking to her. He only wanted to watch, to fully appreciate the precision of her making. It helped that she never spoke or looked at him as she put out a bag of trash or opened the door for a deliveryman.

When her nighttime weeping began, he was blindsided by his vision having grown complex and animate and tried to will the noises away. The stroke had left him cold, and sometimes slowed reactions to other people's pain, but the sounds coming from her body were without rhythm, impossible to become accustomed to and ignore, and he quickly felt moved to mollify them.

The first time he knocked, he heard the strangled stifle of a sob and the hurried footsteps to switch off the light. He burned with embarrassment at a rejection so obvious, but the next night found him at her door again, listening. He did not bring his knuckles to the wood, only crouched and slipped a note under the door: *I thought you could use a drink.—Apt. 3A.* When he checked a half hour later, the mug of bourbon and lemon and honey had disappeared. In bed that night, he thought of her lips on the porcelain, and his skin grew tight, his pectorals and hamstrings newly awake, tensing under her image. He arranged his dead hand on his abdomen, then slid his other under the elastic band of his boxers and moved it forcefully, repeatedly, until every part of him ceased to complain.

What followed was like some archaic dance, one that required mastery not only of the steps but also the nuanced system of nods and glances that marked its transitions. After ten days, Thomas realized with mild panic that he'd sacrificed all of his cups, the university mugs and the gifted beer stein and the ridged water glasses. He hadn't left her with any instructions as to their return, of course, and she hadn't offered any communication beyond the simple receipt of his nightly gifts. He thought about it with pain throughout the day until the ritual hour passed. After several hours of sleep, he woke with an urgent feeling and drank several bowls of water in the kitchen, surprised by how the act of sleeping had induced such a thirst. He looked out at the unlit room as a thief might, scanning for value and an unhindered escape.

Two nights later, the knock came.

"The little bell's been going off and I've been salivating, but the Russian scientist in charge has forgotten me," she said. Her eyes remained somewhere to his left, and it was unclear whether she was seeking his laughter.

The mass of her heavy hair was pinned up and swirled above her face, and her chin jutted from a crisp lilac linen that buttoned all the way to the neck. Though he hadn't considered what her voice might sound like, the reality of it, scratched and thick-throated, still seemed incorrect. It was that of a tollbooth operator, worn in by rote speech, eroded by fumes. The door of her apartment remained open behind her, and one of her hands clung to its knob as she straddled the hall.

"I—I ran out of glasses," Thomas answered. He emphasized *glasses* as though discussing something irreplaceable and watched with resounding discomfort as her fine face flushed, her body retreated homeward by an inch, then two. He heard the measured voice of some nature-channel narration and tried to push it away, but the black humor nagged at him: *meeting the rare creature out in the open, should he play dead, or offer his food, or wave his arms and yell?*

"You can—" she began, gesturing towards her apartment's rose glow. "Bring?" He understood, with a thrill, that the exchange made her nervous, and he nodded as though they'd done this before and knew their parts, and went to retrieve the bottle. The smell of all her things, fusty and smoky and dense, had already reached him.

S HORTLY AFTER their father Seymour's hair had grown so white and downy that Paulie took to calling him Sir Dandelion, he'd suffered a coronary during an early-morning walk, binoculars around his neck and a grocery list in his pocket. Claudia had selected an oak-stained casket for the viewing and baked gingerbread cookies for the reception; she had picked up her three-quarter-length black dress from the dry cleaner and twisted her hair into an unmoving knot at the back of her neck; she had thanked people for coming and accepted their condolences; she had repainted the stairwells and appointed a real estate broker; she had met with Seymour's lawyer and accountant and wept in each of their antiseptic bathrooms; and, imagining that the death of her father would install in her some compassionate wisdom if only she waited a few weeks, she had left the question of Paulie for very last.

Though she and Seymour had discussed a number of assisted living communities in which well-trained aides and social workers would see that Paulie lived his fullest life—and Paulie had even visited some of these places with his father and enjoyed chatting with the staff and residents, as well as testing the bounce of the mattresses and the texture of the food—when it came down to signing the last of the forms, Claudia could not put pen to paper. Having witnessed both of her parents reduced to dismayingly small boxes of ashes, remembering Paulie's insistence upon singing at both services and how tightly he'd gripped her hand, Claudia had decided to take her younger brother's life into hers as closely as she could.

Made anxious by suburban Connecticut dusk the day after the wake, she had prepared an excess of stew, something with the potential to feed many more people than their family of two. When he had stopped slurping, she raised the question.

"Paul? Where is it you think you'd most like to live now?"

"Dad and I visited some places—"

"Could you imagine yourself living there, though?"

"They were real clean, with chefs. I could imagine so much, Claude. I could imagine it is an okay place to be. I could also imagine walking for a long time until you found exactly the place you wanted. There are so many homes, I think, and you could spend the wrong kind of life following them."

Various aging aunts who phoned had clucked their tongues and expressed concern, emphasizing repeatedly that no one could judge her for placing Paulie under the care he needed. But she had helped her brother pack his things—the long-beloved crescent moon lamp, with a cherubic face and a half-smile; the quilt their mother had embroidered over the course of a year, with a panel for the forest, the ocean, the desert, and the town— and she urged him to imagine the fun they might have in New York.

"We'll have picnics on Sundays when the weather's nice, and clap at the men who play mariachi on the subway, and go to museums of sound and art and transportation and history and police and science. You'll have your very own apartment, right near mine, and we'll paint it whatever colors you like." Her breathing had become uneven, as though her safety was the one being discussed offhandedly in a nearly vacant house.

"Okay, Claude," Paulie had said. "Okay, Claude!" He had pulled her to where he sat on the bare mattress and taken her hand, formed a brief O of suction on each of her fingertips as he kissed them. Claudia had brought his head to her shoulder as though he weren't thirty years old and three inches taller, and closed her eyes so as not to look out the window at the yard, now empty of the peeling red picnic table that had stood there for thirty years, Seymour's much beloved barbecue, the hammock where their mother had read her mystery novels and spread coconut-scented tanning oil on her thick calves. The tree Claudia had climbed to peer down at her family remained, but appeared to understand its obsolescence, and drooped.

T HE DEGREE TO WHICH the space expressed Adeleine, the fact that she had found and touched and arranged all these things—this alone made Thomas happy to be there each night. The supply of treasures seemed endless, as did the gentle exuberance with which she presented them, though he noted the bowed shelves, the lack of counter space, and wondered about the difference between pleasure and need.

Adeleine smoked out the window with a frequency that worried him. She cycled between a standing ashtray with a marble top and another, disc-shaped but thick, which spun to receive butts in a hidden underbelly. She had a record player and a whole wall of albums and invited him to run his fingers over them and choose. With her projector they watched movies on the one bare patch of wall—a tipsy Clark Gable stroked his mustache and charmed his way out of corners, Harpo Marx absconded with someone's hat again—and as the hours passed in the monochromatic and jerking light, he felt peaceful, saturated. He caught her laughing and turned to see her mouth open. Adeleine had a past, but it was distinctly absent from the display.

On a night when she seemed particularly pliable and garrulous, giggling at and mouthing punch lines like a sugar-addled child, he resolved to chip away at her mystery. When the film ended, he crossed his legs Indian-style, willing confidence.

"You know, I was wondering. How did your parents give you your name?"

"With a great deal of hope and fear, I guess." She grinned. "Like anyone faced with accounting for the life they've unexpectedly created."

"I guess I meant—"

"Was it a family name? Did it appear to my mother in a dream? Did an old woman place her hand on the bump that was me and divine it?"

"I wasn't betting on those situations, exactly, but—"

"My father drank a lot—drinks a lot. It was a good choice for slurring. Can't really fuck it up. All soft consonants. I'm sleepy. Are you?"

She exaggerated a yawn, patting her fingertips on the oval of her mouth, and walked him to the door, where she gave his arm an avuncular squeeze before locking herself in.

Though Edward had taken to dressing like someone who spent recreational hours outside a small-town 7-Eleven, he showered and shaved and dressed up for therapy: cardigans buttoned up his chest and crisp collared shirts of muted blues and pinks, corduroys ironed and creased. During the sessions he was painfully conscious of his facial expressions, eager to convey an intelligent thoughtfulness, a willing openness, a sense of humor despite it all. He found Mariana's frequent nods erotic, the cross of her ankles too much to glance at for long.

He tried to find the brand of tissues she kept in her office—they were the softest he'd ever touched, slightly scented with aloe and something else probably only people like Mariana knew the name of—and even the health food stores, the places where imported peaches sold for two dollars each, didn't carry it.

Mariana identified Edward's late mother's behavior during his childhood as wildly inappropriate, and urged him to understand that cultivating forgiveness and assigning accountability were not mutually exclusive. It was no wonder, Mariana said, that being kept inside and overly protected from all hypotheticals for much of his childhood had led to a great deal of wildness and experimentation later on. Mariana's speech was peppered with words like *choice* and *self* and *journey*, and much of the time she spent talking, Edward spent trying not to think of how he might arrange her naked form, how all the firm parts of her might move together.

He wanted to kiss her until she no longer resembled the upright and incisive figure in the chair, to erase the wall behind her and the three framed degrees from liberal arts schools that sounded like poisonous plants, to upset the precise arrangement of pins at the nape of her neck. Afterward, he would tell her, "That was a thoroughly positive and expansive experience," and take her out for cheeseburgers, in jest spurning the sparkling probiotic drinks he'd seen in her mini-fridge.

He wanted to feel that the distance between men like him and women like her was not so great, that he hadn't been doomed from birth to struggle, to run from one dysfunctional corner to the next while another stratum of people functioned gracefully and fell asleep easily.

Sometimes when these visions floated across his brain, the thought of her sock on his floor or locket on his nightstand, his face betrayed him, and Mariana would pause and say, "Well, Edward, you're smiling broadly now—can you tell me what that's about?" He would reply, "Oh, sure. I think I just made a breakthrough. Several, in fact." So far, therapy had cost him $42,563. His money was disappearing, running from him like some feral animal.

Y OU'RE AN EMPTY BAG of a person and I know you have it!"
Edith, at the door of Edward's apartment, dressed in a
polka dot dress with misaligned shoulder pads and a bowler hat
that obscured her forehead entirely, lurched forward, gesturing
menacingly with a ballpoint pen. "Let me in!"

Edward, woken that day by a particularly crippling fugue of
melancholy, could not contend with the figure at his door. He
could barely even follow the sounds and images of his television.
He'd been dreaming of Helena again.

She'd been waiting for him for hours in a Victorian green-
house, ready for a road trip they'd planned carefully, her evenly
worn leather bag packed and her hair tightly braided, but he was
stuck in a club, trying to squeeze in one last gig: he'd been sweating under the lights, telling the audience about how his mother
used to lock him inside for days, and tasting the blood that was
filling his mouth.

"Have what?" he mumbled, reminding himself that the day
was happening to him, despite his brain urging him elsewhere.
He found it laughable that anyone could believe he possessed
anything of transferable value. In his long-unwashed corduroys,
lacking the crucial fly button and permanently tented open, with
his beard that grew in temperamental patches and smelled of

inexpensive soup, he stood and waited for her to clarify her accusation. He felt a pathetic thrill at the opportunity to expound upon how little he had.

"You've got my checkbook," she hissed, pointing at him. "I know you do!"

"I do, huh?" He knew it was wrong to indulge her, but something acidic in his body had turned over. "Is that how I've managed to finance this luxurious lifestyle of mine? Cars and women, all the time? Why don't you come in! View my collection of expired milk and secondhand sweaters! Gilded! Rare!"

Unfazed by his teasing, Edith shuffled closer with the determination of a prospector, her elbows forming sharp angles.

"Woolworth's called. You're buying up the jewelry department on my dime, you big-nosed faggot!"

"Listen," said Edward. He found that the nastiness he felt towards himself shifted easily to another target. "Why don't you just head back downstairs in your crazy hat and fix yourself a cup of bathwater tea, pick a fight with one of your moldy couches—"

Edith's invented anger coursed through her thin body and she shoved him, but the reality of her lunge was slow, and Edward easily backed away. In a moment that felt much later and unbearably quiet, he looked down at her form laid across the doorframe, watched her hat as it lolled on the floor in a slowly diminishing half-life: he could understand time was advancing only from the movements of the felt brim on the hardwood. Edith's open mouth made little gasps, and a thread of saliva trembled and played between her lower and upper lips.

"Thief," she breathed and repeated, in and out, the false word finding lodging in her body.

TEN MINUTES LATER, Edward had arranged Edith on his chest and bent his knees in preparation for the first step down. He had determined that nothing was broken, but she refused to ambulate on her own, had remained bubbling the beginnings of sentences from her prone position in his entryway. His left arm cradled the blues and purples of her legs, and his right tensed against her shoulder blades. Her hat, which he had placed back on her head, obstructed his view as he felt his way down the steps, and her breath sounded in strained puffs from her unevenly pink-frosted lips. She began to sing.

Pardon me boy, is that the Chattanooga Choo-choo?
Right on track twenty-nine, boy can you give me a shine?

Edward knew this song. His mother, though pathologically joyless, used to play this 45 as if to say, I was once a person who wore dresses, took trains, looked out windows.

I can afford to board the Chattanooga Choo-choo,
I've got my fare and just a trifle to spare.

He whistled with her as her voice traveled down to the foyer like a recording slowly warping, the notes faltering in their execution.

You leave the Pennsylvania station at a quarter to four,
read a magazine and then you're in Baltimore;
dinner in the diner, nothing could be finer,
than to have your ham and eggs in Carolina.

On the landing, finally resigned to the absurdity and the necessity of it, he shuffled his feet and put his throat into the next bit of song—*Shovel all the coal in, gotta keep it rollin'*—and raised up the dust from the maroon runner in several waves. Edward surfaced from his performance to see a man who appeared composed of only sharp angles standing in the foyer, where the light caught his gold-watched wrist. He removed the sunglasses from his bronze cheeks, folded them into the top button of a crisp pink shirt and sighed, even that sound precise.

"Mother," the man said. His presentation of the word was hard, useful, as though he'd addressed a gas station cashier, asked for ten dollars on number six. Just inside Edward's line of vision, Edith's cheeks filled with blood. On the back of his chilled neck, her nails dug for a better hold. The brass mailboxes glinted, and the agitated air smelled like a garage thrown open to meet the street.

From his top-floor window the next morning, Thomas saw Owen and Edith climb into and emerge from a black cab several times, watched as her son helped her out the door, his face fixed not on her but on the building. Owen ran his hand over the metal fence that bordered the property, then shook it with controlled vigor, testing its solidity. Edith, dressed in polyester slacks the washed blue of a sun-faded Easter egg, moved with small steps in white Velcro sneakers Thomas had never seen before. She looked vaguely in the direction of his window but lost focus, and Thomas saw her mouth form a new, tight line. Owen held her elbow as they ascended the stone steps: she jerked it away and he caught it again, all without so much as turning his body towards hers.

Later in the afternoon, Thomas snuck down the stairs, stood listening for a time before he knocked. Owen answered, wearing a white cotton V-neck that revealed both his years and the physique that resisted them. He had a rag draped over one shoulder, a measuring tape peeking from his front denim pocket. Surveying the well-earned masculinity, Thomas felt the alarm of a phantom itch on the inert parts of his body.

"Can I help you?" Owen said, blinking out of blue eyes that shone as sharply as his crop of gray-blond hair.

Thomas immediately understood Owen's identity as a man

who'd been attractive and powerful since childhood, and put out his hand in a show of goodwill. "Thomas—" he began.

"Thomas Farber," completed Owen. "Apartment 3A, correct? How can I help you?"

"Oh, I'm just—just stopping to say hi. Edith and I are—"

"Oh yes." Owen cut Thomas's speech short with the flash of a palm. "She's mentioned you two are friendly, but she happens to be napping right now—a long day at the doctor's."

Owen offered a smile that lasted just long enough for Thomas to see his perfect teeth, milky and even, and Thomas recognized it as one picked for the occasion. Behind the muscled breadth of Owen's shoulders, light poured onto the kitchen table, lingering on a glossy spread of brochures. All Thomas could make out were silver-haired people, photos of trimmed hedges, bodies of water so blue and round they must have been engineered. Four of them lay on the table, which was otherwise uncharacteristically bare.

"I'll let her know you came by," Edith's son said, and closed the door.

Thomas lingered, defeated. He heard the muffled protests of Edith, the aggression evident, and the studied calm of Owen's speech squashing hers. "You're making this difficult."

"I'm not leaving my home." Her voice yowled, cracking at its edges. "You made her but you won't make me."

The next time Thomas saw them, crossing the foyer at the fullest possible distance from each other, Edith's frame held her left arm like a box of mementos, with fright and care, and Owen let out a low, flat whistle as he unlocked her front door.

N o one expects to find devotion where they do, and Adeleine liked to think she wouldn't have sought him out, wouldn't have chosen his life as the one she'd like to inhabit. Whose fault had it been that she'd wandered into the kitchen of her first apartment in New York, a railroad flat with a revolving cast of roommates, and N—— (now a name she tried not to even think) had been standing there making breakfast? Whose fault had it been that his worn T-shirt had hung from his shoulder blades just so, hinting at the unblemished almond skin beneath?

Certainly not hers. Neither could she claim responsibility for the winter, which was already descending, though they shared a few brief moments on the stoop in the sun; for the sense of quiet that surrounded him and nestled comfortably into hers; for the sanctity of his movement when he got up to change the record; for the face he made when he pushed his cock inside her, determined like a person building something slowly by hand. Never had she longed so specifically for a body, spent so much energy imagining the arrangement of the parts she had memorized.

When people asked his name, he blushed, knowing they'd ask him to repeat the foreign syllables as though they were a code or password. For a month he didn't mention to Adeleine that his father had been a monk in the Himalayas, his mother the free-spirited American who'd coaxed him away from the monastery and quickly become pregnant. When he did tell her, while they passed a cheap bottle of red wine that stained her pale, chapped lips but not his soft brown ones, he moved over the information quickly, eager to cast it as anything but remarkable. He'd spent the first two years of his life in Los Angeles, attached to his mother by a cloth papoose as she completed a graduate degree, and the next sixteen homeschooled in the northernmost parts of California, where as a teenager he made cash as a river raft guide, a job in which his pathological stoicism went unnoticed under the deafening mountainous current.

In the months before he appeared, Adeleine had been flailing in a waitressing job, crying in the restaurant kitchen where she often escaped to hear the thick warmth of spoken Spanish. "Oh *mami*," they would say, "why you always look so sad!" Sometimes they'd sing to her: *"Ay ay ay ay, canta, no llores.* Sing, don't cry." But the commanding nature of the song had seemed to trap her, and she had only smiled feebly. Once he surfaced, she moved through her shifts happily, cleaning silverware and anticipating coming home to him and talking very little, to the commute from her bedroom across the hall to his. All she could say to friends who asked about her new companion was that he seemed good, incapable of concealing or manipulating. Whenever she had asked him what he thought, about a book he was reading or a childhood memory she had shared, he had scratched at his elbows and scanned the room as though in yearning, mentally arranging his most earnest response. He was also, she had told girlfriends on the phone with a surprised laugh, the most beautiful human she had ever personally seen.

The pills, at least initially, had appeared as afterthoughts. She had convinced herself that he received them passively: it was true that someone at the parties he took her to usually placed them in his hands, and that he had shrugged with each swallow as he began his slow disappearing act. Later Adeleine remembered the view from over various shoulders, chiffon necklines and sheep's wool collars and dangling lightbulbs, the strain to see into the next room and the next, the search for him. The people at these places were attractive but removed, their attention spans short, and they parted easily as she passed through their conversations.

She'd find him nesting somewhere, looking more comfortable than she'd ever felt in her life: propped up by dingy pillows on the corner of someone else's rumpled bed or arranged carefully in a chair while people stood around him, his eyes hardly moving. *Can we go home now?* she would say, and he would nod, eventually, after remembering that he had one. Would he notice if she left, or just go on grazing at the edges of consciousness—the thought crossed her mind more and more often, and always she pushed it away. Eventually, she had started swallowing the same things he did, painkillers that produced everything from a slight and pleasant hum to near-paralysis. They found an apartment together, furnished it with a low center of gravity: a ground layer of cushions; long, squat black tables; photos hung a few feet up the wall; a coffeemaker on the ground next to their mattress.

Adeleine had taken to the drugs with the same wandering attention that had steered her through a series of talents but kept her from any lasting passions. N—— would grow twitchy without the anesthetic assistance of various opioids, but she had proved to be the rare individual who did not develop an addiction. The times the pills made her vomit, Adeleine took a certain pleasure in it, a scouring her body needed on occasion.

She was, habitually, the caretaker. They left their apartment unlocked, and often she'd push the door open, find him lying on top of the bed, eyes fixed on a point visible only to him. She would wave to the two or four friends or strangers in various positions of detachment in the room, and change the record if requested. At the end of the night, she would slowly nurse those who had passed out awake with a maternal hand.

Adeleine had known—or had told herself in the beginning—that it must be wrong to adore someone who spent his time tending an artificial happiness, but the way he blossomed when drugged blinded her. He would release the caged-in quiet that was synonymous with his sobriety and flow, describing all the parts of her he admired, wrapping every limb of his too-thin body around hers, telling her stories of the little boy he'd been, speaking with conviction of the life he could imagine for them. They would make a home in the country, grow their own beets and cucumbers, call to silver dogs who swam across rivers, watch their children as they napped in the garden. He would shiver as he fell asleep sometimes, and though she had understood this as a consequence of the narcotics, she relished the opportunity to meet his repeated request: "Keep me warm," he would whisper, "please will you keep me warm?"

They had still managed some kind of domestic cycle, kept eggs in the refrigerator most weeks, pulled the hand-knit afghan up in neat corners after they had drunk in enough sleep, left handwritten notes of private amusements on the counter, tenderly passed the soap and shampoo in the shower. There were five good months, in which he flickered but remained recognizable, and Adeleine continued to defer practical questions to some later point, a milestone that she felt she would recognize once it arrived. One night she stayed late at work and came home to find him particularly soft, particularly cold. "It's you," he had said, blinking as slowly as the lone traffic lights that hung over intersections in the small town she came from. "Come sleep with me." He had held her that night with more vigor, as though making a point, and in the morning wasn't sleeping in bed or sighing in the shower or smoking on the fire escape.

She had waited two weeks, skulking about the apartment, trying to catch his shadow around a corner, although after the first she had filed a police report and spent scrambled hours on the telephone with friends who had no answers. After a month his phone was shut off, and the social pages on the Internet he had passively monitored grew graffitied with confused mourning, the pitch of the posts becoming panicked: *Where are you we love you / Please just come home / Please just say you're okay.* And then, after his vanishing had settled, pieces of eulogy—*I'll always miss you man, you lit up everything / Sweet dreams baby / We always knew you belonged to somewhere else*—and she had stopped checking them. She couldn't spend another hour scrolling through the images of him she had long since memorized, hoping they might deliver a message, or respond to the digital sympathies bestowed on her by friends and acquaintances. The distance between their bland online attempts at condolence and their averted glances when she ran into them in person—as though grief and abandonment were an airborne contagion—was too great for her to reconcile. She had deleted as much evidence of herself on the Internet as was possible, wiped her laptop's hard drive clean, and placed it one night on a bench at the West 4th Street subway station. Dressed in whites and blues, quiet and pale, she had caught the first train that heaved into the tunnel and had begun, in her own fashion, to recede.

As a child, Thomas had looked forward to the science fair all year, to the long tumble of the day when his project put the clumsy baking soda volcanoes, the childishly lettered diagrams, to shame. He had labored on his poster board endlessly, trained his hand to produce letters in shining replica of the fonts he'd found in a large, musty book in his parents' suburban garage. The experiments themselves were often abstract in nature: "The Effects of Weather on the Mood of Ms. Kalsie's Third Grade" (age eight), "The Behaviors of Songbirds in the Presence of Different Members of My Family" (age ten).

Thomas tracked instances of laughter and found that the females in Ms. Kalsie's third grade experienced a twelve percent decrease in glee for recess during periods of rain, while the same cold months saw a thirty-one percent decline in male enjoyment. He hid a tape recorder in the trees of the backyard and made his brother, mother, and father sit outside alone on rotation in the afternoons, and reported that the robins seemed *far* less likely to croon with his brother Jarrod around. "The birds just don't find Jarrod inspiring or deserving," he explained to his family. "It's science."

Throughout childhood and into adolescence, Thomas approached most human interactions imagining himself as the scientist studying them. He found many rituals strange, so he absorbed the information carefully, tried to map precisely what the different kinds of burning silences his father sent towards his mother at the dinner table meant. Two beats of quiet—*one Mississippi, two Mississippi*—after she laughed, for instance, meant "not funny," while three beats after she'd told a story meant "not important." At junior high, he watched the patterns of body language in both sexes and came to find their predictability amusing: a girl, when approached by a boy considered attractive, almost infallibly placed a thumb in her jeans belt loop and tucked her hair behind her ear.

Thomas had understood perfectly well what was to occur to him around age twelve, had acquired a comprehensive education on the matter, and he handled the changes with poise, keeping track of the increasing amount of pubic hair in a small graph paper journal, monitoring his armpits and applying deodorant as required.

It was sometime after these shifts assailed him, around his fifteenth birthday, that his attitude changed. He no longer enjoyed watching the patterns unfold, found no pleasure in sensing the exact moment during his mother's banter in which his father's eyes would glaze over, the certain phrase of his father's Jarrod would cull to mock. Not only had he stopped relishing the fulfillment of his speculations, but also every time he was correct, he felt guilty, as though his having foreseen a bitter response or cold glare was the same as having extended one.

He had turned out rather sparkly-eyed and broad-chested and naturally athletic, and it was no relief. He couldn't help but excel at basketball—he felt the intricacies and translated them to his body—but the smells and sounds of it, the squeal of rubber soles on the court and the rough talk between teammates in the locker room afterward, felt like a long life in prison. He would go home and put on Billie Holiday and press his improbably clear teenage skin to his pillow and weep. But soon he would rise and go to his desk, where the sharpened pencils lay arranged by length, and put one to paper. The thought of his tears muddling a line he'd pulled at so carefully disturbed him, and that formed the pattern of his next seventeen years, work chasing away any excess of feeling like a car that sends deer leaping back into the green.

THE BOILER IN THE BASEMENT, ancient and tall and dust-covered, gave its last hiss early one mid-January morning. Sometimes Adeleine grew so absorbed by the story of Miriam's life, her perfect cursive and the talk of dinner parties and operas, that she forgot to eat. Slim and forever sensitive to the cold, she became more so on these forgotten afternoons, so the first day without heat she could only understand the chill as a failure of her own body. The thermostat, mounted on the yellowed wall of Edith's living room and typically kept at a sturdy sixty-five degrees, crept backward into the evening. The snow outside piled on and obscured bushes, trash cans, bicycles, until they looked only like suggestions, nebulous shapes drawn by small children.

Distracted by a young Miriam's description of her son's first Christmas, the escalators in the department stores and how she accidentally forgot him under a rack of red felt coats, Adeleine put on another pair of wool socks and finally crawled into bed after fetching an extra quilt and afghan from the overflowing linen cabinet. She never had guests but always vaguely expected them, kept piles of folded warmth clean and ready, and when she slept that night, she dreamt of arrivals, doors opened and ready, mouths kissed and embraces shared.

At 2:15 she woke from shivering and saw her breath in clouds around her, the multiplied snow out the window through the thin ancient glass. She crossed into the living room and stood below the heating vents, spread her hands and finally realized. Her teeth clattered as she moved across the hall, and she knocked more loudly than she'd expected. As the creak of his mattress and lean rhythm of his gait sounded, she was surprised to find that the tremor the cold made in her body was nearly equaled by the thrill of his approach. When he answered, his face admitted a struggle: in opening the door with his good hand the blanket he'd wrapped around himself had slipped.

"Come here," he said, wit and effort gone from his speech. She understood he was as glad to offer his body heat as she was to take it, and pressed into his shoulder a while before they spoke.

"I called her at six and knocked at nine—no answer. I think she was exhausted after that visit from her son—she's finally catching up on sleep. Probably she accidentally nudged the tab on the thermostat in a hurry to lock the door." His speculative optimism was like that of a mother attempting to diminish her own worry.

"Either that or she was scheming up a way to finally get us in bed together."

His startled laughter at her bold joke lasted a while, and then she followed him through his apartment—bereft of life's clutter, gleaming, dusted—into his bed. The whole night, they practiced various combinations, linking their bodies at an endless series of points. They were too cold and tired for anything but this, though still she felt briefly the stutter from between his legs. When the sun rose glacial and early, they absorbed the suggestion of it as filtered through four layers of blankets, but didn't move to watch it. She never released his limp left hand.

Midmorning he grunted, spoke directly into Adeleine's skin: "All right, enough. I'm going to find her."

THOMAS KNOCKED with the volume of a man with a full body: nothing. He pressed his head, lightly, to the doorframe, and wished angrily to return to thirty-six hours before, when the situation hadn't yet demanded he assume a position of competence. Or eight hours before, in the locked position with Adeleine, the moment so flawlessly lit and enfolded he believed he could bear the chill forever. The prospect of what might happen next exhausted him, brought a leaden weight, and he leaned still more heavily on Edith's door.

It opened, had been unlocked all along.

He found her in the bedroom, hands tightly clasped in her lap, sitting in an unevenly stuffed armchair, covered minimally by a cocktail dress, which, he realized with dread, he could smell: the odor, like the damp underside of rotted wood, rushed in and out of his nostrils. Its blue lace, variously faded, held a raised system of wrinkles, and from under it came forth a jagged spray of tulle. The back, undone, struggled to remain on the shoulders, and her flesh fell slack, in lumps, to the root of the zipper.

"Oh! I've been waiting for you," she said with a choked warmth, as though practicing words recently acquired in a foreign language, emphasizing syllables arbitrarily. "A little chilly for summer, huh!"

Thomas moved closer, aware of his irregular heartbeat.

"Dear," she said. "It's about time we make it to the market, or they'll be out of the things you like."

He finally understood, with an uneasiness that made his ears ring, how lost she was. Thomas crouched down and began to speak, articulating each sound.

"Edith." She leaned forward and clutched her elbow around his neck, placed a tremor-ridden hand on his cheek.

"I knew you were just down the street the whole time—"

"Edith."

"And I *said* that to June, but she said, 'Oh, probably out carousing again, charming the world and leaving his own house empty.' *Long distance* she calls to say!"

"*Edith!*"

He put his arms around her and whispered the facts in her ear—"It's me, Thomas, I live upstairs, it's Thomas from upstairs, you're Edith and we drink tea together sometimes on my sofa by the window, I ask you about your life, Declan isn't here anymore but I am, it's me Thomas"—and continued in spite of her warbling, gripped the limp, gelid skin, the bones of her shoulders, tried with every portion of available energy to focus. Finally, she stilled and looked up at him, horrified, as though surveying a car she'd just crashed from the driver's seat. On her nightstand was a dingy legal pad, open to a blank page, and a sponge and some keys; around her feet were a series of shoes, a lone violet heel, vinyl yellow rain boots, braided leather sandals. He pulled a faded rose blanket from her unmade bed and wrapped it around her.

I N THE DAYS THAT FOLLOWED, Edith arranged for the boiler's
quick repair, and asked Thomas not to phone her son, though
he assured her it had never been his intention. She apologized
recursively for the "incident," as she liked to refer to it—her language for catastrophe made mild by the era she'd come of age
in—and branded it a onetime slip, simply the product of too
much time on her hands. Indeed, she seemed, in some ways,
renewed; she moved with new agency and a brand-new hot-pink
feather duster, lifted vases and pots to get at their other angles.
But he sensed an uptick in her speech and body that nagged at
him: where was the slowness about her that had so comforted
him before? One afternoon she put on a Bobby Darin record and
insisted on dancing. The formal pose of the waltz was stiff and
foreign to his body, but familiar as a prized memory on her light
hands and proud back. Her eyes traveled with unfocused brightness as she pressed herself closer.

When that shark bites, with his teeth, babe.

"Oh you," she murmured. "Let's make a party!"

T HE NIGHT EDITH HAD WONDERED blithely about Declan's whereabouts and the heat had fled the building like a reluctant visitor, Edward had taken a rare stroll in Manhattan, determined to find the city that had once embraced him, and ended up on an old friend's doorstep. He and Martin had told stale stories and drank most of a fifth of whiskey, and Martin insisted, in a maudlin show of brotherhood, that Edward sleep on the couch. So Edward had not been there when his neighbor came to the door in his Santa-red full-body pajama suit with buttons up the back, at which point Paulie had called his sister, who had not answered. Paulie then set to fort building, hanging blankets over couches and tables and layering pillows on cushions, and told himself out loud not to worry. The winter moonlight that managed to slip into his creation was a wonder, and the fact he'd managed to construct himself any kind of new home had cheered him, but it hadn't been enough.

In the hospital six hours later, Claudia hung from her chair with guilt and told her husband, Drew—who had offered brightly that pneumonia fatalities were nearly nonexistent in the Western world—to go fuck off to the vending machines. At Paulie's side she followed panicked thoughts in circles until she settled, after a long exhale, on a conclusion: Paulie would live with them, and if her husband didn't like that, she would move in with Paulie.

Drew, whom she'd met and married within the dim year that followed Seymour's death, had told her he wanted to be her family. Slowly, with a feeling like coming home and realizing she'd been robbed, she had understood that he meant: *me, and no one else.* He treated her brother like a feral animal, cautiously tousling Paulie's hair and then hurrying to the bathroom to scrub his hands. They had eloped at a rambling Victorian resort that straddled the Catskills, sat out on rocking chairs that faced the lake and giggled with the splashes of oversized trout who seemed haughty and bored by performing. "Do you see how simple things can be?" he had said.

Underfed and sleep-deprived in the hospital, Claudia began to picture the elaborate dinners she would cook Paulie: pork chops with apricots and red wine vinegar, fried chicken with orange zest batter, salads with Brie and spinach washed in the coldest, cleanest water. Looking down at the perforated plastic bracelet on his wrist, the paper gown, she thought of his tendency to eat with slapdash enthusiasm, food ending up in his eyebrows and hair, and she began to cry with such force that several nurses gathered in the backlit doorway to watch her body refill and empty. She passed the rest of the morning like that, and when she finally rose, fastening her hair at the nape of her neck, the shadows on the bleach-scented tiles were lengthening rapidly, trying to reach something up ahead. "I'll be back so soon," she whispered to Paulie, who napped with a hand placed demurely on his cheek, as if hosting a tea or judging a dog show.

She found Drew in the cafeteria, where a few nurses took mid-shift breaks, bringing cartons of orange juice to their lips with gold-ringed hands and tapping at their phones with artificial nails.

"Hi!" he said, rising from the plastic table, his arms spread to catch her. "Are we ready to go?"

She sat and he followed. She put one hand on his and another over her eyes.

"It depends on who you mean when you say 'we.'"

"Oh. Well, how much longer do they need to keep him?"

"Oh! Well! I guess I'm not only talking about *today*, Drew." She had meant to conserve her anger, spread it as a foundation, but instead she had shown herself immediately.

"What is it now, Claudia? Huh? I came here with you, I held your hand, I waited here in this godforsaken cafeteria—"

"I need to be with him—"

"And he's going to be fine, as I said he would. Very soon he'll be calling you at all hours again to read you the weather report—"

"We need to find a bigger place, one where we can all be comfortable."

"And then what, Claudia? And then you spend the rest of your life, *our* life, mothering your older brother? How do I fit in there? How about kids? What will you do when our children need help at the same time he does?"

"This isn't a choice. Some decisions are made for you. This one was made a long time ago. You knew this when we met."

"Claudia, when we met, you had your therapist on speed dial and a pharmacy of anti-everythings in your purse. How was I supposed to rank your priorities in the middle of all that?"

"I'll be at my brother's house if you need me."

Drew worked his jaw and brought the heel of his hand to the table, the thud of the impact quickly drowned by the industrial hum of the room, the commercial refrigerators' whir and the soft ticks of the row of neon soda machines. As Claudia turned onto the wide hallway, the floors so clean they reflected the recessed lighting and passing gurneys, she felt as she had when exiting an important exam, the answers, wrong or right, left behind in the room where she'd decided them.

E DITH PUT UP the invitations soundlessly and happily early in the morning, despite the stairs feeling somehow longer and taller, and recurring episodic flashes of the train station in hyper-color, and waking as she had today into questions of *why* and *how*. It took her most of a minute, sometimes, after gaining consciousness, to name all the objects in her room, and she did so ritually: *Bed. Tongue. Lamp. Window. Fingers, lily plant, blood pressure pills, black-and-white photograph of Jenny on a bicycle.*

Armed with tobacco-yellow Scotch tape and a quiet feeling of use, Edith approached each of her tenants' doors and eagerly pressed her thumb against the aged adhesive. She had decorated the lilac envelopes with stamps she'd found in the hall closet, a space cluttered with Declan's tools and odd minutiae that remembered her children: Jenny's beloved watercolor set, most ovals of color now craters that revealed white plastic bottoms; a rigid wooden archery kit, the green felt pouch and birch arrows, Owen had saved up to buy.

The inkpad had sprung back to life once she'd added a little water, which pleased her disproportionately, and the designs of the rubber appeared in clear and perfect reproduction. One, dating from the early sixties, said *Friends!* in a bubbly font—her daughter had pressed this on letters in middle school—and another featured a heart made of curling ribbons. This she had favored on Valentine's Day, on which she had, for years, composed a rhyming poem for Jenny and for Owen and for Declan.

She'd been so thrilled to find them that she had stamped away to excess; *Friends!* appeared in no discernible pattern all over the purple trappings, and the hearts, which she'd meant to form a border around the edges, ended up glomming together and resembling an overgrown vine. Inside she had stuffed the invitations, written in her once-perfect calligraphy and angling upward as they moved across the page.

A Party!
You are formally invited
to an evening of
food, dance, and play
at Edith's
(Landlord and Friend!)
Tomorrow
At Seven O'Clock

Edward was the first to find one, having woken uncharacteristically early and pulled on ratty, de-elasticized sweatpants in which he imagined he might exercise. He frowned at the note and left it hanging askew, but the uneasy slant of it came back to him on his jog, as he panted up hills, trying to locate some version of his body that was clear and refined. He clucked his tongue as he approached his door afterward, and realized, with the astonishment of someone recovering a long-shrouded memory, he would be attending. He remembered her arms roped around his neck, and he knew.

PAULIE, WHO HEARD EDWARD return and popped out to greet him, was next. He adored formal invitations of any kind and quickly attached it to his refrigerator with a saxophone-shaped magnet. He fingered the two objects, looked proudly at the life they represented, and called Claudia at work: Would she come? Did she think there would be punch? How exactly was punch made anyway—with fists or what?

Adeleine and Thomas, who had slept next to each other most nights since the first, opened her envelope together. Thomas's expression moved from heartened to concerned, still marked as he was by the sight of Edith lost in another life's dress. Adeleine began to feel nervous at even the prospect of a social gathering and closed her eyes.

"What is it?" he asked, then felt the patronizing potential; he knew full well what it was, could guess at how long it had been since she'd spent time outside her trinket-filled seclusion. But then she looked at him with newly scavenged poise, and bit down on her cheeks in mock anguish.

"And what will the recluse wear to her first outing in months?" she asked. "Sequins? Fur? Tinfoil?" He was touched by her humorous handling of her condition, and felt a small hope bob in his throat: if she could laugh about it, maybe the task of wrangling it was possible, and near.

THE AFTERNOON OF THE PARTY, Edith wrestled with the paper streamers she'd found in the closet. The meeting of the crepe, stiff with age, and her fingers, less agile by the day, made for a difficult task. Her initial plan, a network of twists and turns that would crown the apartment, was forgotten in favor of more simple designs: she wrapped paper around the bowls that held appetizers, hung it in vertical strips from the windowsills, formed an X on the bathroom door. She imagined herself making an "X marks the spot" joke to a warm reception, pouring drinks and recounting anecdotes in equal measure, as Declan had always done. As she set out various bottles of liquor her husband had left behind, most of them untouched since his death, Edith remembered the parties they'd held decades ago: her daughter skirting her ankles; her son carrying trays as though they were frangible artifacts; Declan always changing the record, hunting the perfect song for the moment; their guests, couples arm in arm, the men and women dividing more and more throughout the evening to talk about their spouses; the few people still single, a little more tipsy and loud, reminding those married of what they'd given up and gained; the phone calls to babysitters, requesting another hour; the good-bye of the last guest; the cleanup of stray peanut shells, half-drunk cocktails hiding in the bathroom, on windowsills, the beds of potted plants. How she and Declan held each other those nights after the parties, proud of their lives, how in the morning they laughed through their headaches, retelling the night before, asking each other, *I said* that?

IT WAS PAULIE who ultimately convinced Edward to come. "You know I love being friends, Eddy," he said, leaning against the hallway in a neon-green sweat suit belted by a strip of bright blue pleather that held a pair of drumsticks, "but maybe you could use some more!" Paulie had reached out and touched the tip of a drumstick to Edward's nose, and it was in that repulsed moment he flinched and agreed.

Upstairs, Thomas reasoned with Adeleine, who had become skittish again, had begun taking things off shelves, souvenir pennies and brittle bonsai trees, and setting them elsewhere.

"You won't even be leaving the building. If you start to feel like screaming, all you have to do is walk out the door and up two flights of steps."

After a time she nodded and moved to her closet, where she stood vacant and inert, as though waiting for a late train.

Three blocks away, Claudia took privacy in the bathroom, a small space made smaller by the clutter of scented creams and violet sprays and aromatic candles that clung to every surface, and began to compile the essentials in a shoe box she would take to Paulie's. She tried to ignore the leaden steps of her husband, who had hardly spoken to her since the hospital, and had walked around agape as she packed her things. "Whatever it is you're telling yourself about me," he had said in their darkened bedroom the night before, "you can't edit out how much I wanted a life with you." Claudia hadn't contested this, and it was the last thing she'd heard before falling asleep.

She wound her hair in the bun she wore to work, nursed wispy flyaways into cooperation, and thought about the coming evening. That night, she was sure, she would corner Edith, puff up her chest, demand a change in the management of the building. The bar of light above the mirror buzzed softly, as though listening, considering the holes in her argument.

THE EVENT BEGAN with a great deal of circling, a recurrent rearrangement of positions that would have looked, from above, like a natural disaster drill. Paulie, too excited for his own good, bounced between dusty walls and gray windows, from Edward to Edith to Claudia. Music was his idea: watching Adeleine, who wasn't speaking, and Edward, who was never more than a foot away from the crumbling crackers Edith had set out, Paulie thought everyone could use a song. He sprang laterally to the shelf where Edith kept her records and tried to control his excitement while he touched them, these things that breathed music in their rare way. Once he made his selection, he requested Edward's help, knowing that the compelling alien arm might prove beyond his grasp. He had never touched one, though he had watched his mother, in her melancholy floating moods, get up from the couch where she sat with feet tucked, reading, flip the record and realign the needle with an accuracy and control he envied so much that he had felt starved.

Edward sighed and narrowed his eyes. "Did you *ask* her?"

"Well no, but—I promise!"

Paulie held up *The Muppet Movie* soundtrack and Edward groaned, covered his face with a hairy hand and peered at him through two fingers. He gave a lackluster rendition of Miss Piggy's trademark *Hi-YA!*, and Edward removed the perfect black circle from its sleeve, paused to secretly covet the soft colors of the album cover. Time had faded the pastels of Kermit and Miss Piggy, in a rowboat under a rainbow, supported by clouds and the suggestion of water. Edward had loved this record, and he held his breath as it opened and broadened: that familiar precipitous static, the first notes of "Rainbow Connection." Paulie, the self-appointed minstrel of all things gleeful and airy, approached Adeleine with a mock-solemn pout. He bowed modestly and stretched out his hand. Thomas, trying not to laugh at the visible contraction of Adeleine's frame, gave her a squeeze on the shoulder.

As it turned out, Adeleine was a practiced dancer, confident even with her eyes closed. She moved without hesitation, understood the relationship between the music and the body, allowed no delay between the first and the second. The rest of them watched as she and Paulie twirled and retreated. Thomas felt a loosening warmth, and when the song ended, he welcomed her return with an embrace that betrayed his longing. Claudia, sitting in the corner with a Vodka Collins—the viscous mix, she suspected, long expired—seemed more confident each moment of every tenant's insanity, and returned the winks that Paulie, in a powder-blue tuxedo he had worn to a family wedding, kept sending her.

Edith, feeling girlish and opened as she never was in her memory, sidled up to Paulie's sister and kissed her, wetly, on the cheek. "Move over, Muffin!" she said, settling on the couch, adjusting her knees and hips. Claudia, shocked and curious in equal measure, examined the source of the sticky saliva: she saw the slow turn and aim of the eyes, noted the misaligned buttons of the stiff shirt, and saw this was a woman with a rapidly receding grasp. Suddenly empowered by a feeling of goodwill and forgiveness, she took the gnarled hand and brought it into hers. "Declan and I just love a party," said Edith, and Claudia nodded. She could hear but not see Paulie laughing. "Thank you for giving us this," she said. "Edith."

IN THE END, everyone drank enough to see double, except Paulie, who had altered his vision anyway with a pair of tortoiseshell prescription glasses found in a kitchen drawer. The light appeared to hold all the bits of old life unsettled and suspended by their dancing, so that a haze hung over the new circles of movement. Claudia and Edward sat on the musty couch making cruel fun of each other—his sullied sweatpants, her giant purse—before solidifying their bond and moving on to the ridicule of the others. Paulie taught Edith a dance he'd invented called The Slimiest Worm!, and Adeleine sang with the songs coming from the stereo and eventually, in a momentous impulse, fetched her guitar from upstairs and led them all in a sing-along, her thumb and index and middle fingers tugging gently and confidently at the steel, as though beckoning someone shy closer. Thomas drew caricatures of everyone with his right hand—which was more talented than he believed—and taped them to their backs. Edith disappeared into her bedroom for a while and cried until she forgot why, exactly, and emerged wearing an enormous Sunday-at-church type hat, a monstrosity ringed by swirls of gauze that resembled a naive rendering of Saturn. Edward insisted on trying it on, and affecting a smug New England tone, dragging out his syllables. "I come from a long line of honorable Protestant people with sticks far up their anuses," he said. "And as it happens, my family has culled those sticks over the years to build a lovely summer home on the Cape!" Claudia's fingers dug into his wrists, begging that he continue to delight her. In that untouched space of four and a half hours, no one missed them and none of them missed anyone, and the sun went down and the streetlamps went on, and the phone never rang.

E DITH'S SON APPEARED again the next weekend, emerged
from a taxi and paid the driver with pieces thumbed off the
thick fold of his wallet, and soon there were men in the building,
barrel-chested figures who took stairs two at a time and measured everything and nodded at Owen's every word. Despite the
gray of his hair and the wrinkles near his eyes, he moved through
the space with the spry authority of someone young in the world.
He pointed an arm in one direction and all the men followed,
retrieved tools from their belts and pens from their breast pockets. He leapt towards points of interest and they mirrored
him, pushing their faces close to imperfections in walls and door-
frames and grunting, bringing stubby pencils across notepads the
size of their hands.

Once an hour Edith surfaced, called to them where they
spoke with their hands on their hips in front of a crack in the
plaster or raised board. "What kind of people are you? Can you
not hear me? I own this place! Stop!" she said, and more quietly,
"Who are you. How could this have—Declan will—"

At first they looked back, but after several episodes they
didn't turn at all from where they trailed Owen, quoting figures,
running their hands over the banisters. "Mother," Owen said,
when she stationed herself halfway between the first and second

floors, sitting with one arm against the wall and the other against a spindle, and keened.

"You need your rest." He went to her and sat a step below, so that her face was above his, and he looked up. The blood vessels in his eyes branched violently, and he appeared, briefly, like a beggar not yet desensitized to the act of asking, extending a cup and saying, *anything.*

"I'll rest when it's safe," she rasped, and pounded the flat of her palm on the warped line of the stair.

W HEN IT FINALLY HAPPENED WITH HER, it felt to Thomas so circumstantial that he mentally thanked every minuscule factor involved—the plants for needing tending just then, the finicky shower for only supplying hot water in the afternoon. They had been sharing a bed, arranging their bodies together intricately, but still he didn't know the clear shape of her, had never seen her bare hipbones or tasted her saliva or speculated about the likeness of a birthmark to a comet.

She opened the door in a towel, her nose and cheeks scrubbed and red, her hair wet and thoroughly unconsidered, the whole of her bold and undone as he had never before witnessed. The curtains, as always, were drawn, but the windows let in a breeze, and the bits of moisture that remained on her shoulders trembled. She didn't linger in greeting him but returned to the united voices of a Carter Family record, sang along as she traced the room's borders with a red tin watering can, checking the hidden angles of the plants, turning leaves gently to find and nurture any fading green. The precision of her hands, the slow path to gold that her hair waged as it lost water and gained light, compelled him to kiss her.

In an action he later classified as specifically unlike himself, Thomas removed the can from her hands, felt the heavy thud of water against its sides as he placed it on the windowsill, unfastened the towel from its tenuous grasp on her body, and began to move the rough cotton over her head. At this she began to breathe differently, as though adjusting to a higher altitude and the vantage of familiar things made tiny.

In her bedroom he moved slowly, aware that a future version of himself wanted to remember this. He showed her where and how to lie, tried to cover as much of her skin as possible with his mouth, placed his working hand beneath her chin and tilted it once in a while to make sure she knew he was looking at her. Naked with another person for the first time since the change to his body, Thomas listened to himself carefully. He discovered that the inability of his left side lent an urgent creativity to the act, that leaning into her from his good side left him humming. Magnified and daubed with the glow of sweat, the colors of her grew vivid, and he saw finally that under the champagne and brown of her hair was the suggestion of red, that her shoulders retained a secret smattering of ripe, peach-hued freckles. Her hips accommodated his movements with a slight delay and a buck, each of them an assent, a continued urging.

After, she examined him, the soft tufts of armpit hair and his jagged collarbone, with a laugh in her throat and her pupils dilated.

"Where did you come from?" she said, her head on his bare chest.

"I'm a private investigator," he said, and formed a monocle with his thumb and forefinger. "Came to find you."

They laughed a little at his meager, placid joke, at the assured banter the situation had temporarily afforded. The sliding shadow of a passing car appeared on the wall and advanced over them. After a while she sat up, her elbows locked and hands splayed, and scanned her bedroom rapidly, as though expecting to find it rearranged.

P AULIE FELT BADLY FOR CLAUDIA, all crumpled on the couch for weeks on end. He wanted to help, didn't always understand, knew that. Seeing her like that left him electric in the bad way, opening all the cupboards and closing them, throwing the pillows off his bed and then placing them back, running his hands under the hottest water he could stand. He had no idea what it was like to be her and didn't know if this meant his love was insufficient. Once, when she came back from work and said it'd been a rough day, he started doing jumping jacks, told her to try, thought the funny waggling of the body could help, and she started to cry. He was confused and so he just kept going, faster and faster, and she wept harder, sounding out like a whale across a dark ocean.

She was staying with Paulie for the time being, she said. To take care of him. Also because she and Drew were fighting. Paulie asked why.

"Are you mad because in the morning he doesn't ask you what your dreams are like or tell you about his?

"Does he forget to call at lunch?

"Does he talk over the ends of your sentences?

"Does he not take you to the zoo enough?"

"Some of that."

Paulie could see her face doing an impression of a smile.

"He definitely does not take me to the zoo enough."

At this, Paulie grabbed the head of lettuce that was sitting out for the dinner Claudia hadn't yet started to prepare and got down on one knee. He held up the bouquet.

"Claudia, I've wanted to ask for a long time. Will you come with me to the zoo?"

Her head bowed in assent, then connected with the fan of green, the cool droplets of the water on its outer leaves attaching to her eyelids.

"I can't hear you, lettuce head. Are you trying to get back into the ground or what?"

He remembered the end of a joke then, one that begins when a refrigerator door opens: "Lettuce alone! Lettuce alone!"

Claudia pushed her face deeper.

"Lettuce alone!"

Between moments spent wrapped around Adeleine, Thomas sat with Edith and tried to believe or recognize her. He moved like something deflating down the stairs, then rapped with the tops of his knuckles, breath held, hoping that she wouldn't be home, would be out shopping with her old creaky bustle of efficiency.

Most days, she sat at her kitchen table, hands firmly planted on the soiled tablecloth, and spoke in platitudes. Nowhere was the nodding or eye fluttering that had meant her thorough listening, the careful gathering of information that had made him feel seen.

Thomas spoke to her at length, described the strange relationship that had grown up around himself and Adeleine—thick and ragged, hard to see out of—and how much time they spent together but how little they spoke of their lives before. He wanted Edith to cast a suspect glance in his direction, to get up and fiddle with something as she picked out her thoughts, but she only said, "Oh, wonderful! Marvelous! Very, very good."

Thomas tried gently to explore the topic of her children, whom she'd mentioned only in the past tense, and her mouth became a strictly measured line.

"My daughter," she said, and waved her hand above her head like *poof.*

"Dead?"

Her head wobbled in what seemed neither confirmation nor dissent.

"And Owen?"

"Can't be bothered. Very, very busy."

He tabled the issue, but it ate at him, the thought of their desertion in her decline, of Owen surfacing just to shelve her in some facility, and his idea of Edith's past life acquired an unsettling tinge he grew afraid to address. What kind of children had they been, to leave her so completely, and what kind of mother had she been, to let them go?

Thomas grew determined to engage her in some new way. He took out the media of color and shadow late one night, unlocked and removed and wondered at the paints and the bristles and charcoal nubs spread out wide. He would make Edith feel like an agent of her body and brain again, show her what it was to look back at your own effort. Perhaps, he thought wistfully, caught up in the dusted-cocoa smell of a sable brush, he would remember his own relationship with production, find the lesson there. Could the wisdom he'd acquired from all those years of making really have vanished with the abilities of his left forearm and long fingers, like an ex-lover who vows never to speak to a certain chapter of her past?

A year and five months had passed since the stroke had entered him and left him changed, and nearly as long since the days he shoved so much of his life into closets: limp rolls of unstretched canvas, folding cotton cases of pencils, a wooden box of acrylics covered in half-inch tests of blues and grays. Thomas had not told anyone what he was doing, suspecting they would protest and intervene, and so he'd strained to carry the boxes of rulers and pastels and oils, the bouquets of pencils short and long, the paintbrushes of varying thicknesses, and shoved them in whichever way he could manage, sometimes with his temple, sometimes with the arch of his back. He had collapsed, damp, on the floor, admired the smooth lines of the hardwood planks leading out and away.

So much later, used to the quiet of a space free of clutter, when he finally released the doors of cabinets and closets, he held his breath for the inevitable tumble and crash. But the instruments, pressed together so long, came out shyly, adjusting to the newly available space with small sounds, like the creaking of frosted branches, the meeting of utensils over a plate.

The brown paper grocery bag, which Thomas cradled with his arm and chin as he descended the stairs, held a modest sampling: a watercolor set he'd never used (he thought Edith might like to just see colors bleed into each other), a set of crayon-pastel hybrids whose smears always felt forgiving, some glue to accompany a number of rice paper scraps of emerald green and pink and cyan he couldn't remember acquiring. Feeling confident and duplicitous both, Thomas strode purposefully into Edith's increasingly chaotic space and set the bag down on the tablecloth, which still held stains from the party, clouds of oil that had spread and set.

"Edith!" he said, grinning. "It's art day!"

As he'd hoped, she blinked but believed readily, and brought her palms together as in prayer.

"Oh my: oh my oh my oh my."

Edith's hand gripped the brushes and sticks as though she had limited experience in manipulating objects towards her will, her fingers curled but not tensed, so he coaxed them. She would get distracted by a blue once she picked up a gray—her focus broad, as though surveying an ocean—so he asked her to tell him the story of each. And what is that one doing? Where have you seen that green before? What will that orange become?

Edith liked this very much: at least it kept her pressing on the paper, at least it kept her talking. But then he took it too far. And what will they all do together, that washed blue and that sharp emerald and that ripened yellow? Edith halted her shaky but expanding line and looked down at the page as if it were inaccessible, a codified to-do list written by someone else.

"Dear?" she said. "I'm tired, now."

Thomas suggested that he help. He wrapped his right hand over hers. He looked at the lines she'd put on the page and simply went about solidifying them, feeling the familiar movement of his wrist as he matched curve for curve, created thicknesses of hues that scored the thin paper. He did not see how she leaned in, how her eyes grew wet as she reached for a dangling memory, and they sat there like that, orbiting each other.

B ECAUSE HE HAD A DIFFICULT TIME looking right at him, or acknowledging the way Paulie made him feel, which was happy and panicked both, Edward started filming. Capturing Paulie in a frame, no less keeping him there, was a task Edward met with varying dedication. So often the footage took the pattern of Paulie on-screen, his bright and tiny teeth exposed and shining, his body forever batting like a moth to keep up with his wilderness of thoughts, and then the picture instantly as empty of him as it had been full. In one of Edward's first attempts, Paulie discussed Canada geese.

He's sitting on his kitchen counter, dangerously close to the plastic vase of fresh flowers Claudia places there each Monday, wearing a turquoise zip-up sweatshirt with the strings pulled taut so that the hood forms a circle of tension around his cheeks and chin. ("Like an Eskimo," he says earlier in the tape, when Edward asks about it, "with a new style.")

"They fall in love only one time, Eddy. These guys and gals are for keeps with their feelings. Once they know, they know. But if one of them goes away, and by that I mean dies, Ed, the other says, no way can I abide this"—here Paulie spreads his arms to indicate the wingspan of lone eternity that lies ahead, and the camera zooms out to reveal it—"and instead of staying with the gaggle, which is what their friend group is called, Ed, the sad goose flies alone for the rest of his life. He stops grooming so his feathers get to looking like monsters, he moves over all kinds of trees and lakes without ever getting to say, again, 'Hey, do you see that? Do you see how green that is?'"

Paulie lets the strings of his sweatshirt go slack; his face opens while he considers the gravity of this, and the camera hovers on his eyes and lips again. Then the great hole of his mouth flaps open and in a flash he's gone—"*What is that bug?*" yelled from just off-screen—and replaced by a peeling patch of paint. The camera, exhausted, remains in place while exclamations continue. There is, inevitably, a bang, a silence. Edward's sigh fills the sonic space. The film cuts.

Over weeks and then months, the cache of recorded bits of life accrued. Paulie in full color, making his way down their street in the first hints of spring, backpack so high it almost meets his head, stopping to crouch at chalky, budless flowerboxes and yelling, *"Hey in there, unborn motherfuckers!"* and the sound of Edward's sniggering at his influence on Paulie's vocabulary. Paulie in a quiet moment on the stoop, leafing through *Popular Science* with eyes wide: "Ed, do you think you could really trust something that reproduced with itself?" Paulie prone on Edward's visibly lumpy red cotton couch, asleep, one arm dangling off as though to exhibit his watch, the arms of which forever circle a miniature Aldrin and Armstrong taking a giant leap for mankind. Paulie on his thirty-third birthday, wearing a conic and glittering hat as well as the tie Claudia has fashioned him from streamers, standing at his keyboard, triumphant, hammering away.

Late at night, when he couldn't sleep, Edward let these play back, sometimes stopped to edit, trim a life down to its brightest core. Other nights he turned off all other sources of light, the standing lamp and the screen of his phone and the microwave display, and just watched.

B EFORE THOMAS HAD HEARD HER CRYING, he'd heard her
singing. He hadn't mentioned it when she had first begun
taking him in, reaching across his chest and squeezing as they
slept, but sometimes when she spoke to him it recalled the strain
of her voice, through the wall, reaching a note, of the guitar rising to meet it. Only two or three sung words had ever reached his
apartment from hers, few enough that they could have come from
the street, or a film played at a low volume somewhere in the
building.

He was curious, wanted to hear her, but there were so many
other unanswered questions—Who had she been before this?
What had driven her to a life so compacted?—and so he had not
asked her about the sounds, which trembled high and faded
slowly. Dustless old guitars, steel strings taut on smooth wood,
leaned here and there around her apartment, and he looked at
them with something akin to lust, knowing they'd interacted so
closely with the pulsing of her throat and the pursing of her
mouth.

After seeing her play and sing at Edith's party, he'd begun to
feel greedy. He wanted to experience that sound alone, watch
her long fingers curl and move up and down the neck, to hear her
voice without the interruptions of drunk people. So when he
found the bulging notebook wedged between the thick novels on

her nightstand, the careful lists in her inconsistent handwriting, he was hungrier than usual, less gentle, more insistent.

"Adeleine," he called to her where she stood in the kitchen, boiling water in a faded tin kettle and soaping some mugs. "What is this?"

If she was angry at the invasion of privacy, she didn't let on, save the way she tugged gently at her left ear. "Oh," she said. "Just songs." He urged her to go on, appearing behind her, gesturing in tight circles with his index and middle fingers, smiling slightly to relax her. She sighed and settled on a high kitchen stool covered in dark green, beaten leather.

"They're songs about the things I've found. I try to give each of them a story."

His eyes scanned some of the titles on the page.

Rolodex (red)

Photo (three children, one lawn chair, 1962)

Jar of Marbles (19)

Circus Music box (chimpanzee and bicycle)

Beneath them were lyrics in her tight, variously spiked hand, many words crossed out.

"Are you trying to tell me you've written songs for all the objects in your house?"

"Not quite all of them."

And then, as though in defense of some weaker life form: "They deserve it."

Thomas sensed her resistance spreading and tried to remove the judgment from his voice. He wanted to find the noble aspect of her motivation, to justify it as she had. Where had she found them, he asked. Did she mean to repurpose them, or tell their original stories, or try to imagine the people who had owned them?

She dismissed him curtly, crossed one knee over the other and glanced somewhere over his left shoulder. "It's intimate."

He wondered in blazing silence whether cradling her in her volatile sleep, pushing his tongue between her legs, holding down her hips while she came, did not quite meet that classification. He felt that the elasticity he'd afforded their relationship—to unfold without the usual expectations of reciprocity and honesty, to continue only under her exacting requirements in her cluttered apartment—had been a mistake. He angrily promised himself to stop giving her so much, but he still couldn't get up to leave.

In what he would come to understand as her concerted generosity, sometime after midnight she roused Thomas from her bed. It was late enough that little light came in from the street, and he could barely make out the strap of her guitar across her chest, the angle of her arms holding up objects that sent several teetering shadows. She brought light to the dusky mauve lampshade on her lace-covered side table and placed the items on the bed, kept her eyes low.

"Pick," she said.

Still fuzzy from the dream he'd just been having—Adeleine in a taupe cotton shift and rubber boots, backlit by pink sky, pointing at something far up in a tree, another in a series of fantasies he'd had of her outside—he selected an ivory comb. Her breathing was arrhythmic when she began, and her fingers flew between the strings quickly, like insects to sources of sugar. The song concerned the rituals of daily presentation, the careful grooming for an empty job that paid too little. She started into the next without being asked, briefly indicating the object before she began: a Polaroid showing the spectral spaces on a painted wall where framed photos had once hung, a broom leaning against a wall. The words she had composed in honor of it were quiet and kind, and they wondered: will the house remember us when we're gone?

When she stopped he removed the instrument from between them, caught her flushed face in his hands, mashed his nose against hers. As their eyelashes met briefly, he saw that she was proud, and he tried to determine if what he felt about her was pride. He wished he could see her behind the wheel of some long and gleaming American car, could watch the circle of leather spin under her hands as they made wide, elegant turns. He fell asleep teasing that want, following it to the image of Adeleine at some peeling picnic table, setting cheeses and apricots on little napkins, placing her hands at its edges and swinging her legs in, settling down on the bench and calling to him, insistent, eager.

THE THIN STRUCTURE of the building ensured that no sound was contained by the apartment that produced it: the three floors gave and received heavy-footed trips to the refrigerator and unsnoozed alarm clocks and the burst-and-whoosh of bath faucets and late-night infomercials in a reliable cycle. Living with the proof of other people's lone domestic movements had become a kind of comfort for the tenants, a telephone that didn't require they speak into it, a letter that didn't ask for a reply. Several bleak sunsets and seasonally ambiguous days into March, just after four in the morning, the sound of Edith in the stairwell bounced up and down, with increasing depth and urgency, until they all decided to meet it.

Paulie emerged first, in a blue terry cloth union suit with one back button undone, carrying the lamp shaped like a crescent moon with a cherubic face smiling from the center. He joined her where she sat, exactly halfway between the second and third floors, and plugged the light into the nearby outlet. Still waking from a dream of a doomed romance between a Labrador and a Roman candle—the dog catching the sparks in its mouth and yowling—Paulie did not ask her why she was crying, just laced his right hand's fingers in hers. Claudia, with her sixth sense concerning his whereabouts, appeared shortly after, having awoken to find him gone. She settled on the stair below them and

admired the way her curly-haired brother took naturally to the
care of others, considered in her half-sleep how strange it was
that she and her parents had spent exasperated lifetimes asking
Paulie to conform to the rest of the world.

"I don't want to go," Edith said. "I want to go home." Her voice
sounded like the decline of a music box, gasping but still percus-
sive. Edward, who had lain awake eavesdropping for a good ten
minutes before joining them, lingered with a palm on his doorframe, caught in a role familiar to him. He was saddened by the
proof of someone else's pain and embarrassed by the open acknowledgment of it: he had perfected the art of devising clever
ways to describe his inadequacies but felt like an unwelcome
guest around those who wanted to dissect their own. That night,
he knew it was wrong to remain there listening, so he washed his
face and clenched his body and ascended the stairs.

He stood over the three of them, feeling too large for an event
so delicate; Claudia, sensing his discomfort, tugged the sleeve of
his sweatshirt and urged him downward. Edith's sobs had paused
but her shaking continued, and Paulie, in a gesture Edward could
recognize as noble, continued to wipe at her face with his sleeve.

Thomas and Adeleine came last, floated down the stairs clasp-
ing hands, still groggy from the rich sleep of people new to sharing a bed. Dressed in cotton pajama sets in different shades of
blue and blinking rhythmically, they appeared somehow synthetic, like projections of slides or photorealist paintings. From
where they sat above her, Thomas made circles on Edith's back
with the palm of his hand, and Adeleine began to braid the scant

fluff of white hair behind her ears. Edward wondered when everyone had agreed upon such silence, and with a jerk like a quarter horse outside a bodega suddenly brought to motion, he narrowed his eyes and put a hand on the very tip of Edith's left foot. Edith's body continued to buck, though in incrementally smaller movements, and Paulie began to speak. He tried to whisper, to suit the hush of shame they all felt at their inability to reach her, but delicacy of volume was a skill he had never mastered.

"I think we all need to give our friend Edith something she can take back to bed with her," he said. "We are all going to say one thing we like about Edith. I'll start. *I* like how she lets these monster sounds out. Okay, Eddy, you go."

Edward had closed his eyes in the hope of disappearing, or encouraging Paulie's swift span of attention to move past him. His sweating feet caught the low light and glistened.

"Maybe you should hold my moon for help."

Edward opened his eyes and saw the glowing thing coming quickly, almost violently, towards his face. He received it as though it were covered in mold and held it with four tensed fingertips. "Oh god. Okay. One thing I like about Edith is that . . . is that she hasn't raised the rent in fourteen years."

Claudia gave a swift but robust pinch of Edward's ear and began. As she spoke, she focused her gaze on her brother. "I like how Edith appreciates all different kinds of people."

"I like the way Edith respects time," said Adeleine. "And also privacy."

Paulie nodded with violent enthusiasm, sending a bounce

through his hair. Thomas fixed his vision on Edward's awkward cradling of the lamp.

"The more I know of Edith, the more I like," he said, and bent and kissed the wilted skin of her cheek, which blanched, then tensed. Her closed eyes opened and she looked repeatedly from one face to another, blinking like a late-night traveler under the fluorescent lights of a gas station. "I'm so glad," Edith said, "you could make it." She brought up her hand and rotated it with some wonder. "It's so nice of you to come."

PAULIE REMEMBERED it like this: He was the only one not mad at his mother for leaving. He was the only one who told any good stories about where she was and why the phones there didn't work. He missed her too but it bothered him how his father and Claudia just sat around on the couch. It bored him terribly. Paulie didn't hate many things but he could say he did not like laziness and they just lay there. He was no good at doing all the kinds of housey things his mother had always done in her apron colored like the Fourth of July, and for a month Seymour and Claudia didn't bother. He had always liked the phrase "dust bunnies" until he started to see them around all the time. A trail of ants moved up a cupboard and became an angry parade on the counter.

They were too sad to clean the shower and Claudia's hair stuck to the walls in shapes like countries on maps. In the kitchen the area by the coffeemaker radiated long-set spills and raised crusts of grinds. Most of his shirts had several kinds of dinners on them and there was a smell like milk left out that followed him up and down the stairs.

He had been everyone's favorite at the hospital and the nurse said maybe he should work there and so had his mom grinning in the white gown in the white bed in the white room. He sang and sang. Seymour and Claudia asked him to please keep it quiet pal and so he went up to his mom and he sang soft but right into her mouth. *So that way it lives in there* he said. Her teeth didn't smell right. He kept expecting his mom to cry like everyone else but her face hardly ever changed, so he surprised her with his best impression of a Christmas tree. Arms spread to make a triangle with his head as the tip and eyes blinking on and off like lights. She used to love it but she had said *Paulie, Paulie, please stop honey, you look like an epileptic,* and that was the first time Seymour and Claudia laughed and he left and did the thing where he took off his shoes and slid down the shining tile in socks but it wasn't fun alone and the people in the rooms didn't have real clothes just the paper kind and the rooms didn't have any colored quilts and the whole vast hospital didn't have one place not one where you could talk loudly about how the bottom of the ocean felt or how the neighbor's baby with the starfish hands looked like he knew more than everyone not less or why some people needed their radios and TVs on while they slept. All that light and sound to protect them from what.

B ECAUSE EDWARD MISSED the cramped spaces and the accumulated smell of hundreds of comics sweating onstage, and because Paulie had been begging him, and because Edward saw this look in Claudia's eyes that was like searching for a missed turnoff in a rearview mirror, he began taking Paulie to the clubs where he used to perform. On the train the first time, Edward heard each breath he took, heard his heart's percussion magnified by a mocking echo, and without looking up at him took Paulie's freckled hand.

The first acute betrayal, a reminder of how far from his life he'd run, was the bouncer, a man he didn't recognize and who took long seconds sneering at their IDs.

They sat in the back, past the spill of spotlights. Though he hoped they would be there, Edward didn't want anyone from his old circle to see him, and he wore a slightly malformed baseball cap that spread shadows over his nose. Paulie took no hints, laughed at almost everything, ordered nachos from the waitresses that came around with sour looks and outdated hairdos, consumed them with such force Edward struggled to hear the punch lines over the crunching. He wasn't eating so much as pitching them in the general direction of his mouth, then letting his tongue and incisors go crazy trying to harangue them. Following the catch came a great deal of slurping, which did nothing to keep their profile low, and at one point Edward returned from the urinal to find that Paulie had ordered him two pints of beer in a giant glass boot.

Edward, who painfully remembered the abuse that flowed off the stage to hang viciously over all the little tables, felt concerned that his companion might become the butt of one of the comics' jokes, and attempted to hush him. But it was like Paulie float in some bubble of munificence, or exuded chemicals that inspired goodwill. Everyone seemed happy to have him there: the tourists in line whose photos he took happily when they asked, the waitresses who winked at him. Those comics who noticed the insane cackle coming from the back of the room acknowledged it jovially, sometimes saluted him as they crossed the room to leave.

During a droopy-elbowed comic's bit about boring marriage sex—"and I'm like one of those robot vacuums on toppa her, shoving into wherever I can"—Edward drifted off, towards memories of himself onstage during the pathetic denouement of his career, post-Helena, and imagined Paulie into the room, inserted him in the audience. He saw the kid right up front in the toxic orange shorts he loved, totally engaged by Edward's infrequent and deeply morose sentence, even at the set in which the only words he uttered were "Time. *Death. Time.* Death. Time. *Death.*"

Edward was smiling broadly at this, at the ridiculous juxtaposition, when the act finished, and he didn't even hear the moderate clapping, reemerging only when Paulie put his hand on his shoulder: "I knew it. I knew you still loved this!" Only then did Edward realize he'd been laughing, his eyes and nose wet from the lengthened pleasure.

B EFORE EDWARD and before the accident, Paulie had liked nothing more than going one floor up and watching Thomas in his world. Thomas had colors in small tubes and colors from thin pencils and colors from dusty jars. There were orangey reds and reddy blues and bluey greens. "Why go outside when I can see any color on the earth right here," Paulie liked to joke, and Thomas always made a happy sound at that. Nubbly strips of cloth lay on every surface and their job was to clean up extra color or to keep a pink from bleeding out of its place. There were gleaming scissors and six rusty tins of paintbrushes and crumbling half pastels like the stumps of a forest in miniature and leaves of paper that floated around marked with unfinished sketches like secret messages. Tacked to the wall were glossy full-color photos of outer space and sepia maps and intricate inky drawings of ships and black-and-white photos of women and men in friendly hats and maps of trains from all over the world, all layered over each other so that the wall was hidden. Paulie liked to ask Thomas about the images and Thomas would say they were all possibilities. Paulie started saying that, sometimes just to himself: *everything is a possibility.*

Before the accident Paulie had gone up most afternoons and sometimes handed Thomas the things he needed and tried not to breathe very loud and watched the pieces get bigger slowly and sometimes poured tall cool glasses of water and carried them across the room as if in religious procession. In Paulie's very favorite piece Thomas drew a whole life in figures that grew and then shrank. Every afternoon he watched. Egg zygote toddler kid teenager, all the way to a bent-over old man. It took four months and more kinds of whites and creams and blushing pinks than Paulie had ever seen in concert. The change from day to day was never obvious and that was what he liked so much about it. Even if he concentrated and stayed very quiet he couldn't see everything, only the tuft of hair or the underside of a foot that Thomas was shading. It made him feel that waiting meant more than how it felt in the moment, that little seconds often combined and became something of weight and worth.

When Thomas took breaks from making his marks he would clear a space on the kitchen table as if cleaning a window to see out of and spread out a lunch of celery pieces and carrots and dried fruit, everything small enough to hold in their hands, and they would eat. Thomas asked Paulie questions about music and said things like "I could hear you playing last night, and it sounded a little bit like seaweed moving in the ocean" or "It made me feel like making a mess." Paulie sometimes thought he loved Thomas more than anyone else, and it made him feel desperate and occasionally very quiet.

After the accident it was hard to know. Paulie saw him in the hall and Thomas explained that a stroke had done something to him. Paulie tried to hug him but Thomas felt like a dirty sponge slick with oil that wouldn't take anything he tried to give it. His body was hanging wrong and it scared Paulie to look at it.

Paulie would go up to Thomas's at the usual time but the door was always locked. He would do their usual knock that was just for them three little knocks plus scritchy-scratchy nails and then call out, "Tommy Tommy" but the sounds turned to ghosts in the hallway. Once or twice Thomas came to the door but didn't open it and said, "I'm sorry, pal, not today." Paulie wanted to say, "What about the seaweed, what about the music that feels like the right kind of mess, what about what you're building and what about lunch with friends?" But Thomas wouldn't even look through the milky peephole that changed the size of everyone outside.

In the afternoons when he missed Thomas he played music especially loud. He learned Randy Newman's "You've Got a Friend in Me," and he did that between four and six times a day. One night he got out the Christmas decorations Claudia had asked him to please leave in the closet for the rest of the year and he pulled out the string of white lights that pulsed. He brought them up to Thomas's floor and bunched them into a knot and put them in a big glass jar and plugged them in right next to his door. He thought Thomas would like how he had put everything bright in one place and tangled all of it together.

But nothing happened and even his ribs and teeth hurt, and Paulie asked Claudia, who said, "Friendships are more like oceans than rivers. There are high tides and low tides but not a steady rush. You're up against a lot of currents, not just one." Paulie was wordless at that, so Claudia said, "Sometimes people have a hard time looking out of themselves and need to just be alone and listen to all the conversations in their head."

He waited months. He felt proud and brave and thought: a number of currents, some unseen. Then one day he went up and knocked, and Thomas opened the door all the way and said, *Hey, pal*, and the crow's foot by his right eye did the crinkle Paulie remembered, and he invited him in.

The tin cans with the brushes reaching out like strong arms were gone, and the layers of maybes on the walls were gone, and there were no slips of paper anywhere, and not even one color where it didn't belong and not one idea growing. "Different, I know," Thomas had said, and shrugged in a way Paulie didn't recognize, and offered him tea. Paulie kept looking around the room for the easy way the two of them had been. He didn't go up after that and had to make loud noises when he thought of Thomas surrounded by all that white and said hi in the hallway but not much else. In dreams he still balanced glasses on his long fingers and floated towards the wilderness of colors, eager to cure his friend's thirst, to listen to the water slide down his fine throat.

A FTER TWO MONTHS of cloistered nights spent almost exclusively in her bed, surrounded by the encroaching assortment of archaic coin banks and cardigans embroidered with glass beads and shell-colored moth-eaten lampshades, Thomas prepared himself to broach the issue. It was, he decided, a matter of phrasing.

Do you ever get out of the house? was obvious on top of insensitive, he thought, but something that merely circled—*Do you prefer to stay home?*—was the kind of inquiry she would cleverly deflect. Her intelligence, unlike her sanity or income or background, was never in question.

In the end, he framed it as an announcement, took her face in his hand late at night in the dark and gave the words with guilt, as though returning something long borrowed to its rightful owner. "You never leave your apartment."

"That's true," Adeleine replied. "And you've got scars up and down your arms, ones I assume not placed there by the grace of God, or any accident except yourself."

Thomas had expected her to crumble at his examination, and the surprise of her competent reversal made him laugh.

"There's plenty," she said coldly, as if stabbing at a contract on a long, polished table, "that we haven't discussed. Did you think I didn't notice?" Instead of turning away, like he'd witnessed so often, Adeleine leaned over to switch on the golden light, then placed her excessively ringed hands on his shoulders.

"What would you like to tell me"—she ran her fingers down the scars—"about these?"

Her confidence had arrived without notice, and Thomas found the narrative he expected upended: she forged ahead on some mountain, beckoned him to hurry towards the view while he struggled with the bulk of what he'd carried.

"I haven't," he said, filled with quiet fear, "since you."

Adeleine remained above him, wiping at his eyes without fanfare, pulling the blanket closer around them. "Would it help," she said, "if I told you about me?"

THEY WATCHED the streetlamps going off, the doors on the street opening, the precision of morning sharpening the colors of leaves and fire hydrants. She explained to him about the perfectly placed pillows of psychoanalysts' couches, and pills of different colors meant to regulate a spiked range of crippling emotions: they had told her she was bipolar but not about the specific horrors that made up a life swinging between the two extremes. Not about the manic afternoons in which she would change her clothing sixteen times, or the sheer cliff of the other side of her condition, the slide into bed and the passing of hours there only indicated by the light's shift from gold to blue to black.

He wanted to know about before, the years preceding the saturation of lithium and various benzodiazepines, and she told him: about the tactical mechanics of waking up amid the belongings of someone months gone and in all likelihood deceased, and how afterward the Internet was filled with the pages he'd abandoned, the snapshots he'd taken of comical typos on deli signs, images of him laughing on stoops with a bottle of wine in one hand. The dissonance between the two, the manifold evidence of his life and the unrelenting fact of his absence, had become untenable to sift through anymore. Thirteen months after, finally gone from their apartment and in her own, armed with or destroyed by the new diagnosis, she still found herself looking for him whenever she left the house, and it was about that time, she told Thomas, that she began on her own kind of vanishing. It was then she began to pile up her nest of glittering curios and nonperishables, her angora sweaters and sundresses meant for extremes in weather she wouldn't see again, and about that time she stopped leaving.

A memory came to him, teasing at some understanding: his grandfather dying in a mustard armchair, his mother whispering to her sisters, "He's not eating, he won't eat," as though it were a political stance the old man had assumed with sudden conviction. In Adeleine's bed, remembering this, Thomas knew, then tried to un-know: that trying to lead her outside, talking to her of spring, was like his mother crouched by her father, a fork in her hand, convinced that if only she could sneak in a little food through the clamped line of his mouth, the slow drift of his eyes would sharpen. She had stayed there days on end, failing to discern his total inability, speaking to him of the herbed meat loaves she had brought, the tangy quiches and rhubarb pies.

THE NOTICES, affixed with double-sided tape at all four corners, were smoothed and aligned so precisely that they nearly eradicated the tenants' memories of the doors without them. It was Claudia, who had been unofficially living with Paulie for two months and four days, who saw them first. She slid down the door and remained there, leaning against it, unable to enter and tell her brother that she no longer knew what to do, that Edith had been the only landlord who hadn't grown alarmed by the possible liabilities of Paulie living in a place alone. That the best solution she had designed, so far, had been to sleep on his couch and wake with pillow lines on her face and try to do her best at work and entirely avoid the question of her husband, who had stated in too many ways tacit and then not that the care of her frenetic and disabled brother had not featured in their vows.

In these hamstrung moments, she remembered how their mother had looked when she thought no one was watching, how she had peered out the window, a dishcloth hanging from her slack hand, her mouth parted as if to speak out to another life, as if to say, *I could pack very quickly, I could be ready to go very soon.*

Upstairs, Thomas used the arch of his back to push his door open. He barely managed to hold the items he carried: a voice recorder, a fifth of Scotch, and four tiny oranges. The latter items were meant as gifts to persuade Adeleine into letting him use the first, and they sat tenuously, the clementines lolling in his palm and the sweating glass wedged between his forearm and chest. The fruit was first to hit the floor, their waxed skins revolving on the dusty wood as he read of his imminent eviction.

He felt sure he could not enter the only space she had and inform her that soon it would cease to be hers, and so he didn't; he placed the recorder and the Macallan on the floor, slid his fingers under the paper until it popped off: his door, then hers. It crossed his mind that by removing this piece of information in a minor way, he would need to excise it on a larger scale. He had two months. The thought settled and adjusted itself, scanning possible solutions, the question buzzing at his joints as he moved around his apartment, setting out ingredients for the simple meal that would fill him.

OVERNIGHT IT HAD TURNED to thick summer. The smells were large—chalky baked soil, barbecue smoke, discarded plastics, rush hour excess—and they squabbled and rivaled for dominance. Thomas and Claudia and Edward sat on the stoop together in light clothing, looking for the youthful feeling the setting and season had once suggested to them, as though soon they might jump in a taxi and pay the driver and meet someone singular and change their life in one night, as though any of them could sustain that kind of mobility and reinvention. Edith's son had temporarily flown back to whichever place he came from, and it afforded them a short window in which to discuss things, develop a plan if there was one to be had. Thomas was the only one intent on action. Because he sat there full of thoughts of Adeleine and Edith and their need, his convictions were stronger than any that would have developed on behalf of his own well-being.

"Really, I could just move," Edward said in a clipped voice. "We all could."

Claudia released the sigh that had been growing, lowered her shoulders, and dragged a palm down her face.

"Right now," she offered lowly, "right now I can't—" She didn't finish the sentence, and it remained unclear what it was she couldn't do, but the hazy answer seemed to arrange itself in the clotted air between them: possibly anything.

Thomas wondered which angle to dance around first: his somewhat-reciprocated love for an unstable person who had cultivated a little false universe on the top floor, the deconstruction of which would mean a swift blow to her sanity, or his belief that the old woman with a bittersweet fever in her brain shouldn't lose her last years to a son who didn't care about how she lived them.

He chose the second, hoping that the people who shared the decaying staircase possessed the decency he suspected. He mentioned Owen and the loveless way he looked at Edith, reminded them of the open-door policy she kept for her tenants, how she had welcomed all of them for a bit of conversation or understanding silence, depending on what their lives were lacking. Did they remember that six-day blizzard, how on the fourth day she'd been the only one with groceries left and brought them all downstairs for dinner? Hadn't they all relaxed in the circle of her generosity, the jingle of bells she'd hung on the door, the forgiving wave of her hand when rent was late?

"Listen," interrupted Edward. "I'm not going to sit here and say that the old lady deserves to die in some home, playing nonsensical checkers with incontinent zombies. Or that her son's a fantastic guy for rooting for her bucket to kick so he can put in granite countertops and make a cool several million. Clearly the man has a Laundromat for a soul. But I don't see what we can possibly do besides put our little tchotchkes in little box-kes."

Claudia, who had been hiding her red face in her dry hands, laughed loudly, and Thomas watched as any control he had over the conversation faded like the sounds of ambulances passing nearby, the urgency that turned to a whine before disappearing.

She sighed and spoke up with ironic brightness. "Paulie doesn't own much but a set of coasters shaped like bugs and a couple cookies, anyway. Won't be hard to pack."

Edward snorted and brought his hands together, brushed them in two opposing up-down motions, the gesture that signified *Our work here is done.* The crags of his face, the sharp hook of his nose and the protrusion of his brow, were softened with the remaining light. Claudia leaned her head on his forearm and sniffed.

"We could fight him," said Thomas. "We could—" He felt the acidic tension in his body dissolve. The defeat felt like the ten minutes after swimming, the leaking of warm water from the ears and the adjusting of limbs to a different way of moving.

Edward announced that he needed a beer. He got up and Claudia followed. Thomas watched them make their way down the street until they turned, wondered at how quickly he had failed to sway them. There was no one else on the street, no sounds save the ticking of the watch he still wore as though he were a man who didn't let hours pass like the endless parade of cars on the Brooklyn-Queens Expressway.

I T HAD BEEN EASY for Thomas to overlook the resemblance: only three photos of Declan as a young man gripped Edith's walls, obscured by hanging plants that fell down from the ceiling in curls.

One showed their wedding, Edith shy on grand stone steps and Declan leaning in as though to prop her up, and another a tinseled Christmas, the grinning father supervising his son's solemn assembly of a train track. The third photo, skewed somehow, showed the building freshly painted, the sky diluted, and Declan. Settled on the stoop, his slacks high on his waist and his white shirt crisp and his hair combed back, his cigarette between left thumb and forefinger like he learned in the war, his eyes met the camera as if in a brief nod of acknowledgment, decent but curt, eager to get back to a thought.

Thomas's jaw, he saw now, was shaped like Declan's, the soft lines leading to a broad dimple; his lashes similarly long and feminine; their eyes the same scratched brown, like a worn belt. They both carried all their strength in the shoulders, pursed their lips slightly instead of smiling with their teeth.

He could feel the tips of the plants brushing his shoulder blades as he lingered by the photos, as he waited for her while she fussed with something in the kitchen. She had denied his offers of help several times, and the apartment filled with sounds of cabinets opening and closing and her outbursts, spit from her mouth like cherry pits—"Curses!" and "I'll be!" and "Jiminy Christmas!" Finally, she emerged with a dull silver tray, on which sat two jagged pieces of chocolate-dipped biscuits, four unevenly cut slices of cheese, one bruised apple, and two cups of iced coffee adorned with faded blue curly straws.

She had insisted on feeding him. He had arrived, for the third time that week, with a brown-bagged selection of art supplies, and he had promised himself that this time he would pin down a sustained conversation: about her will, her son, and possibly her daughter. Each time he had tried, he'd instead fallen quiet at the sweet cyan and maroon watercolored circles she was fond of making, and only reached out to pat the pale back of her neck. On the last occasion he had laid out brushes and acrylics and the paper to receive them, and Edith had painted a hammock suspended from a telephone wire on which four little birds sat singing to one another. Behind them, a pink sky relinquished its blush as it moved towards the edge of the page.

"What's this?" Thomas had said.

She had seemed surprised at the question, then shocked that she knew the answer. She had pulled at the bunches of her slacks and looked out the window.

"That's what it's like when you think of your whole life. You're fairly high up, and the lines get crossed and there are lots of little voices chirping, and you're hanging from that and you try to find sleep."

Today he could tell immediately: it was one of her off days.

She was wearing too many colors, and spoke as if she'd just been dropped off on this planet, in this apartment.

"These things are delicious," she exclaimed, waving the biscuits as though trying to keep the attention of a baby.

"And I like those too!" She pointed at the hanging plants that she herself had raised from tiny seeds.

"They're beautiful, Edith," Thomas said. He wanted her to know about her effort, to remind her about the little chair she stood on to water them, to present the proof of time she'd spent and cancel her forgetting. "You should be so proud at how they've grown. They need much more than light."

He heard the lilt of his sentences and the sweetness in his tone, as though he were speaking to a worried child, and felt sick. He missed the woman who so calmly separated his life into pieces he could understand, and he needed her instruction.

"Edith," he said. "Can we talk about Owen?"

Her lips grew hard and she sucked at her teeth. She hurled the stale cookie in her hand at the table.

"I don't want to talk about him anymore!"

"Edith, I only want to help you—do you—is he—"

Strings of saliva dangled across her lips, over her bared teeth. He could smell her breath—like tea bags left out for days, the sweat of poor sleep—from where he sat.

"Declan! I've said it too many times! The boy doesn't care for us and he's got no interest in us caring for him. And that is that!"

Thomas didn't think about what it meant not to correct her, only swallowed and took her hand and hoped the words might come out in a way that she could hear.

"Edith, I need to know what you want to do about the building. Your property. I have to hear you say it. Do you want Owen taking it over?"

"Declan," she hissed. She clutched at the edge of her table, its dirtied lace tablecloth brown next to the bright moony white of her knuckles. "How many times. How many times did I say. Nothing of mine will go to him. It's Jenny's. It's my sweet Jenny's. It's in the will and there's nothing he can do about it."

Thomas felt his resolution gathering, all parts towards a desperate act, remembered the dead man in the photograph and quietly begged his forgiveness. *It's for her own good*, he tried to explain to Declan across years, and laced his hand into hers.

"Dear," he said. "Where is the will?"

EDITH NAPPED while Thomas searched, lay facedown on top of the covers as he took apart the many years she had packed away methodically. He had kissed her forehead, damp from summer humidity, and brought a thin cotton sheet over her slowly vanishing body. She dreamt like a dog, kicking often.

On the hunt, in and out of boxes he found on shelves in the highest points of the apartment, he stumbled across various mementos that confirmed the great tenderness he held for her: a photo of her and Declan in one of those two-person horse costumes, the colors warm and soft like baking things rising.

They each wear a cowboy hat and a Western shirt, and stuffed cloth legs dangle beneath their torsos, comically short. Edith, at the head, wears the suspenders that hold up the mare's comic snout and mane with pride and has a thumb slipped under each strap; she is just about to laugh. Declan, behind her, holds a can of beer in each hand and winks. The people around them, in Halloween costumes much milder and more comfortable, look on at their glow, the obvious volume of affection, with jealousy and apprehension.

Behind this, Thomas found a photo of them applying glue to strips of wallpaper with a solemnity meant for churches. He continued to move through the stack, his thumb light on the upper corner as he flicked, and stopped again on a photo of Edith holding a giggling baby up to the husky afternoon light on an unmade bed. It was the same room, he knew, where she lay now, managing ragged breaths.

When he found it, a stack of duplicates in a beige vinyl box, he passed his fingers through his hair in some wish to appear presentable. The words *Last Will and Testament*, formal and exclusive, kept him still a moment longer. He fought hesitation with the remembered moments of Owen and Edith, his sharp angles and the flashes of his gold watch as he grabbed at her elbow, then the image of Adeleine, looking out at him through the crack of her door, her eyes wild as though she were being chased by her end. The conjured images lent his fingers some electricity, assisted them in separating a leaf from the pile.

His tongue made a soft sound against the roof of his mouth as he surveyed it, a whole lifetime of days laid out in plans for divestment, as if the physical things weren't tied to memories or moments, as if they had never quite approved of their human ownership and the bonds attached to them. Her clothes to the

Salvation Army, her novels to a literacy foundation, her kitchen things to a homeless shelter.

When his eye reached the page that concerned the property, he saw that she had been correct, had not in her confusion of decades forgotten the legacy she meant to bestow. The address that had housed the last decade of his life was meant to go to Jennifer Whalen of San Francisco, and the date of the document was more than ten years prior, shortly after Declan's collapse. A vision came to him, of Edith alone for the first time in fifty years, adjusting her hat in the foyer of some lawyer's office, ready to regulate the details of her own demise, and the heat left his body. He had never so badly wanted to protect someone, and never felt so thoroughly incapable.

PAULIE WAS IN FORT GREENE PARK and there were fireflies and he thought possibly they were the same ones that had winked at his mother in Connecticut and brought her outside on so many sunsets. He wondered if maybe each time they lit up they were remembering other places they'd been. Like, *fwoosh*, light, and here is the meadow that swelled around a little house left behind: *fwoosh*, and a real broad garden where the flowers reach out however they please just like the people sitting around growing into the grass: *fwoosh*, and the lake where reeds grew up tall and lived half their life underwater and half out.

Paulie knew the word *bioluminescence* and wished he could use it more, that it showed up in recipes, on the checks Claudia scrawled for his rent each month, on the change-of-service signs in the subway. *How are you doing today? Bioluminescent!* He would say this all the time if his body made light you could see. He would blink and blink for Claudia, he would summon all his bioluminescent friends and surround her.

For years Paulie had been begging her to take him to see a natural phenomenon in Elkmont, Tennessee, which he knew from maps was in an area called the Smoky Mountains, which he definitely liked the sound of. Thousands of male fireflies lit up all at once and did a kind of dance for the females, who hid near the ground and flirted with little flashes, and it went on a while, all of them listening to each other, filling the sky with light all at once. It happened only once a year, and in two places in the entire world, and Paulie suspected if he got to see it his whole life would open. But he knew that Claudia became quiet and wet-faced at night, saw in the morning how she slept until the last minute she could. He tried not to mention it.

T HE INFORMATION SAT with Thomas like a poor meal hardening in the stomach, resisting digestion, as he lay tensed on
the couch in his apartment. He couldn't determine whether his
impulse to find Edith's lost daughter in California was more
rooted in his wish to save others or in his desire to see himself as
capable, the kind of man who followed an idea down, clearing
obstacles to make a path for it. Even with the full agency of his
body, Thomas had never known himself to be a man of action.
He had spent parties in low armchairs, allowed the conversation
to drift to him, charmed people with the opinions he shared
minimally and stoically, poured his time into canvases that he
manipulated exactly as he wished, and cared little for the work
of human relationships. The women he had fallen in with were
always those slinking around corners to find him, prodding at his
reticence, showing up late at his door without asking. He had
given up on his parents, their silent TV dinners and failing bodies
and shared misery, discarded an active connection to them as one
might some faulty appliance.

A sharp, acrid sentiment bloomed in Thomas. His understanding of himself—that he'd grown cowardly since the stroke,
had forsaken some former virility and honor—appeared, finally
and absolutely, as a lie he'd told himself for comfort. Knowing
this felt like watching the sand at his feet escaping and returning

to the ocean, feeling the divots grow deeper and his balance melt, understanding that soon he'd need to move. He looked around his apartment now, at the few things lying around—two mugs left unwashed; a failing row of potted herbs; a box of childhood photos his mother had sent, which he'd never unpacked—and wondered what kind of life they indicated.

He got up and moved to the kitchen table, where his laptop sat open, displaying articles he'd only half read: an economist's half-baked ideas about what the on-demand consumption of pop culture meant for minor artists, a biographical entry about a middling starlet, the obituary of a childhood acquaintance who had drowned. He brought the computer screen to full brightness and began his search for an airplane ticket, and the immediacy of it, the options rippling open in new windows, moved through him like a chill.

ON THE AIRPLANE Thomas brushed thoughts of Adeleine away like mosquitoes in a high-ceilinged room, their buzzing becoming softer but never vanishing. He looked out at the modest oval of sky and considered Edith, who'd been so kind in the months after the stroke, who had brought him meals without any mawkish sympathy and hadn't stared while he taught himself how to use his body in a different way. Later, she had taken grocery bags from his unsteady grip without discussion while he unlocked the front door or checked his mail, and when he blushed had told him, "Thomas, helping you with what you need isn't embarrassing for me, so it shouldn't be embarrassing for you."

Turned confident by thoughts of his newfound generosity, he had made the mistake of reaching out to his parents to tell them of his plans. He was interrupting a sports game—he was, infallibly, calling in the middle of the competitive event to end all competitive events—and his father had grunted and handed the phone off to his mother. He heard, in the interim, the fumbled transfer of the phone, her surprise at the contact from her faraway son, but she'd called him "honey," asked how he was doing. He had perched on his locked suitcase and spoken without interruption, bubbling with the wild enthusiasm of a child with money to spend however he pleased.

"I'm just the person to help them," he offered in summation. "It just sort of . . . *aligned* in a way that rang out." He knew he sounded like someone who waved around tarot cards and looked to crystals for guidance, but the prospect of such concrete usefulness had left him upbeat and serene.

"Dear," his mother said, "if you need another place to live . . . isn't it easy online, now? You just put in your specific, uh . . ." —a pause as a cheering stadium filtered through and washed over his parents—"you just enter a price range and an area."

"That's not—"

". . ."

"Thomas, we've got—this game is about to—"

"That's okay, Mom. I've got a plane to catch."

"Take care."

THE CONVERSATION CAME BACK to him like an infection, worse and larger in its return—the distance between them amplified, the futility of his belated attempt to connect obvious—and he tried again to focus his head on the possibility of Jenny. He removed the photos he had taken from Edith's box and saw, again, a child with a long braid who turned from the camera, her face always directed away: towards a window, a hot dog stand, the flat and gray Atlantic Ocean. Then a teenager wading into a subculture: as the dates scrawled in cursive on the backs of the pictures progressed, Jenny appeared in looser clothing, sitting on the opposite end of the couch as Declan and looking up with eyelids painted blue; on the edge of her unmade bed, surrounded

by dried flowers in mason jars and carved wooden incense hold-
ers and pinned up photos of people yowling into microphones.
On the back of the last, in which Jenny stood on the stoop of the
building with a hand gripping a suitcase, looking directly into the
camera as though daring it to capture her accurately, Edith had
scrawled *San Francisco or Bust.*

Thomas was rereading the final report from the private investigator Edith and Declan had hired, dated more than thirty-five
years prior, when the pleasant ding of the seatbelt sign sounded
and the flight attendant chirped of impending descent into San
Francisco. The brittle paper revealed nothing more in Thomas's
fifth or sixth review: The man had found several people who had
known Jenny casually, and one who'd slept with her once, but
none had any idea where she'd gone. The document closed with
a quote from one of those interviewed:

> *She was around a lot, sure, but I couldn't tell you who
> she was close to, really. We shared drugs but not much
> else . . . that girl was either out of her mind high and
> dancing all over everything or curled up in a corner or on
> the fucking move . . . I would see her walking all around
> the city. She never talked about any kind of past—I
> didn't know where she came from—and I don't think she
> had any eye on the future.*

E DWARD HAD SET OUT cardboard boxes preemptively, to tiptoe around the idea of leaving, so that when the time came to pack he could rise to the occasion without much effort. Meanwhile, he stepped around the empty cubes and cursed, sometimes sent them wheeling with his foot and felt satisfied watching their failed attempts at flight. He had bawled at the thought of moving and run his hand over doorways and faucets, remembering the person he'd been, nearly twenty years before, when he'd first signed the lease.

In those days, he'd spent most of his time in a T-shirt on which he'd drawn, in Sharpie, an empty pizza box. He'd moved in with little furniture and found two orange school chairs on the street, their nubbled plastic coating marred with profane carvings. He had sat on one and rested his feet on the other while he wrote his jokes, blissfully happy, happily alone.

For the first time in his recent memory, Edward was working on something, and the boxes around him, empty but designed for transitions, seemed to urge him forward. He had spent the first day trying to assemble a title for his memoirs and emerged with several possibilities: *Friends and Enemas; Not Funny: A Life.* The prospect of summing up his years had left him largely in thought-driven repose on the couch, periodically taking breaks from doodling tits to stand barefoot by the open fridge and shovel cold pieces of turkey into his mouth. He knew nothing about writing save the hustle and brevity of the screenplay, but his checking account held enough to pay the rent on possibly a bathroom somewhere in New York City, or to purchase a bus ticket to the Midwestern town where his brother sold life insurance, and so he had decided perhaps it was time to write and sell a book.

He was struggling to nail down words, already exhausted, when he heard the sounds in the hallway. He could tell from the approaching steps—the arrhythmic stabs of high heels worn by someone better suited for all-weather hiking boots—that it was Claudia, and when she knocked he rose from the empty screen, arranged his face as one pleasantly overwhelmed by too many erudite thoughts before opening the door.

Claudia settled her substantial frame horizontally onto Edward's couch. They had drunk with each other until three in the morning the night before, and he had found himself talking again, in excess, about his late mother, and she had described what it meant to be the sister of Paulie.

"Because honestly," she had said, gesturing on the crooked back patio of a local bar, a long-thriving dive where the money was always damp and the chairs slightly broken, "why should someone who does the most convincing impression of a Christmas tree, who calls me Rosebud right after I've lost my temper and wants to tell me he loves me through the bathroom door even while I'm shitting the worst shit that's ever been shat—why should that person ever have to be alone?"

At that Edward had snorted into his meaty fingers and chucked her under the chin and cheered his fifth bitter ale at her;

they had laughed all over the bar, out the doors, and all the way home. He remembered this fondly as he looked at her now, slumped in the work clothes that clung in unseemly shapes to her body. Two people in the bar had asked whether they were brother and sister, and it was true that they shared a stockiness, as well as deep-set brown eyes and a way of tipping up the chin to smile. Today in his apartment, the afternoon made her hangover visible: the side zipper of her skirt a few inches undone, the bun on her head dramatically crooked.

"I have to talk to him, right?"

"Who."

"My *husband*."

"Claudia," said Edward, "did he give you a ring or a life sentence in a marriage-shaped prison? You know, Hitler had a gentle side, too. He *painted*."

"He wants me to put Paulie in some kind of assisted living community. He won't let him come live with us. My reaction thus far has been to ignore the issue entirely and sleep on Paulie's couch which has, as you may know, three pillows shaped like daisies."

With one hand Edward rearranged Claudia's legs so that he could share the couch, then sat and sighed. "Not once," he reasoned, "have you given me any indication that this guy is someone whose bullshit is worth sticking around for. Why stay?"

Claudia's face was pressed between two cushions that muffled her speech. Her words moved through them slowly, traveling in thick surges to convey their message.

"He wasn't always—he was softer. And, you know, our parents are gone and he—he wanted to be family."

The admission set her whole body rippling. Her fingers worked the rounded edges of the throw pillow, searching for a steadier hold, and her lungs emptied themselves into the worn material. Edward lifted his hand as if to catch a fly; the motion's inappropriate briskness struck him, and he remembered the slowness required by solace, lowered his palm to Claudia's back and saw with shock that he had begun to rub it.

As Claudia's bellows changed from uneven gasps to steady sobs, as though sliding from verse to chorus, he knew or learned to tuck a strand of hair behind her ear, to go to the sink for water and offer it without speaking. It was a strange moment to realize how glad he was she'd forgiven him for a blunder he'd made the night before, fueled by a surplus of stout and the thrill of making a woman laugh. In their hallway she had begun a search of her purse, first shaking it near her head to detect the jangle of keys, then emptying it item by item. Finally she had held them up, the grin on her face like that of a Labrador with a retrieved ball, and hiccuped, and thanked him for listening.

"No," he had said. "Thank *you*," and reached out to touch her nose in a way that was meant to be avuncular, and folded her into a hug. The embrace, made sluggish with beer, had lasted longer than it should have, and Edward had made a miscalculation. His right hand shot up under her shirt, only the first knuckles making it beneath the taut underwire of her bra and becoming trapped there, wiggling a little, unsure whether to tunnel ahead or turn back. While he clumsily deliberated, Claudia squinted at the ceiling as though retrieving some once-memorized fact.

"I don't think—" she said.

"What is *completely inappropriate?*" Edward asked, feigning the earnestness of a *Jeopardy* contestant, then the heartening, fatherly reply of Alex Trebek. "You are *correct!*"

"I'll see too yamorrow," she had said, laughing, waving off the gaffe. "You, tomorrow." From across the hall each had heard the other's clumsy preparations for sleep, faucets going off at full strength and hands slapping at the walls to kill the light.

E VEN THOUGH HE WASN'T SUPPOSED TO, Paulie believed there was nothing wrong, not really, with going down to visit Edith when Claudia was off at work; if at first she was surprised to see him, he knew she enjoyed their games. Paulie had never witnessed anyone else play Go Fish so rigorously: she clapped and she slammed the stern kings and mischievous jacks on the table, she said *fish* like she meant every last one, of every size and color, in all the five oceans.

On a bright day that didn't soften with afternoon, the sun at four still white and the heat closely packed, Edith's attention to their game dwindled. Her fan of cards loosened until they slipped, one by one, onto the floor. She leaned into the table and wheezed.

"What do I look like to you? You haven't got twenty-one," she said, "not by a long shot!"

"What? Um?"

"Give me back that money!"

"Edith, please—I'm not—this isn't—"

Her gnarled fingers made a fist that she waved as though it held a ticket, and she looked at him and saw a man she didn't know: he had curly hair long enough for braids and a shirt printed with images of constellations, and he was crying from huge eyes.

She turned away from him and bit the sides of her cheeks. The temperature felt like punishment.

They sat in silence for fifteen minutes. The last of Paulie's tears emptied onto the galaxy of his shirt, and Edith focused on her surroundings, tried to place herself in them, burning all her energy in the attempt to recognize a chipped teapot or spiked plant or open door.

"We could play something else," he said finally. "Let me just visit the men's room."

Paulie had loved the phrase "the men's room" for as long as he could remember; it felt like a password into the world of suits and cars and wives that had otherwise rejected him. He closed the door behind him and splashed water on his face, sat down to pee as he'd been taught by the mishaps incurred by standing and aiming. He observed the shelves in front of him, their mysterious spectrum of jars and boxes and tubes and brushes, some dusty and some never used, the colors ranging from bright to earthy. He forgave Edith for yelling. The inflexible losses of games, the rules you couldn't reason with, upset him too.

Back in the kitchen, with the cosmetics spread across the table, he kissed her forehead before he smeared on the first splash of blue.

When he finished Edith's face, Paulie stepped back and regarded her with a hand on his chin, surveying his work from several angles. His hand-eye coordination had never been exquisite, and he had employed an abstract approach, marking Edith's pores with meandering paths of red lipstick that met lush fields of green eye shadow. He felt particularly proud of her nose, an isolated bridge of shimmering cyan, and moved in and out of the late sunlight to observe it.

"It's your turn," he said finally. "Now you do me." He pulled up a chair in front of her and closed his eyes. "Jungle cat preferred!"

An hour later, the people returning from jobs in the city paused to glance at the sight on the stoop: an old woman in an oversized sun hat and a grown man who sat with his legs splayed like a six-year-old in a sandbox, their faces altered by a mess of pigments. Beside them sat a time-yellowed cream-colored radio, the taped antennae resting on the lip of the stone step above, and they mouthed the words of the songs that came in over a base of static. The last of the commuters saw the nest of white hair bent into the neck of the man, who stroked the head and sang a thirty-year-old commercial jingle for squat, rounded figurines marketed as untippable.

Weebles wobble
Weebles wobble
Weebles wobble but they don't fall down.

Multicolored and projecting a two-headed shadow, they were still sitting there when the streetlamps came on.

I n Thomas's absence, Adeleine felt a distinct anger: at the way he had entered her home and classified it as strange, at how he had decided her relationship with her possessions needed broadcasting: the night before he had boarded the airplane, he'd set up an array of recording devices and urged her to catalogue her songs.

"They should be heard," he had said, posturing with an authority she found obnoxious. "The creation is only ever the first part of it. The next is letting it go." She had started to buzz, was still buzzing, with the familiar anxiety that used to sound when someone urged her to do something with her talents. Songs were fine and good, she thought, but they were not the water that turned seeds to plants, or the materials that built steady houses, or the ointments that healed a wound. Once, when she had voiced concerns along these lines to a psychiatrist, he had asked her why she hadn't become a farmer or a carpenter or a physician. She hadn't had an answer, and had hated him for asking.

In an attempt to smother the old temper in her stomach, she washed the dishes and scrubbed the perpetually grimy bathtub, but the activity only heightened her heart rate. All she had ever wanted, she realized, since she was a little girl who turned away from doting cameras, was to be left alone.

Lying on the floor with her palms up, hoping to receive some wave of calm, Adeleine could hear, layered under the fluttering notes of Paulie's keyboard, warped, feral sounds. She pressed her left cheekbone into the hardwood until it ached and listened until she recognized the noises as coming from Edith. Without further thought, she rose and approached the doorframe, watched her wrist and palm rotate the knob.

THOMAS HADN'T VISITED San Francisco since losing his old body, but there was a time he had flown out once or twice a year: he would casually tour the spectacular heights and views, stay with friends and spend unfocused hours on foggy rooftops. He had always arrived with no definite plans and found a city that didn't require any. As he looked away from the airport's organic grocery store, its rainbow bounty of produce, as the escalator carried him down from ARRIVALS to GROUND TRANSPORTATION, he reminded himself of the wholly different shape of this visit. Imagining himself as he'd last been on the same steel moving walkways—his linen thrift store slacks, his military-green duffel bag, his carefree stroll towards the line of cars outside and the warm way he'd greeted the friend who'd picked him up—he constricted and grabbed for the handrail.

There was no one pulling up in a car for him out front, no one waving and grinning: he hadn't let anyone know he was coming, couldn't imagine summing up the last two years or explaining his total lack of plans for the next few. He followed the signs to other transportation, fumbled with the unfamiliar ticketing system, pulled his rolling suitcase into the train car, and waited for motion.

————

HIS PLANS WERE VAGUE, loose as algae. He had wished—so hard that he'd begun to expect—that he would divine some clue or plan from the sea-brined air, the Victorians that seemed to lean crookedly uphill. Instead he was a man in a city not his own, holding the decades-old mementos of someone's lost daughter, standing at the exit of an unfamiliar station with no itinerary besides a stop at the library. He had smothered such hatred of himself since meeting Adeleine, had distracted himself with the unfolding mystery of her, but now he felt the creep of fog under his light sweater and tugged at his sleeves, furious with himself for failing even to look after this basic aspect of survival.

He narrowly skirted an argument between two bearded homeless men but not the thick odor of urine it seemed to agitate, pulled Declan's cardigan against him, and cut a path towards the library, a seven-story building of angular granite that abutted its neighbors' stone reliefs of angels. The automatic doors acknowledged him and opened.

Three hours later, on the top floor, where the city records lived in quiet decay, Thomas had found an excess of nothing concerning Jennifer Faith Christine Whalen, save the small fact that she had attended, or at the very least signed up for, a class—on what the registrar didn't reveal—at the city college the year she arrived. It was as though she had never assumed an address, or cast her ballot in an election, or subscribed to a journal, or taken any of the measures that mean inclusion or community or home.

Why, he wondered, in all the photos of her, did she seem uncomfortable in the world of domesticity and people: why had she seemed to hover over the couch rather than let the cushions receive her? Why hadn't she reached out to hold the volunteered crook of Declan's elbow? Why had she only packed such a modest suitcase on the day she left, forsaking the playthings of childhood and pinned-up photos of idols so easily?

Thomas's frustration with the lack of results nudged at his aching for Adeleine; the smell of browned papers and the creak of century-old book spines in the records room had irritated it, reminded him of all the antiquated things she worshipped so stubbornly. The sound of the chair as he pushed it back reverberated, a loud screech in a room full of things still and near soundless, and he took the stairs down at a clip, determined to hear her voice on the telephone.

Outside, settled uncomfortably on a ledge that barely accommodated his body, Thomas listened as her phone rang but she didn't answer, and vividly pictured the worst. She had recounted to him the psychiatrists and the pills, those prescribed and otherwise, and he had grown to sense her need for him, had seen her darken when he told her about his plans to travel. Three thousand miles away, he imagined the mass of her orange and beige anti-anxiety pills emptied out, the sleeping agents spread in lines, or her water-pruned body drawn in a tight shape in the bathtub where she had hid for hours, murky, loose as algae. His imagination, he considered as he withdrew from the fantasy, had never lacked ambition. Looking up towards the inscrutable gray of the sky, which hung low and concealed distance, he dialed another number.

E DITH'S VOICE RANG OUT so firmly when she said hello that Thomas, on the other end, could almost believe her as capable as she once had been: he could fly back at once, let his mind flow into calm under her maternal reassurance, grow tired by the hiss of her worn blue kettle. It was mid-evening there, and he imagined her stroking the tufts of her hair, rocking slightly as they talked.

"You're in San Francisco!" she chirped. "Why, that's where our wild Jenny went off to." The careful conversation he had led, informing Edith of his purpose, begging that she rummage for any more information about her daughter, quickly diverged.

"Yoo-hoo," she giggled. "You wouldn't believe who has joined me this morning. Ad-e-leine! And she's got the loveliest house-dress on, and I think I'm going to take the train into the city and find one just like it at Bergdorf's!"

Standing upright, newly chilled by the fog, Thomas watched a homeless man in a shrunken sweater listlessly rearrange the cans in his shopping cart, and forced a chuckle.

"Listen, Edith, do you think I could speak to her?"

"To whom, dear?"

"Adeleine."

The phone emptied of sound.

"Oh—yes," Edith warbled.

Adeleine greeted him girlishly, with forced and uncharacter-istic affection. He wanted to warm and unclench at this, at being addressed intimately for the first time in days, at being recog-nized, but her chipper tone bore a suspect echo.

"What are you, uh . . . *doing?*" It was not like her to get out and socialize with the neighbors, no less the demented and capri-cious landlord. He supposed he should congratulate her, but the suspicion arrived first and made its demands like a guest at the table too hungry for manners.

"Edith was having"—she paused while she searched for safe language—"a bad day, you could say. I heard it from my apart-ment and I came down." She offered this information blithely, as if she were not someone who received her groceries exclusively by delivery, who had turned defensive and morose when Thomas suggested that she might someday join him on a camping trip.

"You could . . . hear her bad day?"

"Yes, well. I was on the floor, so. Anyway, I've been writing down some memories for her—she was upset because she said they were sort of losing their foundation, like they were flooded and pushed into the wrong rooms."

"Flooded?" Thomas remained astonished. He didn't recog-nize the uptick in her voice, or the assertive clip of her intentions; he tried to imagine her eyes focused in the muted lamplight while she urged Edith on in her remembering, while she pushed a pen across the page with a strong wrist, but couldn't.

"Point is, I thought I should help. How are *you?*"

"I miss you."

That was all he could manage. He had never had a talent for

speaking on the phone, was always hovering over the conversation's true purpose or cowed by the speed of the interaction, reacting too slowly, forgetting to assent with his voice as well as his face.

"Okay," Adeleine agreed hesitantly. "Me too. I think I'll get back to Edith now, but I'll talk to you soon."

"Okay," he echoed, but she had already ended the call. How could it be, he thought, that the people he had gone galloping off on this fool's mission to help were so comfortably supporting each other in a warm room? He felt glad for them, for the idea of Edith's chatter being caught and held, but the phone call had left him more and not less lonely, and he knew that every passing hour was another in which he hadn't earned his way home.

THOMAS SLEPT LATE in the exorbitantly priced hotel room, succored by the white anonymous space as he dreamt, slowly, of untouched earth. Even as he walked through the dream, he knew it was strange that his mind, so accustomed to an urban setting, would conjure rivers rapid and green, footpaths curving under the grand theater of forest. When he woke, he thought of water. He wrapped the plush, bleached robe around him and crossed the empty hall, where he stepped into the washed glow of the elevator.

The pool possessed a certain type of lavish 1920s grandeur: the curved glass ceiling demarcated by thin white panes, the pale tiles and plush lounges immaculate, the verdant fronds tall and loose in each corner of the room. As he willed himself to float, he looked up through the glass at oxidized copper roofs, at office buildings pulsing with light, and marveled at how his liquid surroundings rendered the paralyzed side of him just the same as the other.

In the late afternoon, dry but still drunk with the sensation of floating, Thomas stepped out of the lobby and walked. He carried the last photo of Jenny in his pocket, studied it on various benches, patted it while he ascended and descended the hills that seemed impractical for the purposes of a city. Why build on such angles? But he admired them, enjoyed the performance, the way they routinely hid the next mile from view and surprised with an abrupt path downward. After two hours of walking he realized what he'd known but ignored: that the city wasn't as large as New York was, wasn't a place that offered getting lost as a gift. Through some unconscious set of lefts, he had already begun to return: to his scant luggage, the pennies and dimes on the night table.

He walked down Market Street, the early stretch of it still dominated by strip clubs and SROs and the woven dens of the homeless, constructed of scraps of cotton and cardboard as though designed by earthbound birds. Thomas dodged a handful of requests for change that varied in tone and volume, stepped over a half-dozen sleeping bags, and then he saw her. Her out-stretched hands, her skin that appeared to have experienced flood and drought in an unending cycle, her eyes unchanged.

HARDLY FEELING THE DIP between curb and street, he glided towards her. He was sure, or nearly, that this was the child Edith and Declan had lost. She was standing with a foot on the concrete ledge of an angular fountain, working a denim pant leg up with one hand and holding the plastic handle of an overflowing shopping cart with the other.

He approached and stepped into the fetid scent, understanding too late he was interrupting her bath.

"Jenny?"

The woman wrinkled her forehead to regard him, and the dirt on her face realigned. She was worn in the way of broken things left out in brown yards, stretched and sun-bleached and sagging.

"Who are you to ask," she spat. "You a cop?"

"No, I—"

She pulled on his sweater and tilted her head to the side. "No, you're not a cop."

"I came to talk to you—"

"I'm hungry," she barked. "You gonna get me some fuckin' food or what?"

Before he could answer she was shuffling off, pushing her cart against the light through protesting honks. He tried to keep up, weaving through traffic and raising his hand in thanks to the drivers who let him. In front of a McDonald's she acknowledged two hunched and gaunt men pinching cigarettes between diminished lips and leaning against the intricately scratched window, and parked her rolling pile of possessions there.

Inside, she told Thomas what to order, grabbed a booth while he waited in line. She'd brought in four bulging plastic bags, which she examined and sniffed. Thomas looked up at the back-lit photos of hamburgers, unsure if this was how he had wanted to feel when he found her. It had happened too quickly: he had not been prepared: but how, he wondered, could he have readied himself for this?

She didn't comment on the way he crouched to slide the tray, one armed, onto the table. While she inhaled a double cheeseburger and gnawed the ice from the soda, splintering it in her open mouth, Thomas looked for words, aware he'd spent much of life like this, stammering and searching. Wasn't this outcome more likely than any other he'd considered—couldn't he have guessed that the lost child, damaged by an era that chewed up so many, would be somewhere between life and death, growling, pushing her rotting blankets and talismans through depressed intersections?

"I guess I'll get right to it. Your mother? Edith? Is sick. Your brother is trying to take the property from her against her will."

She said nothing, kept eating, opening ketchup packets with her sawed-down teeth and picking at her gray gums with a pinky nail.

"I know it's been practically a lifetime, but—"

"I don't know who the fuck you are, but you must be a lunatic or somethin'," she said, finally. "Don't know why you want to tell me this shit. Like I don't have plenty to deal with. Everything I can do just to survive. City making new laws to illegalize me every day." Her frustration soon became unintelligible, and she was speaking in schizophrenic apostrophe. "Little bitches," she said. "Flying around, not even my own age."

Her cool anger seemed to flash, vanishing from her face before it appeared in her body. Their circumferences like those of dinner plates, her enormous hands spread and hovered over the table, then slammed down. "Fucker. Mother*fucker.*"

"Jenny?" He said it again, though he knew now how wrong he was, and longed at once for all the clean, quiet moments of his life, as though summoning them might give him some power in the barbed present.

"I'm leaving, and I don't want to see you again." She removed a butter knife from one of the plastic bags that swayed from her arm and stood before him, swiping it through the air vertically. Thomas found himself laughing, everything suddenly a well-earned punch line: the carving on the bench that read SUK OR FUK MY DIK, the irate homeless person he'd tried to offer free real estate, the filthy woman's eyes protruding as she gripped the dull, bent knife.

"Lunatic is right!" Thomas said, as she backed away. Freed in some way, he closed his eyes and sank into the vinyl backrest.

He folded his arms on the table, buried his sight in the scratchy wool once Declan's, and found the memories of his past life there: himself at an art gallery, shaking hands with suited men, later sharing their cabs, waiting for the girls in belted linen dresses to come to him, packaging his pieces for shipment once they'd sold, taking a nap in the afternoon, knowing the world would be ready to receive him when he awoke. He sighed and rose and pushed the door open.

Before he felt the force of hands around him, he noticed the scent of old sweat. Then the voice of the woman who wasn't Jenny, skirted by two others, and the coughs as they slammed his head against a wall, searching his body as though it were a cluttered drawer. The greedy push of their fingers was several seconds gone before he opened his eyes, saw them running and the man in the blue uniform approaching.

PAULIE HAD SWUM towards a quiet place within the limits of his condition. He had come to understand that the affection he shared with Claudia was as sacred as any—but still sometimes an alarm went off, all parts of him knocked together. When at the zoo he saw a father hoisting a child to see the wild goats canter, or on the street he watched a pair of sweethearts speaking to the stroller between them, he felt angry at the simple shape of his life: at the meals Claudia helped him prepare and the way she watched him complete the tasks she nervously assigned, at the days he sometimes spent playing music for just himself, at the brightly colored blankets and playful lamps that smeared his apartment as reminders of a permanent childhood. Once in a while he would still plead with Claudia, *But what if I adopted, but what if you helped me take care of the baby*, and always ended up red-faced and tear-streaked.

The conversation had happened again. Paulie had shut himself in his bedroom, turned on the light shaped like the moon and insisted, uncharacteristically, on wallowing in his poor temper. He had fallen asleep in his clothes, slept through Claudia leaving for work in the morning, and woken up with a mood that moved like an injured bee, frantically, from wall to wall.

Paulie thought he might go see Edward, either lie on his couch and ask him questions about what he was writing or convince him to go somewhere with plenty of color and sound, a loud movie or fast train, but when he knocked, no one answered. He sat down on the landing, not yet ready to return to his apartment, and tried to think up a story he liked about staircases. When he heard Edith's door open, he brightened. He called her name too loud and stood waving like a traffic guard, trying to direct her eyes to his voice.

She turned and blinked steadily for most of a minute.

"How is today looking?" he asked. Running her fingers over the peach costume jewels that ringed her neck, Edith squinted up at him. Her face reacted as though to some improbability, a lynx strolling through a bank or a waterfall tumbling out a third-story window.

Her eyes welled. She had gotten dressed, put on makeup, left her apartment with a purpose, but now it was gone. Paulie watched her slow crumple and felt an immediate sense of guilt. How had his cheerful intentions betrayed him in their brief trip from his mouth to her ears? Shoelaces flying, he rushed down to meet her.

Most people he knew, even Claudia, tried to smother any complicated emotions in his presence, and so he found himself in some way honored when Edith didn't try to conceal her crying. The tears drove tracks on her face, snatched up the beige powder from her eyelids and moved it through the unblended pinks and reds.

"Did staying inside with all your things start to feel bad?"

Paulie knew you should ask someone before you touched them, but he didn't, this time, before he cradled her. The swollen pads of her fingers groped at the back of his neck as he lifted her half an inch, and her body's weight left the floor in small increments as his frame received it. When she kept shaking, Paulie searched his body for a solution, then started to lead her towards her door, which remained open, as though she hadn't been sure she had everything she needed.

Paulie escorted her in, mentally reviewing a list of the ways Claudia comforted him, tried to remember how his mother had spoken when he was sick. He placed Edith on the couch, crouched and kissed each of her cheeks, then her eyelids. Then an idea came to him, and he bounced on his knees. "Hold on," he said. "I'll be right back."

Upstairs, Paulie handled the Nesquik as though it were holy. To stop it from trembling, his left hand held his right wrist, which grasped the spoon and stirred. He could smell the froth of the cocoa on his way down the stairs, and he ached with wanting it for himself.

"Chocolate milk!" he announced, near her again, on the dining room chair next to hers. She appraised his offering as if it were an idling, unfamiliar car, so he said, more softly, "For drinking." Finally, he brought the glass to her lips and she pushed out her tongue, touched the milky surface.

"Drink it like a dog!" encouraged Paulie. "I don't care! It probably tastes better that way." It did—he could tell by the way her breathing had changed. He sat beside Edith and moved his hands in what he hoped were perfect circles on her shoulders.

"What now?" He was unsure how long consolation should last. "I have another idea!" He turned so that their knees met in two neat points and put his hands up in a gesture that could have meant stop. Edith regarded him warily, but then the song he sang,

Three, six, nine
The goose drank wine

and the way he pushed his hands forward to meet hers, his right to her left, then both of his on both of hers, then his left to her right,

The monkey chewed tobacco on the streetcar line

called her back.

The line broke
The monkey got choked

Jenny, as a shy little girl in a linen jumper on the stoop, had loved this song, the elaborate hand-clapping pattern, how Edith had trusted her daughter's small palms to meet her larger ones, how her mother's voice bounced, carried all the animals to the safe homes the story kept for them—

And they all went to heaven in a little rowboat
Clap, clap

The song stayed with her, and later that afternoon, as she crossed into the kitchen to put on the kettle, she was mouthing the words to herself, thinking of the mother she'd been in her best moments, when her right foot moved into the cocoa-colored puddle Paulie had left behind. As her legs flew out in front of her, she pictured the tufts of down and fur, the oars pumping skyward.

EVEN ADELEINE—who gripped the frame of the door and kept one foot inside—came out to see the ambulance. Owen stood near the vehicle into which Edith had just disappeared, and gestured elaborately, his hands hinting at the arc of a fall. ". . . Just lying there when I came in," they heard him say.

The four tenants watched him speak with a carefully groomed EMT, who touched a gold crucifix on his chest and stepped back towards the van. "Thank you for your help," came Owen's voice, wheedling, pitching up. The man in all white retreated further, his hands up to brush off the thanks, and hopped up and into the bright interior lights, which were hard and loud on the blues and violets of dusk. Paulie couldn't believe how quickly it vanished— was it safe to go that fast, he wondered—and started to cry almost immediately and asked whether Edith was still alive. Claudia let out a small gasp, and Edward put a hairy hand on the back of his neck. Adeleine shifted the two inches back into the foyer and slipped up the stairs with her milky palm on her mouth. In the summer twilight, the wallpaper that followed her upward glinted.

Owen, with his hands on his head and his fists full of hair, swayed a little. His mother's renters observed as he grew still for a time, then how his eyes came open, newly serene. He brought his wrist up and checked his watch, approached the building and climbed the stairs as efficiently as a commuter at rush hour. As he reached Claudia and Edward and Paulie, he wiped his hands on his khaki shorts and settled on the step beneath where they stood. "It's hard to know," he said, his voice speculative and restrained. "How do you tell someone her life has become too much for her?" Above him, unsure of their position, they transferred their weight from one hip to another, fiddled with the bodega receipts in their pockets. Paulie worked two fingers into the band of Edward's pants. Soon they turned to go, leaving Owen to look down the view he'd been born into, the tall narrow buildings of the same cheerful brown, the old trees reaching for each other above the street. He looked like a child transfixed, face pressed to cool aquarium glass, willing cognition from mystery.

A FEW DAYS AFTER the ambulance took Edith away, Edward and Claudia sat on his tiny couch, dark bottles of beer in hand, their faces lit by a stand-up comedy special. Paulie sat between them on the floor, leaning his head lightly against Claudia's knee and occasionally patting Edward's calf. They passed things to each other wordlessly as they laughed: Claudia handed Edward the carton of lo mein; Edward removed a cushion from the sofa and placed it behind Paulie's neck; Paulie, without taking his eyes from the screen, removed a pinecone from his pocket and placed it on Claudia's right foot. That afternoon, while the three of them picnicked in the park, Drew had placed a trash bag on their stoop: Claudia's dirty laundry, worn underwear and coffee-stained nylon button-ups she hadn't bothered to wash before she left him.

Paulie finished eating first and began silently farting. Edward's face contorted as though witness to a quick accident, a knuckle hacked off in shop class.

"Paulie! What the *fuck*! That smells like if celery were homeless!"

Claudia choked on her beer at this, sprayed it out the side of her mouth, and Paulie's face reddened furiously. They were hidden in the safety of the moment, the comfort of intimate ridicule, when the lights went out.

THE FACT THAT THE WOMAN who wasn't Jenny and her bumbling street colleagues hadn't managed to steal anything made the humiliation worse. A stronger person, thought Thomas, would brush this off with a laugh, the thought of blindly following a homeless woman into a McDonald's and babbling on while she devoured greasy food, preparing to rob him. The way they had wrenched his body left a series of bruises, and on the back of his head he felt a raised welt, but he knew it didn't warrant the two days he had spent almost entirely in the hotel room. He had accomplished nothing, eaten little, felt that he deserved to remain hungry. On the third evening he resolved to rise early the next day, take himself to a museum, and develop some plan in the unfettered mental space a concentration of art almost always gave him.

At the Museum of Modern Art the next day, Thomas wandered through a photography exhibit focused on Depression-era small towns, thought how the dirt-faced children were all most likely dead. Later, he nearly stumbled into a sculpture that took up a whole room, a netting of tied rope that seemed to fall naturally but was in fact hardened with shellac. Signage prohibited venturing in or under it, and he felt a silent camaraderie with the others who skirted the edges as he did, looked a lingering while, perhaps thinking of parts of their life that had once seemed flexible and had irrevocably calcified. He drank expensive coffee on the rooftop garden, which seemed to gather all the heat the gray city had to offer in the bright steel of its abstract sculptures, its polished wooden benches. Nearby a new family talked loudly, their idealism pouring into a high-tech stroller, and from the street below came the sounds of someone with a bullhorn, trying to rally people for a cause that was not quite discernible. Thomas decided to try the library again, if only for the quiet.

At his pleading, Edith had finally admitted, in the benumbed voice she seemed to reserve for protected memories, that the last they'd seen of their daughter was a shot of her tangled hair in a television news segment. He thought it possible that if a news network's team had been there, so had some local reporters, and he resolved to spend the afternoon at the microfiche machine, watching the nicotine-colored celluloid whir by like water escaping a hole. At the base of the library, a sloping lobby that looked up at six floors of smudged glass walls and people moving slowly behind them, Thomas felt a new wave of surrender to the search and followed the feeling into the elevator.

Edith had been unsure of the precise year, had finally whittled it down to two possibilities, and Thomas requested the reels of the *Bay Guardian* and the *San Francisco Examiner.* His hand on the lever, he spent hours moving the blown-up images forward, hastening the speed, quickly absorbing then rejecting headlines about the rare heat wave, the murder of a police officer, the kidnapping of a child. At the end of it all he had nothing; the final strip reached its ends and retracted back to its spool, and the screen, deprived of anything to project, glowed eerily white. Comfort had replaced purpose: the idea of Jenny had splintered and lost focus, but he felt calmed by the dated technology, the rolls stored in their time-stamped boxes and handled by librarian after librarian, the stories they held immutable, and so he requested two additional rolls from later years.

His right wrist, loose, let the blown-up reproductions float by rapidly, and he basked in the therapy of the changing ochre light, the steady hum. He settled back into his chair and imagined soothing, unlikely futures, apartments he and Adeleine might rent and furnish together, children he might have and carefully watch.

And there, unmistakably, appearing for half a second in a photograph that championed most of a page, was Jenny.

Two mornings before all the bedside lamps and televisions went dark and the refrigerators stopped humming, Adeleine answered her door in a half sleep, convinced by the dream she'd just exited that it was Thomas standing on the other side. Owen was in and past her before she'd even rubbed the yellow-green sleep from her eyes.

"I saw you in the lobby when the ambulance came," he said, crossing her living room in a series of little stomps, gauging the strength of the floor. He pushed a curtain aside to inspect the lock on the window. "You're the only tenant I haven't met." Adeleine felt exposed in the yellow lace nightgown she'd answered the door in, looked down and saw the bow at the neck and the gauzy skirt as signs of weakness. She felt the slow creep of a man noticing her, and pulled a throw blanket from the sofa to wrap around her shoulders, but this only seemed to thicken his attention.

"You live alone?" he asked. He already knew the answer, was already busy cataloging her insane collection of objects, turning in slow circles with his fists in his khaki pockets.

She nodded.

"What do you do when something breaks?"

Her anxiety kept her from answering at all, and he grinned.

"I see. You're in it for the historic charm! The claw-foot bath!

The fire escape! The easiest attitude to take in these old places, huh?"

"Listen," he said, announcing his transition into business with authority. "I need someone to pop in on Edith while she's recovering from her little hospital adventure. I'm working on getting her placed somewhere permanently, of course, but in the interim I can't be here all the time playing nurse. I just need you to check once a day that she's eaten and bathed somewhat recently. If you'll help, maybe we can work something out. I won't require that you vacate, as I will with the rest of the tenants."

"I, well—"

"Great," Owen said. "You will. Fabulous." He chucked her chin with his index finger and winked, was out the door. Adeleine glanced at her watch. The whole exchange had lasted less than three minutes, but the safety she usually found in appraising her things—the stacks of books she'd annotated, the gauzy scarf draped over a lamp—was gone, had left with him.

With Helena's curtains tied up to admit the light from the street, the apartment felt larger, like a space human clutter had not yet succeeded in filling.

Edward paced, on hold with Con Edison, while Claudia found and lit candles, then stuffed them in four recently drained wine bottles he had left by the door. Paulie couldn't understand the fuss, was thrilled to see their faces and the corners of the apartment shadowed and defined so differently. He had immediately suggested to Claudia that they all think up their most haunted stories, but she had told him only that ghosts were pains in the ass, unreliable guests who didn't clean up when they came to dinner. Perched on the couch, crossing and uncrossing her legs, she looked over at Edward and swore under her breath. Paulie felt awfully bored and lay down on the carpet, where he demonstrated for his sister all the stretches he knew of, starting with his legs all the way up and straight and his hands clutching his toes. Edward had moved to the bedroom, where he had finally gotten someone on the line, and they could hear the pitch of his voice move up and down in protest and negotiation. After fifteen minutes, he was back.

"Fuck," Claudia said, when she looked at his face.

"They said we can't do anything without her, since she's the account holder."

"Did you explain her brain is fermenting on the floor beneath us? That we can't even get her to come to the door?"

"What do you think, Claude? You think I just spent twenty minutes on the phone with them solving the moral conundrum of abortion? We figured it out! *It's wrong!*"

"I'm sorry," she said. "It's just, how much longer can we . . . ? I can't put him in danger again. I can't."

Claudia sat back with a sigh. She looked like someone who has searched the same small area for a lost object over and over, increasingly convinced the space doesn't hold it but not yet ready to name the search fruitless.

"Paulie," she said, with the urgency of a religious fanatic in a pulpit. "When is that . . . firefly thing?"

"In the Smoky Mountains?" He leapt up onto the cushions, noodling as he tried to find his balance. "It is exactly one week and four days from now, Claude! And it is *highly* recommended that you reserve a camping space before arrival!"

Behind Paulie, Edward began waving his hands at Claudia, half circles that indicated *turn back now*, and shaking his head. Already flying with conviction, she avoided his eye contact and enunciated Paulie's name slowly. Edward watched her tense and refine, her mouth pursing, her spine straightening, like a predatory animal set on action.

"What do you say, pal? Should we finally take that camping trip you've always wanted?" His answer came in waves of yeses, eradicating the hushed air of the room. He sank to embrace his sister and covered her face in pungent kisses, then lifted her in a strained cradle. One neon-sneakered foot danced towards a wine bottle holding a candle, and a nearby Chinese food carton alit with a slow flame. After Edward dutifully doused the thing, Paulie rushed him with a crazy grin, the hinge of his jaw appearing askew. Some previously unprompted reflex opened Edward's arms, and he kissed the thirty-three-year-old on the forehead and sighed.

Paulie insisted on music to celebrate with. He retrieved a battery-powered keyboard from his apartment and pounded out the opening of Whitney Houston's "I Will Always Love You." Edward placed the brown take-out bag on his head and whispered obscenities to himself: *Holy fuck doctor. Ass lunch.*

When he hit the high notes, Paulie turned his face upward like a dog on a rapturous scent. In the dramatic conclusion of the piece, Edward removed his mask, watched Claudia hold up her candle and move it back and forth. Moments later, when Paulie asked Edward if he'd come with them, he slapped a hand to his forehead and nodded. The evening breeze had cured him of fatigue, and the candle flames nagged at the room, an obnoxious reminder of the space's total infeasibility. What could he say but yes?

THOMAS STOOD on the top floor of the rapidly emptying library, dreading exit, ignoring the announcements about closing, printing several copies of the photo.

Jenny and another girl stand in the shadow of a man wearing only jeans and sunny brown hair hanging past his nipples. His hipbones, distinct above the denim's low waistline, gleam. A variety of greenery, spiked and reedy and leafed, moves up their legs. Jenny, on his right, rests her hands on the wooden handle of a shovel nearly as tall as she is. On her biceps is a tattoo of a circle, perhaps something more that Thomas can't make out. To the man's left, the other woman leans her soft face and long braids against his sculpted shoulders. In the unfocused background sit lopsided structures made of waste, bits of crates printed with half names of brands, deformed soda bottles, slices of tire, all of them thatched with twisted steel and strips of faded cloth.

The accompanying article, dated 1973, concerned a group of people who had departed San Francisco, gone farther north, in a return-to-the-land movement characterized by an emphasis on quiet. While they specifically avoided terms such as "leader," the twenty-odd individuals—mostly young women—had followed the man in the photo, who called himself Root, to the property just below the border of the Trinity Alps Wilderness, an area rich in conifer diversity and poor in people. The son of a prominent senator, he had washed himself of his family's reputation and spent their money on three hundred acres.

They spoke only one hour of the day and harvested simple crops, arugula and tomatoes and corn. In what little of an interview the reporter could manage, Root offered few words about their rejection of identity. "We're no one, just like everybody else," he said. "And we're not afraid of it." Regarding their notions about silence: "It's not a hard and fast rule. Nobody is upbraided if they need to talk outside the hour of the day we set aside for it. But we find that the lion's share of verbalization is an unnecessary excess, a vehicle that brings us away from ourselves."

Jenny, who had begun to call herself Song, spoke only when asked about her home—had she come far to join this? Did her family approve?—and she answered only, "I was born in a place surrounded by water you can't drink. Can you imagine?"

WHEN AN INTERNET SEARCH confirmed the community still existed, Thomas felt the return of obligation. Back in the hotel room, he parted his hair neatly and combed it, took a harsh gulp of the tiny mouthwash. He kept expecting to find an out, to follow a selfish wish, and felt some surprise in the cab en route to the nearest car rental, as he spoke clear directions to the driver, and in the moment after the uniformed employee dropped the keys to a bland sedan into his hand and he crossed the parking lot, humming. He hadn't driven a car since the stroke, and some part of him had expected a test demanding he raise both hands and make fists. He pushed away his mounting anxiety until the road was already rushing invisibly under him, then transferred it to the pressure on the gas pedal. The indirect route he'd planned, he hoped, would work to collect his confidence. On the Golden Gate, he ignored the way his left hand wilted across the steering wheel and watched the light perform on the bay. North of San Francisco, the land turned first into a near canopy of deep green, then cow-spotted hills that sloped modestly into imposing height.

C LAUDIA WHIRLED AROUND corners and opened and closed closets with a mania that frightened Paulie. It recalled his mother, who had always taken to cleaning after Paulie's visits to the doctor: all surfaces of the house wet and gleaming so that touching them seemed wrong, the carpets robbed of all the soft steps they'd collected and shampooed to an unnatural sheen, the toilets so bright Paulie had felt guilty using them.

Paulie followed Claudia's laps, shadowed her bent figure as she opened drawers and bumped them shut with her round hip, sat nearby as she unzipped and rezipped outer pockets on the two neon-pink suitcases she had purchased for the occasion. She told Paulie that when they returned from camping with the fireflies, the two of them were going to find a new place together, and that was why she had begun packing up his things. He felt squeezed watching his cymbals and ladybug cups, their shapes concealed by the seedy headlines of the *New York Post*, disappear without fanfare into the plain cardboard boxes. But he said nothing, just stuffed his hands in his armpits and returned every smile she flashed him.

Around ten a.m. Claudia hinted at a surprise in the afternoon, which made Paulie sweat and repetitively swallow to ease the dryness in his throat. He had never been fond of putting off joy, or giving his imagination the chance to inflate possibilities. He worried Claudia was making decisions too fast. In the bathroom, he sang a verse of Cat Stevens's "Moonshadow" and turned on the faucet to obscure the sound he knew was coming, and vomited.

When they finally left the apartment four hours and many boxes later, when Paulie felt the beloved rush of the subway and in Manhattan moved through a crowd of people who all smelled different and Claudia stopped him in front of the REI, he couldn't form the smile that appropriately expressed his excitement. The tall double doors opened and he galloped through Skiing and Running and Swimming before he reached Camping, where he stood taking shallow breaths and deciding what object to touch first. He fingered the tiniest portable stoves and caressed glossy freeze-dried bags of food in flavors from chicken noodle to chickpea curry. Under the supervision of a cheery and vested employee, he evaluated six different sleeping pads in icy blues and sharp purples and mature greens. Lying there, he wondered at all the clunky items of human life rendered collapsible and manageable, efficient and unbreakable. He closed and opened the windows of the model tents, loved the clean sound of the plastic teeth coming together. Suddenly worried by the scale of options, Paulie asked Claudia what he could buy and she said, "Whatever you want. We're going to drive around camping for a month!" He wilted onto a plastic log, where he sat with his hands on his knees, overcome with shock, blinking as he tried to absorb the prospect. He knew what was happening in his ears was called ringing, but it didn't feel safe to hear the sounds of your body competing with the rest of the world, every breath struggling on its long way out.

I'M SORRY for not calling sooner," Thomas began, on speaker in the compact rental car, his phone plugged into the stereo system so that when Adeleine spoke her voice caressed the rearview mirror, the sun-spotted windows, the pristine cloth of the backseat. He turned her soft voice up.

"That's okay," she said, indicating her situation was anything but. "Thomas?"

"Yes?"

"Edith went to the hospital. She slipped. Or something. Owen was back for the weekend it happened and then she came home and he left again. Also, were you going to tell me about the eviction, or did you plan just to let me rot up here?"

"You have to believe that I'm taking care of it. That's what I'm out here doing. Is she okay? How did it happen?" He posed the question as if the information were at all surprising, as though it concerned an Olympic athlete and not a woman in her late eighties with a flailing grasp on the season. It occurred to him that he had counted on the building to pause, an immutable tableau, while he left to save it.

"I don't really know—but—"

"Who's taking care of her?"

"That's the thing." The fear in her voice was evident through the speaker's magnification and lent the dappled light a frantic quality, every fluctuation in brightness a mirror of her manic stuttering.

"He asked *me* to, I mean, he came into my apartment and basically ordered me to! And I can't, I can't. I'm worried I won't be able to leave. I mean, I went down there without you once, but it was the first time in so long that I felt like I could and now, god, the *lights* are off—"

"Honey." He paused, gathered the confidence to swaddle her in while he leaned slightly into the turns of the mountainous road and tightened his hand on the wheel. He resented the telephone, wished just to give her the view of the highway that cut improbably through cliff.

"Yes, you can. Think about it: you're still not going outside, right? And you sounded so industrious on the phone when I called and you were with her! You sounded like someone who could orchestrate a space shuttle launch with the flick of a wrist."

"I think you'd better come home," she quavered. "The *lights* are off," she repeated. "And I think Edward and Paulie and Claudia have left. I haven't heard anything, but I looked down and there are all these boxes on their floor in the hall, and it feels like being the last person alive."

"Adeleine. Can you stop scaring yourself? She probably just didn't pay the bill. She keeps all her papers on her desk, under all the plants. You just call Con Ed and pretend to be her. Go down there and check on her, tell her it will be okay. She needs you." Thomas couldn't believe the gruffness in his voice, the impatience for her shrill worry. Wasn't she the woman whose pathology he had taken such pains to dance around, more or less protecting it? He felt decidedly vexed at her then, her solipsism and odd intelligence, all her resistance to a regular life out in the open.

She hadn't answered.

"Did you hear me?

"Adeleine?"

He heard the soft cluck of her mouth opening and waited for some murmur of assent.

"Okay," she gasped. "Okay."

"It will be all right. I'm on my way to Jenny as we speak—I'll tell you the story next time we talk. Call me and let me know when you've got the lights back on and give me an update on Edith." He didn't give her the opportunity to hesitate again. "Good-bye, love."

His thoughts purified quickly. The happiness that stemmed from tiny adjustments of the rearview mirror, the sharp turns he continued to handle, was large and flexible. The diffuse uncertainty of his predicament washed gently, like a tide eating slowly at firmly packed sand.

S ITTING IN THE DARK WITH EDITH, holding her hand, listening to her breath try and fail to determine a rhythm, Adeleine attempted to think of her condition as others saw it. As though considering a photo taken without her knowledge, she turned it, held it up to light to reveal some previously invisible element of herself. Had Thomas considered just how opportunely the arrangement had developed, the cheap punch line of an agoraphobe taking up with someone just across the hall? Did he see her affections as paltry for how little they traveled, how rarely they were tested? She had navigated the situation far too casually, she thought, had allowed her proximity and availability to stand as an ersatz reproduction of commitment. She may as well have said, *Yes, I'll keep welcoming you in. I'll stay, but how much that has to do with you and me is a little murky.*

On the phone she had wanted to say, *My pillows are losing the scent you left*, but she had only moaned about her various inconveniences and inabilities, added to the tentacled shape of all that required his fixing. There hadn't been any way to tell him, that week in early March when he came down with the flu in her apartment, how much it had meant to drag a damp cloth across his face, to fetch tea and watch him wrap his hand around its warm comfort.

Instead of closing the conversation with an assurance of love or even faith, she had only absorbed his instructions, sat on them for a day before following them downstairs. The bill was right where he'd said it would be, the phone number in bold. She had picked up the cracked plastic cordless phone, and she had dialed.

EDITH WAS THE WORD Adeleine pushed out of her mouth slowly; what she'd intended to say—*Help*—had died somewhere on its escape. The shadowed suggestions of both their bodies, Edith's flattened against the bed and Adeleine's drawn close to her on a nearby chair, stretched across the room when cars passed, threatening to disintegrate. Adeleine liked the idea of confessing to Edith, the guarantee that nothing she mentioned would be long considered or captured.

"I haven't left the house in more than six months. The closest I came was standing in the foyer when the ambulance came for you, and even that made me feel like I was in the mountains with not enough air.

"I used to be better. Brunches on Sundays with other hung-over people in sunglasses. Parties—crowded ones. I always knew the corner store guy. The last one gave me boxes when I moved and kissed my cheek."

The last fact was too much: the shared kindnesses she'd once enjoyed now only measurements of how she'd deteriorated. She leaned hard against the rigid wicker and pushed away images of herself balancing a grocery bag on her hip while she stopped to pet an acquaintance's dog, biting her lip while she listened to a neighbor's story of a hellish Christmas. The truth of her life came from her easily now, and she was freed to speak into the room that was not empty of love but also not quite listening.

"Edith? Thomas is so good to me. I'm worried I can't or won't be what he needs, or that he'll leave me if I don't get better. And that he's with me so he can keep hiding from the rest of his life."

"Oh, June. My sister."

Edith reached her hand, which appeared as rough and inflexible as reef, towards Adeleine's and covered it. She spoke calmly, as though reciting a multiplication table, facts that would never become less true.

"It's not your job to say why someone loves you, is it?"

Adeleine, eyes wide, sniffed and shook her head. "No?"

"And you'll never see the way your skeletons can dance. Not if you keep them to yourself. You've gotta let those bones twist!" Even in the dimness, Adeleine could make out true delight, the glint of silver-crowned molars as Edith smiled.

Edith's grip tightened, and Adeleine watched the slack, spent skin on her arm collect as the muscles beneath it contracted.

"Now," she instructed—Adeleine heard a woman who facilitated long-term plans and kept appointments—"come lie down here, next to me. You need your sleep after a long trip like that."

Adeleine took in Edith's fermenting odor, the brackish taste of her own weeping. Unable to decline even such a confused offer of warmth and rest, Adeleine surrendered and crawled towards her. The two women curled on top of the quilt sewn by hand sixty years before, their backs to each other but their hands linked, and began breathing deeply.

Two hours later, Adeleine woke to the sudden light of the bedside lamp. The living room overhead, the bar above the stove, the bulbs in the bathroom: they came on inch by inch, as though moved by flood, the *tinks* of the filaments like champagne flutes meeting somewhere nearby.

I n the 1966 mint-green Dodge Dart that Claudia had purchased for $4,250 the day she'd quit her job, Paulie sat up
front with the window way down. The wind pushed back towards
Edward, examining the contours of his receding hairline. Under
her foot, the give of the gas pedal galvanized Claudia's already
electric mood; she kept turning up the volume of *Pet Sounds* and
letting her left hand float out the window. Edward, strapped in
by the well-worn seatbelt, wearing his only shorts—an unfortu-
nate pair of bleach-spotted cutoffs—pressed his back against the
vinyl and felt the car's rapid acceleration. He wondered briefly at
how quickly, how myopically, he'd agreed to come, but then his
vision settled on the line of Claudia's arm, now stretched across
the middle section to reach Paulie's shoulder, and he felt proud
and awake.

"Paulie," Claudia barked as she drummed four fingers against
the peeling steering wheel. "Tell us about these fireflies. Lay it
on us."

Edward leaned forward. "Build a house out of facts, brother. I
want to live in them."

Paulie giggled, then cleared himself of humor to make room
for sacrosanct focus.

"They're called synch-ro-nous fireflies," he began, talking

over the rushing of the freeway and furrowing his eyebrows so that he looked, for once, like someone who had lived thirty-odd years. In the rearview mirror, an oversized soda cup danced wildly between cars, willing suicide. Trucks as long as Manhattan blocks trundled past.

"And they only live in two places on the earth. We're going to one of them. Elk-mont, Tenn-ess-ee." He gave each syllable attention; he wanted to honor this information.

"If *synchronous* reminds you of *synchronicity*, then you're on the right track, my friends!"

Paulie told them that the *Photinus carolinus* gathered once a year, that thousands of the males pulsed in glowing simultaneity, competing for the attention of the females that clustered below, watching, each hoping to choose the brightest mate.

For Claudia and Edward, Paulie's babbling crested and receded like the landscape out the windows. During a lull, in which Paulie stopped speaking and Claudia didn't pick out another tape, Edward retrieved his video camera and began recording, moving first through the space between the front seats, bits of Claudia's hair that whipped into the frame, then moved towards Paulie.

"Eddy!" he said. "Is this going to be a movie? Will you make me very famous? Here, get me smiling. Make my little teeth big." In the one-inch viewfinder, close up, the rows of tiny white triangles could have been something else—hills in the distance, calcified shipwrecked things breaking through the sand on the bottom of the ocean—until the tongue broke through, fat and full.

THE COUNTRY THOMAS HAD REACHED boasted of its beauty in a way that seemed to erase tract housing and mini-marts and rat-infested public transportation; the overwhelming height and age of the trees, the loud proof of the river beyond them, nullified his memory of anything else. When the map he'd hand-drawn at the library—a childhood habit and a comforting pleasure—indicated his location on the curving two-lane highway as half an hour or so from the possibility of Jenny, he pulled over on an untended shoulder. He would find his way to the water, which he believed he could smell.

On the silted bank, he accepted the probability of Jenny's being long gone or dead, and he watched as the river, rather than bracing for impact, hurried its pace around the bend ahead. Picking up pebbles with his toes and letting them drop, Thomas waited there twenty minutes, until he felt his breathing had refined. Back behind the wheel, he signaled before he pulled out onto the concrete. He had not seen another car in hours.

At the point in the road where there should have been a turn into the community's property, he searched for a clear demarcation but found none, let alone the hand-carved wooden sign or softly lit path of loose earth he had imagined in his more sanguine moments. The road neatly divided two biospheres, one that tumbled down in sharp angles of rock and trees that grew almost horizontally into the bleached altitudinous sky, the other a level forest dense with age and nearly lightless.

He left the car door open, the sensor dinging and nagging, as he paced back and forth along the road's shoulder, pausing at points to will some divine clue and then blushing at his foolishness. On his final lap, ready to get in the car and scan the next few miles of road, he felt the pang of an approaching aura. Unwilling to embrace the uncomfortable swirl of color at the margins of his vision—*This doesn't help me, not now*—Thomas settled horizontally on the damp and green side of the road with a hand over his eyes and waited for the ache to strike. As the pain descended, he tried to focus on the view, the trees that triangulated in their height and framed the lowering sun.

Closer to him than the wash of sky, thirty feet above the ground, a length of faded mauve cloth stretched from one branch to another. A foot above glinted a section of pink ribbon, taut and pearled with the near-dusk. A slash of green. Orange. Yellow. He gripped grass in his fists and looked, but saw no clear indication of how whoever tied them there had scrambled up, no marks in the tree but those of weather. The aura rippled and bled his perspective of the colors, and he waited for them to clear, his mind renouncing worries one by one, like muscles giving out.

IT FELT DIFFICULT to believe that an hour before, he'd lain curled in the throes of a migraine on the shoulder of the road: now he walked through patches of light where the trees parted their tangled meetings, now he saw—far ahead, but not unreachable—the system of structures.

He momentarily believed, with the kind of unblemished optimism that only accompanies new places, that he had nothing to be afraid of: he would end up with Adeleine or he wouldn't, he would find Jenny or let the blurred idea of her go, he would accept the lost agency of his body and find another use. Fed by rosy resolve, he approached the cluster of buildings set against the forest in ragged lines, and made for the largest, where a slipshod porch cast blue shadows. The shade of a veranda, composed primarily of a drooping sweep of fishnet, was woven with the spines of hardback books, the lone soles of hiking boots, gnarled pieces of wood that varied in lengths and browns.

In the small of his back and the balls of his feet, Thomas felt the men approach.

He turned to witness their congruent outlines, long hair that fell around stern faces, clothing patched and repatched so thoroughly it obscured any original layer. Their ages seemed indeterminable, as if instead of possessing a certain number of years they shed and gained age, as circumstances required, from one great shared well. In one motion, all of them extended their arms upward in Vs. Either like reaching for something hidden, Thomas thought, or preparing for a fall.

"Raise your arms up to greet us," said one with gray eyebrows that nearly met and a tattered rope of violet cloth in his long hair, not ungently. He was trying to guide him, Thomas could tell, attempting to lead the foreigner's first communication.

"But I—can't," said Thomas, pointing at his limp arm with his virile one. "But I *can't*."

LATER, INSIDE, a hardening clustered among the men. He was a stranger, and he had asked to speak with Jenny, had used her birth name as if he owned it. "I'm here," he had said, "on behalf of her mother," as though that would make it better, as though it weren't offensive enough, his arriving there insisting she belonged more rightfully to some other life.

They were seated in what he assumed was a common area, under polished conch shells that sat on foot-long shelves of birch high up the wall. Bags of rice rested on tapestries of crudely stitched images of forests and rivers. Tortoiseshell cats entered and exited, turning corners purposefully. In a specious reversal of power, all the men sat on square pillows they had removed from a pile in the corner and arranged in a half orbit below Thomas, who balanced in a modest rocking chair. Looking at them, he noted they had mastered the art of listening and threatening simultaneously. The door, which leaned slightly off its hinges, was half open and suggested escape, but he understood they would not permit him to walk out.

"Her son is trying to take her home from her," he said, his voice hushed with exasperation. "Jenny's *brother*."

"Song," they said. Every time he said *Jenny*, all the figures in the room murmured *Song* in correction, further contributing to the impression that they were forever collectively processing.

"She was one of the first ones here, wasn't she?" Thomas heard himself continue. "She came with Root." He hoped that this might indicate a respect for their mythology, that he had not arrived to beg without understanding what they risked by giving, but the mention of the lean man in the forty-year-old photographs made them lower their heads.

"I'll take you to see Song," said the one Thomas now understood to be the eldest, "but after, it will be time for you to go." He rose without checking to see whether Thomas was following, used a careful thumb and forefinger to open the door. Thomas, who hoped to express some thanks, stood to speak, but their heads were pressed into their laps, and their long hair in grays and browns ran over their ears and onto the dusty hardwood. The man he was meant to follow was already outside, and the day was already losing its downy heat.

E DWARD AND CLAUDIA took turns at the wheel, slipping in and out of the driver's seat without much discussion: he could tell by the change in her breathing, low and shallow, when she'd grown tired, and she knew when he became quiet, no longer mocked billboards and bumper stickers. Paulie alternately napped and enthused, woke into excitement and wore it out again. He resembled a maladroitly assembled angel under the staticky corona of hair that encircled him, and he glowed with the dew of sleep in the refracted sun. As he drooled on the bright blue sweatshirt pressed against the window as a pillow, Claudia periodically looked over and gave thanks for the temporary quiet. It was as though every time he regained consciousness, he remembered not only their destination and the much-anticipated dance of the fireflies, but also every moment in his life that had amused or satisfied him, every song and birthday and windless afternoon.

First his unnaturally long eyelashes fluttered, then his eyelids snapped up like blinds. His slack fingers twitched, then all straightened at once, like something being turned on, and clapped his face. "Oh my god!" yelled Paulie, so loud that Edward jammed his index fingers into his hairy eardrums. "We're getting there, aren't we!"

In Edward's few moments alone—pissing in increasingly

squalid gas station bathrooms, the rare occasion of focused thought made possible when both Claudia and Paulie had fallen asleep, on stretches of highway shoulder where they stopped occasionally to move their legs and establish some distance from one another—he admitted to feeling a little worried. Claudia looked towards her brother with a fierce adoration, yes, but she also assaulted the gas pedal with the unyielding force of a waterfall, she also seemed unconcerned with the existing flow of cars when merging onto the freeway. He had stopped suggesting she glance over her shoulder, which only made her driving more aggressive.

For the first three or four hours of the trip, her cell phone had rung and shaken at a near-constant rate. She had turned up the stereo and sung louder to *Sticky Fingers*, she had insisted on an inane car game in which one alphabetically listed the fictitious people they knew. Paulie had strained to remember: "At the party, I saw Aranda . . . Bernard . . . Caligula . . . Dan . . . Eloise." Finally, without fanfare, she had turned off the phone and let it slide down her glistening palm, past her chipped blue fingernails, and onto the freeway.

Edward mentioned it later, at a cinder-block marriage of a Subway-KFC-ARCO where eleven-year-olds congregated to suck down cigarettes and a voice bleated over damaged speakers when a rented shower became available.

"What were you thinking? Just get rid of your phone? Think that was *whimsical*? What if mine was stolen! What if—"

He realized his mother and the anxiety he had inherited were glinting in his grating tone, and he recalibrated his voice.

"Claude," he said, unsure of when he had adopted the shortened version of her name, but certain some milestone of intimacy had been stomped over. "Wanna tell me why you're acting like the entirety of *Thelma and Louise* sped up and played on loop? *Mid-Life Crisis: The Musical?* Should we do some screaming in headscarves, cut off our hair, prank call our exes? Is that it?"

Paulie slumped against the passenger window of the car, exhausted after singing to Jagger's yowl, and they could see him napping from where they sat. Claudia brushed some crumbs of fried chicken off the table's oily surface, folded her hands on the plasticked red, and put her head down and started to cry.

"I just want to have this. Can I just have it? Will you just let me have it?" She bolted upright again, and her fingers were straight and quick as knives as she passed them across her wet face.

"Have what? A terrifying sandwich served by a pregnant teenager named Kimmi? You just did."

"Once I go back," she continued, "everything is going to be different. I'm going to do what I should have done and make sure he's always taken care of. I have to get Paulie and me a place together, build a client list and work from home. I have to keep him safe. Drew is losing his shit—who leaves someone not even two years into the marriage, he said, which, who can blame him—and that was him on the phone. He cries in some messages and swears in others. About every third one there's some kind of threat." She spit the words out low and hard, gnawing a tiny crescent of skin from her thumb, and he tugged the digit away from her mouth's nervous bite, held it between two of his fingers.

"Okay. If you need me to support you in your no-holds-barred Spring Break-a-Thon, so be it. I'll attach a boozy IV to your arm once we get to the Smoky Mountains. We can act out a commercial for herpes medicine, go white-water rafting and high-five on mountain peaks. But I have to ask you here to be a little bit cautious, and not drive so goddamn fast, and not start believing this is your very last shot at living. If you don't start being a little more careful with yourself, I'm hailing the first Greyhound back to New York City."

Claudia had never been known as beautiful. She had always dressed in high, flattering waists and dull gold ear studs, kept her brown hair tied and clean, her life small in the service of others. There, however, in the combination Subway-KFC, she loosened. His teasing coaxed her orthodontically corrected teeth into a smile that curved under her still-wet cheeks, and her hair fell tangled around her face, protesting a lifetime of imprisonment. She closed her eyes and began to nod, as though envisioning the cleaning of many rooms, the stacking and sweeping and mopping and finally, the space around her, gleaming.

How long had he been cross-legged on the stiff cowhide rug by the darkened fireplace? What was Jenny's intention, sitting up in the wide sun-bleached bed, looking impossibly old? The tattoo on her arm was the same as that in the newspaper photo—a faded black circle that he recognized now as a snake eating its tail—and the line of the freckled jaw was similar to that of the little girl in Brooklyn, but she looked as though her body had been systematically deserted, memory by memory emptying out in single file. He kept searching for evidence of her taking in or releasing air. The room seemed a near-total void of history or evidence or yesterday or tomorrow: the sheets white, pristine in the way of nothing else on the property; for a nightstand, a slab of unpolished tree trunk; the curtainless window. Just beyond her, a doorframe revealed a small, low-ceilinged room, within it a black woodstove and two simple chairs stacked together. The smells of food, of things warmed by time and by bodies, were absent.

Finally, without opening her eyes, she spoke.

"Edith sent you."

"Well—not—you see—" he answered, although it had been clear this wasn't a question. The woman, once a child on the steps of the building Thomas had come to need, stopped him before his unorganized mumbling achieved any pattern.

"I'm afraid I can't help."

"But your brother—"

She put a palm up with the patience of someone directing the weak and hospitalized.

"That person is named Owen."

Thomas sensed Jenny's language was one half-forgotten, its structure uncharted, the pressure of the tongue against the palate to make a sibilant sound uncomfortable.

"I should not need to say that these people you mention are not part of here.

"However," she continued, "I can and will give you the same option I give others who come to me. You can stay here for a week, and stay quiet. If you still have the same concerns then, you may pose them. But I find"—and here she readjusted the pillow behind her back and put a hand to her jaw—"the questions tend to change."

ONLY THROUGH TRIAL AND ERROR did Thomas learn that Jenny—or Song, as he'd tried to start remembering her—meant precisely what she said. No one punished him for speaking—not when he addressed her, or any of the men who arrived with plates of grainy cornbread and boiled, dirt-caked spinach and fried eggs over brown rice—but his words didn't seem to make it any farther than his lips. They didn't glare at him or admonish him when, during the first twenty-four hours, he continued to ask, "Would it be possible for me to bathe? Could I make one phone call?" But neither did they acknowledge the sound; they only gazed and blinked, as though waiting for some unseen photographer to press down a button. It's either like checking into a hostel where no one speaks your language, Thomas thought, or regressing into preverbal infancy, conceiving that care will be bestowed without even grasping the concept of trust. Neither option seemed ideal, but then neither seemed impossible to master. The discomfort of it was like a pulled muscle, unnoticed if he remained still.

By hour thirty-four, he had consigned his old urgency. He dipped his feet into little pools of memories, walked in and around them, trying to absorb every side. A nameless and cinnamon-scented teenage babysitter guiding Thomas's tiny fingers into pots of primary-colored paints, then across the page. His mother at her happiest, alternately darkened and illuminated by a romantic comedy at the multiplex theater, her hand hovering over an unending bag of popcorn, sometimes squeezing his in delight, calling him *my love*. His high school biology lab partner, a red-haired girl who had undressed in his bedroom while his back was turned and insisted he draw, instead of the assigned feline skeleton, her. The variously svelte and pilled couches he slept on his first months in New York, the friends and acquaintances to whom they belonged. An afternoon he draped himself across the parquet after he had hidden all his art away, trying to forgive it for leaving. His ear pressed to the wall to better hear Adeleine's song. The end of a film moving across her face. He entered and exited these rooms blithely as the hours passed, sometimes dozing off under a thin blanket, sometimes waiting, with a flat, simple hope, for food.

ADELEINE WANDERED through Edith's apartment, determined: the sleep had felt clean and efficient, and she wanted to keep that, bend her body to it. She opened windows and took in scents in all their elements, the exhaust of buses breathing under the loose summer sap, and she ran her hands over bright jars of old buttons and white doilies gone brittle. She turned her face towards lamps, nearly kissed the heat of the bulbs. She tilted an ear to the obsolete, yellowed plastic radio on the kitchen counter Edith always kept turned on but low, and she listened.

She could hear Edith, snoring in the next room, and she settled onto the couch, which had the color and smell of a rose left out and starved of water. She began on the important work of imagining herself capable: by the time Thomas returned, she would have plumped and dusted and shined and scrubbed and generally exhumed the apartment. Edith would grow used to resting under the breezes Adeleine let in, to the cool cloth placed gently on her forehead. As her confused words spilled out and jumbled, Adeleine would nod and rearrange them. If she had committed herself to honoring Edith's life at its end, she had only barely considered that this effort might mean instilling some new worth in her own. Though she knew the power she felt was mania, she thought she could shape it, polish its rampant energy and send it to work for her. When her moods went running, she could dispute them from a frightened distance or turn herself over.

As she dreamed from an upright position, Adeleine wrapped one arm around her waist, remembering how Thomas had held her. It was then that Owen entered, holding a key ring in one hand and a bag of oranges in the other. He cleared a space for them on the kitchen table's stiff lace tablecloth, much of which was obscured by stacks of unopened mail, individually wrapped candies in decorative bowls, a single wool glove left out since winter. As though she were a colleague whose face he had memorized in boredom, he nodded at Adeleine, flopped his hand in a kind of wave. "Come here and have a seat," he said.

I N A MOTEL ROOM at the base of the Appalachians, one they'd checked in to at Edward's insistence, was a television with the sound off but screen bright, the decade-old smell of cigarettes, and two beds covered in faded outlines of peonies. Paulie was in the shower with suspiciously soft plastic walls, surfaces that bent when pressed, audibly enjoying the miniature soaps and shampoos. Edward sat on the end of one mattress, examining the toes of his bare left foot with curiosity and disgust, and Claudia sniffed. The lull of the day enfolded them. Moments were lost, extended in the observation of afternoon light as it stretched in shadows across the nubby carpet.

"Sometimes I wish I had taken up smoking," she said. "You know?"

"Nope."

He flipped the mute screen to its next iteration. An ash-blond reporter pushed her breasts forward and said something about the several ambulances next to her, the cosmetic sheen of her face compromised by the red lights that periodically flashed onto it.

"A vice, you know? But a manageable one. Convenient. Just a quick mistake between meetings. I never really let myself explore, is the thing. Always responsible. Sensible shoes! Early bedtime!"

Paulie had stopped singing, and the pipes of the building hummed and coughed. The water continued in spurts.

"Claude," sighed Edward, as though he had filled this role his whole life. "There is no shame in meeting the expectations of the people around you. In being dependable. Please take this earnestly from someone who once blacked out and pissed all over someone's bedroom and tried to not clean his mess but *absorb* it by shaking baby powder everywhere." Claudia put a hand over her face, her fore- and middle fingers parted so that she offered her distaste and amusement to Edward with one eye. They lay back on their respective beds and played a largely unsuccessful game in which he launched peanuts, underhand, in an arch over the space between them into her mouth.

Claudia, filled with the kind of comfort that comes from conquering so many miles in one day, curled up. She descended into a light doze, released cloistered sleep from her mouth and remained still within the uneven ring of peanuts that surrounded her.

When he saw her inert at last, Edward exited the room with attention to the door's gentle close. He padded down the dingy, porous cement stairs, carefully opened the gate with the sign about pool hours, slipped off the drugstore flip-flops he'd bought ninety miles back, and descended the submerged steps into the glowing green-blue.

Paulie, now seated, brought his folded-up legs ever closer to his chest, quivering and murmuring half-words. The shower ran over the empty space of the tub, beating it with uneven sound.

He didn't know why he was crying, or why the space seemed impossible to exit, just that something wrong had set up a home in his body. One moment there he'd been, excited by tiny hotel toiletries, and the next his chest felt smaller, and the room didn't look like a place a person could ever live, and he couldn't remember what he deserved or why. Now he whimpered for his sister, and then Edward, and received no reply; now he reached for a phrase in the cache of those he knew and loved, but it wasn't there.

P LIABLE IN THE HEAT, still softened by the rare optimism that had come her way, Adeleine had not been able to deflect his questions, and soon Owen had known: that the building was empty save the three of them, where Thomas had gone, for whom he was looking. The information had seemed to occur to him in stages, first sharpening the movement of his eyes and hands, until he was bloated with it, and his limbs just hung from the chair where he sat. "I need to move," he had said. "I need to look at something else." He'd led them up to Adeleine's apartment with one hand on the back of his neck, one on his mother's.

Edith took to fits of cursing and forgetting and sleeping, and her son remained collected, occasionally sighing out a bright, focused note. He sat hunched on a chocolate linen ottoman, his legs splayed. The women perched on the brocade chaise under the cracked parlor window, listening to the small sounds of his thumbs on his phone. Every few minutes, a breeze from outside tickled their bare necks.

"Oh, Mom. I wish we could just talk about it. Do you think I like to be here? Think my time is best spent in this strange woman's apartment? Edith?" He wove his fingers together into perfectly tanned Xs and pressed them outward, stretched then straightened the curve of his back.

"This can be an easy conversation."

His mother's jaw worked violently; she looked like someone deep in a casino, lost in obsession, absorbing only the changing light of slot machines.

"Edith, you can sign the house over, or Adeleine, you let me know where your boyfriend has gone to converse with my vanished sister, and we can all go somewhere we'd rather be."

He turned his body in the direction of Adeleine, tilted his head and considered her as though she were selling something. "Of course, your hands are not tied. You're free to go. But something tells me you won't."

THOMAS SAT on the uneven slats of Song's wooden porch, observing a lone chicken cross a patch of dirt in a jagged line. He didn't know where his shoes were. It was morning, and already warm, but with the extended absence of language also vanished observations about things like temperature and time. It had been seven days, although he didn't know that; he'd stopped counting, or forgotten to measure, at four. When Song emerged and situated herself on the handwoven chair behind him, he reached to squeeze her left ankle, and she patted down the unruly parts of his hair. Pale as the early light, the chicken paused to investigate an unfamiliar plant. Two men appeared at the crest of the hill; Thomas and Song watched as their faces became clear, and nodded. The wood creaked to accommodate two more bodies. Mugs of tea, carried a mile, changed hands. The chicken moved in its rhythmic way, a step and a pause and a gawk, a step and a pause and a gawk, into a patch of cedars. Water rushed nearby: they could hear it.

O WEN WAS A MAN accustomed to administration and power—having most recently developed a circle of debt-collection agencies that took a "modern" approach, hounding their targets through e-mail and social media—but he had long forgotten how to earn it. Adeleine could sense his impatience building, observe how he stored it in his shoulders and forearms. She felt unsure of which role to play, given her lack of concrete theories about Thomas's precise location and long-term intentions. He had stopped calling several days before, like an appliance that ceases to function without fanfare, leaving memories of its usefulness fresh, its malfunction confounding.

For the twentieth time since Owen had escorted them upstairs, a grandfather clock she'd found and restored rang out to signify the hour. Owen took a blue silk scarf from the closet and daubed it along the back of his neck, plucked a red whistle from a bookcase and slipped it in his pocket. The women sat on the chaise while he moved about the room as though it were a museum, pausing frequently at pieces of interest to lean and squint.

Edith's command of language seemed to have vanished with the sleep she and Adeleine had shared in the still, dark hours before he'd arrived. The only communication she offered her son was an occasional gob of spit, which she gathered in the back of her throat with visible effort and launched with a quick, deep grunt. After wiping the phlegm away, Owen would retrieve the whistle and blow wearily, a kid bored with a game, producing a shrill note that cowed his mother.

A detainee in her own home, Adeleine paid circumspect attention. She couldn't determine whether it was tenacity that drove Edith to spit at her son again and again, despite knowing the consequence, or some aspect of dementia that named all moments independent, unsupported and unaffected by those that preceded and followed.

Adeleine had never felt any tug of clairvoyance, had generally lived by passively observing the present and only in the fallout of disaster looking for the parts of the past that had led her to it. But in this instance, the quiet that begged her attention, she sensed the impending: eventually, Owen would swivel his attention upon her.

Losing interest in his mother's outbursts, Owen placed the whistle on the coffee table in front of them. When she hissed or bellowed, he only closed his eyes and exhaled. Tension played at the pulse points of Adeleine's body, which felt as though it were filling and hardening.

Owen approached Adeleine and crouched before her, like a gardener inspecting a pattern of decay.

"You and I both know," he said, "that this way is getting us nowhere. I just need to know exactly where he is, and after you tell me that, we can all part ways." His gaze fell down her ancient crinoline blouse, the finicky top two buttons that had slipped halfway out of their enclosures. After he frowned and adjusted them, he cupped her shoulders with his supple palms.

"You are a pretty girl. Very strange, but very pretty."

The phlegm struck his face with the sound of things joining, like the commencement of some dramatic chemical reaction. Edith spoke for the first time in hours, and the words escaped in slow jolts. "Don't. Owen." That his mother had spoken his name seemed to touch him, and he looked her over, the wobbly jaw and milky eyes, before he returned to Adeleine.

His index finger stiff, Owen traced the crinoline where it met Adeleine's linen skirt, the tight line of her waist, then hovered his right hand over her torso, as though waiting for the kick of a baby. "Leave," he said. "Why don't you just go?" His palm reached the underside of her jaw, and his eyes closed and his mouth parted, and he looked to her then like a person finally alone. She took his suggestion and stood.

Halfway to the door, Adeleine looked back at Edith, who had her hands folded, her head down. Her recent protest had evaporated: she was swimming in her own head again, immersed in it, far from air.

As Adeleine crossed the stairs' halfway point, she tried to ignore her nausea, what felt like the revolution of every organ, and ran her fingers across the familiar wallpaper. With the wrench of the heavy front door came the soaring sound of her own blood, and with the descent of the stone steps the refusal of every bone and ligament to cooperate any further. She knew she should develop a plan right then, and tried to remember the order of subway stations on a Manhattan-bound train, just the words themselves and none of the people that would spill from the cars, hurried and hostile. The unmetered air, the confluence of smells, felt like a rough examination of her whole body. *DeKalb* was first and then was—

Huddled on the last step with her angry temples between her knees and her hands full of her hair, she heard Owen cooing from her apartment's window. Soon he was next to her, cradling her, collecting her stiff limbs in his arms. "Come inside, now." A gray-haired woman passing on the street stopped, mulling over the possibility of alarm, and Adeleine heard him say to her, "Bad day. Happens to the best of us."

The woman clucked her tongue and continued on her way home, satisfied with his answer.

J UST AFTER DAWN, on the walk from the pea-colored emergency room lobby to the parking lot, through the two sets of automatic doors and across the quickly warming concrete, Claudia kept her arm hooked around Paulie's waist and refused to look back at Edward. Still dressed in the thin motel robe, the regrettably undersized cutoffs, and the orange drugstore flip-flops, Edward gave a range of sighs aimed specifically at the back of Claudia's head.

She opened the passenger door for Paulie and kissed his forehead as he settled in.

"Hey," Edward said, before she'd had the chance to slip around to her side. "You really think this is such a good idea, to keep going? You don't think he's maybe had too much excitement and change for three days?" He was careful not to gesture in Paulie's direction, to keep his image through the windshield calm.

"He had a panic attack, Edward, not a total breakdown. His condition comes with the occasional anxiety issue. He used to cry every time the trash went out because he didn't want us to lose anything."

"Claude. Have you forgotten the last five hours? I had to pry his hands from the bathtub. He said his heart felt like a drum march. The doctors had to sedate him."

"I've been his sister for about three decades longer than you've been his weird misanthropic neighbor," she said. "Travel freaks him out, but he's been talking about these fucking bugs longer than you or I have talked about anything." She indicated the conversation's conclusion by sliding into the driver's seat and slamming the door.

Edward leaned on the hood and looked out at the lot. Three silver-red hounds left behind in the cab of a peeling green truck barked up a chorus, trying to crowd their mouths through the just-cracked window. He closed his eyes and felt the car start, all the parts beneath stirring towards purpose.

THE STRETCH OF THE DRIVE that followed, free of sound save the occasional zoom of a speeding car, seemed to reject any passing of time, presenting the same fast-food billboards and roadside crosses in triplicate again and again. Paulie kept his hands in his lap and sometimes pressed his mouth against the window, forming bubbles of spit that broke almost as quickly as they formed. Claudia, her posture improved but fossilized, as though her shoulder blades were sewn to the seat, sent hard looks to Edward via the rearview mirror. Made restless by the silence, Edward dug into the backpack at his feet and removed his camera, trained it on Paulie, and called to him gently.

"Oh hi Eddy," said Paulie, with a deflated inflection.

Claudia sensed the presence of the device immediately and asked Edward to place it far within a body cavity of his choosing.

"Ass could be good, but why not try—"

"It's okay, sweet pea," said her brother, looking straight ahead. "Let Eddy do what he wants."

"Hey, pal," Edward said. "How you doing? Last night must have been rough on you."

"To be Mr. Frank, I feel like an octopus in a . . . math class."

"Yeah? Feeling weird? Like, foreign? Alien?"

"I guess so, Ed. I guess you could say alien. I guess *I* would say I was worried I was accidentally living on the wrong planet."

"You know what, though. An octopus in math class could work on a number of equations at once with all those arms."

Paulie's face, as represented through the viewfinder to Edward, began to twitch upward in small ways. "Wow, Eddy. Wow. I bet you're right."

"Just a different way of working."

Edward repositioned himself. Up on his haunches, twisted behind the driver's seat, he filmed from a slight height. Paulie retrieved a pen and paper from the glove box and began to sketch the tentacled creature in question. "Oc-to-pi," he said, exhaling air from his open mouth rapidly. "Oc-to-pi."

Claudia slipped on her neon-green gas-station sunglasses and began looking for a radio station, turning the knob at the first hint of static.

I CAN WAIT for a long time," he said, but Owen, Adeleine could tell, was made uncomfortable by silence. He jerked his thumb across the screen of his phone until the battery died, ran his index finger along the spines on the bookshelf and pulled down a 1930s Boy Scout manual. He grew briefly engrossed in a series of yellowed diagrams titled "How to Build a Snow Tent," delicately lined images replete with pastel-cheeked boys in uniform. After he closed the brittle pages, Owen gravitated towards the records, delicately set the needle down on a Robert Johnson recording and settled on the floor. Adeleine watched as he drew his knees upward and tucked his face, like a hiding child trying to make his space in the world diminutive. He started to speak, and the spite in his voice, refracted through cloth and limbs, seemed softer, washed of grit.

"This isn't how I imagined it happening, you know. I didn't intend for this all to play out like a crime movie. I only came to get what's owed me. Right, Mom?"

Owen turned his face, his coloring now blotched like a much-used eraser block, towards Edith, but she didn't move. His speech was absent of its regular pattern of hard consonants, syllables doled out with restraint. It had adopted a reedy lilt, and Adeleine could imagine him very young, begging: for another hour outside, for dessert, for uncompromised attention.

"You have any idea what it was like growing up here, Edith? Mom? Dad throwing parties all the time while I tried to sleep? You painting all your attention on Jenny, praising her every weird ritual and sudden mood while I brought home perfect grades and made my bed? I spent all those summers helping Dad with the house, I worked to pay for school myself, I never asked for a cent—meanwhile you two blow your money on gin and private detectives: Where's Jenny? Where could Jenny be? And I could have told you for free—getting fucked in the back of some car in California, getting high, losing what was left of her mind. I was never mistaken about what I meant to this family. I wasn't a part of all your embarrassing excesses and I never wanted to be. I'm just here for what's owed me." The repetition of the phrase— *what's owed me*—seemed to comfort him, break happily from his body.

As he droned on, Edith closed her eyes and began to whisper, her dehydrated lips moving against her teeth rabidly, as though physically locating the words she needed. Adeleine recognized the words as a prayer, and held her breath to listen.

Count not my transgressions,
but rather my tears of repentance.
Remember not my iniquities,
but my sorrow for the offenses I have committed
    against you.
I long to be true to your word
and pray that you will love me.

By the second recitation, Owen had quieted, and by the fourth, he was breathing in large heaves that moved up his back, broadening it. The needle had reached its center point and the record went on spinning, sounding out once a second with a modest, crackled thump, a reminder of how quiet it had become.

BY THE TIME Song finally opened her mouth to speak, Thomas had long since stopped expecting it. The unfamiliar travel of human speech confused him, and he looked around the small house, at the peak of the ceiling and the slanted gap beneath the door, as though to find where the word had landed. It was afternoon. He sat cross-legged on the floor, sorting through rocks the color of long-circulated money, and she watched him from the wicker chair by the room's one window.

"Hello," she said. They had grown so comfortable with each other's silence that the greeting seemed unnecessary, even foolish. Not quite ready yet for whatever it was that language might reveal, Thomas kept his fingers on the stones, thumbing the smoothest stretches, admiring dramatic variations in shade, and nodded. "I'm prepared to speak about the issue of your friend Edith," Song said. "I trust you now. We grew that."

"Oh," he said, searching himself for a feeling of concern for their conversation. "Well?"

Hunting for the pivotal speech he'd filed away, he played back images and sounds: the locked door to Edith's apartment and Owen's impatient words behind it; the rigid form of her body in her son's presence. Adeleine on the top floor, every object placed to amuse and comfort her, the safety that finally played across her face as she slept. Paulie at the keyboard, the clamor refining into pristine patterns and flying up the stale stairway. Edward, whispering something to Paulie as they made their way down the street, towards the park and the last of the sun. Claudia waiting for them on the stoop with overflowing grocery bags, heads of watermelon, ears of corn, smiling at Thomas with a muted, infectious contentment.

"It's the house," he said to Song. "She left it to you."

"To the person I was, once, a long time ago."

"Okay, yes, to who you were. But Edith is sick, and Owen is trying to put her in some retirement facility against her will. He wants to get rid of her and take over the property, push us all out of our homes and rent them for six times as much."

Song's face had not turned. Her peace rivaled a houseplant's.

"He's rough with her, Song. He herds her around like she's his inmate."

"Oh." Her eyes closed briefly, and he could sense her muffling a response, pushing memories down as they surfaced, like things in a basin of water not yet clean. She gripped the arms of the chair, and a bellicose purple stood out in the veins of her throat.

"Please present your purpose."

Thomas went to Song and knelt, as if positioning himself like that might let him catch some of the unwanted, unhappy recollections that spilled from her.

"You have to take the house, Jenny," he opened gently, careful about how he called out to her past, careful not to send it scurrying away from the light. "You have to save her like she wanted to save you."

She released a ragged sound, as though some long-struggling part of her body was trying to open.

"Jenny," he said.

"*Jenny*," she said.

Almost as soon as her moan filled the room, it seemed replaced, eliminated by the atmosphere's familiar muting of extremes—the structure never too cold or warm, the sun always filtered by trees, only the necessary words spoken—as if snatched up by some invisible maid who didn't prefer the messiness of suffering, and swept back out into the wild. Thomas couldn't locate the moment before, the split second when he'd connected her to who she had once been, and her eyes, placid again, revealed nothing.

"A sweet person," she said, with apparent regret. "The girl you're looking for doesn't exist, don't you see? I gave up my past when I came here. I made a commitment. I was born *after*, do you understand? I don't have any right to that place. In fact, the system we built here precludes ownership."

"But—"

It felt as though his blood were moving through him at a perilously slow rate, but he continued, even knowing how little power he held. "But she was your mother. She was your mother and—" His voice broke as he thought of the photo, of Edith on the lumped and sun-strewn bed, holding up the tiny new human to the concentration of light; then he recalled his own mother, throwing an arm across his chest at sudden stoplights, the bashful smile she always gave him after.

"She never stopped missing you, do you understand? She was sorry her whole life. She never stopped *looking*."

Song turned away with a long gaze, taking in the horizon in no hurry, but Jenny's mouth softened and quavered. In an expeditious series of motions Thomas wouldn't have thought her capable of, she was up and at the door, lacing up her boots, reaching for a hat.

"I'm going for a walk," she said without affording him a glance. "I have some listening to do."

As he moved through her home, picking things up and letting them drop like some machine sent to methodically dismantle, Adeleine practiced her ability to live remembered moments in full detail, to focus on the greens and whites of other days and forget her current circumstances completely. After he had carried her up from the street, he had arranged her back on the chaise and flashed a palm across his mother's field of vision, as if to alert her to his upcoming performance. He pulled the curtains open, one by one, with his thumb and forefinger. Although Adeleine had bucked as he placed her there, sent her legs up in a few frantic kicks, her body, spent from its failed escape and stunned by the brightness and volume of the outside world, soon collapsed. Adeleine had not replied when Owen had asked her whether she would let him borrow a few things, had not watched as he approached the bowed bookshelf as though it were an infestation he intended to eliminate. She was already recalling a former life, sinking into another time.

He tapped out a jar of skeleton keys, and the rusted browns and grays fell like birds that dive into water; he held up records to read their labels, then sent them into flight; he removed a stack of age-bloated postcards, their backsides filled with tight, extinct cursive, and he flicked his thumb across each as he dealt them onto the floor. With a fine moisture growing on his upper lip, he shifted his focus to the rows of books, lower down: he took some poems by A. A. Milne and tore off leaves of the plain ink drawings, the verses about introverted mice, the place halfway up the stairs, the vanishing of glamorous mothers. His vision snagged on the stacked Pyrex and skillets of the kitchen, and he crossed to touch them.

With a snap, the stuck knob of the oven reached its highest setting, and on the middle rack he placed her ceramic coin banks, tiny dachshunds that leapt through hoops with pennies in their mouths, hand-painted golfers forever poised to putt. In a brief, cheerful stretch, he bent his knees, then moved to the bathroom, where he raised the toilet seat, pissed for a full minute, and jiggled himself dry. He turned on the bathtub's hot water with a flick of his wrist as purposeful as a plumber's, and he made several trips to the living room, forming aslant stacks of novels and journals that he wedged under the stubble of his chin.

Submerged under the steam, the books resisted a minute before releasing inky gasps of black and gray.

Adeleine, ankles crossed, eyes closed, was visiting a place she had been with her parents as a child on vacation: a summer cottage in a small Massachusetts beach town—a modest structure, made mainly of windows, that stood on stilts above an overgrown lawn. To counter the sounds of her life combusting, she replayed the moment when her mother finally pronounced the dusky light insufficient and flicked the switch, spilling yellow through the mesh windows and out onto the uneven grass. Adeleine had insisted on sitting outside to watch this, the whole house suddenly so bright, as if built then and there, the round wooden dining table and blue painted chairs and overstuffed couch appearing as if summoned by a magician.

She could sense Owen growing still, surveying the room he had laid to waste, but she remained in the tall blades of grass, eleven years old and very thin, devouring the smell of wet dirt, an odor that was in equal parts the determination of growth and the languid pace of rot. She knew that soon she would stand, say good-bye to the chorus of fireflies that lingered in the bushes below the house, make her way up the uneven stairs, past her parents where they sat reading, down the low hall to the bed with a time-softened quilt. She would lie quietly with childish dreams of bicycle rides, of the pink-cheeked boys who might kiss her.

By the bell she had hung there with a brief, fleeting optimism for a future full of comings and goings, she heard the apartment door of her adult life close. Adeleine sat up from the twin mattress in the wood-paneled room, heard the laughter of her family nearby, saw the clear rubber sandals and fluorescent-thread bracelets of girlhood. She put them away in her past, and returned to the vestiges of her home.

Adeleine could smell her books, the aged scent of them more pungent with moisture, like a futile weapon dispatched to combat their drowning; she could feel the heat of the oven, her precious items roasting and cracking. Around her feet were pieces of things she'd loved, the gilded circular plate of a rotary telephone, the wheel of a wooden airplane, splayed strings of violet and oak-colored yarn unspooled from their perfect globes. A herd of marbles lolled, mapping the slant of the floor. Next to her, Edith repeated the ends of sentences, pieces of conversations that twirled in her head like wind chimes, revealing one glinting part and obscuring another. ". . . About two blocks down," she said. "Expensive side," she said. "And what a view."

Adeleine positioned herself gingerly on the edge of the cushion and leaned in to touch Edith's uncombed, colorless hair. She was acutely sad to smell the hour-old sweat on her own body—an odor stiff like the air of a revolving door, the perspiration she had worked up just by thinking herself away—and she reached over and up to unfasten the peeling white latch and let in the weather. She had feared for her body, but instead he had exposed the tableau she had built to protect her mind, the tokens she had appointed as mediators between her and sanity.

With the window open, she felt the change in pressure as though it were some communication, a phone ringing or a package slipped under a door.

AFTER THE RATTLE of her exit ceased, Thomas listened for the last sounds of Song on the porch and crawled onto the great blank bed. He didn't understand what he was searching for until he knew it was missing: it was not in the snowy wool blanket that lay folded at the foot, or in the folds of the enormous down comforter, or lying on top of the pillows. He discovered no odor, no stray hair, no impression of a body's weight resting. The lack of evidence of her gave him a feverish chill, and then fatigue settled, vaporlike, around his collarbone and temples. He had come all this way and failed: she felt nothing for the property across the country or the woman decaying inside it. He wanted sleep the way the terminally ill finally turn their curiosity towards death and begin their small negotiations with it.

When he awoke, he saw the men's faces arranged around the bed like beads on a shared string, moving in one line, secured by Song's place in the center. He gathered the blankets around him, and Song smiled without showing her teeth. From the lilac patch of sky through the window, he knew it was the hour in which they would use their saved-up speech.

"We hope you slept well," she began. "I've done the listening I need to, and think I've found a bridge of a kind." Thomas looked up at the woman, her white hair backlit by dusk, and realized his position in her bed would make disagreement absurd and impossible. Though she spoke in gentle peals, and glowed the pink of a long walk, she had not arrived in the spirit of compromise, but rather to offer one firm solution. The men now bowed their heads, and he saw, for the first time, the shared aquiline nose, the eyes the color of alpine lakes. These were her sons.

"We don't have any right to that property, unfortunately." They nodded. "Or interest." They tittered. "However." Their heads dropped again.

"I've come to believe that your friend Edith and I might enjoy meeting each other. Reuniting, *you* might say. We could forgive each other for who we once were. She could live out the rest of her identity here. She would rest. She would be safe."

Presented with the possibility of Edith in this strange place, all of Thomas's repressed intentions for her appeared in vivid presentation. All along—on the airplane that had crossed the Midwest in the middle of the night, in the darkening library where he'd looked for any meager trace of her daughter, around the curves of the narrowing two-lane highway—he had assumed he would be the one to protect Edith. He would be gentle with her when she was furious, would keep her mind at ease with whispered comforts, preside over the moments in which her febrile confusion became fear, bring her water with decorative straws and simple games in subdued colors. He would hold the crook of her elbow and guide her through the neighborhood, naming the streets she had known much of her life. *It was supposed to be me*, he thought, and knew, simultaneously, that the reality of the task, the hushing and the spoon-feeding and the laundering of soiled sheets, would have been too much for him to hold.

The only word of protest he summoned was weak, led nowhere.

"But—"

"Of course, there's the matter of the house. I cannot accompany you back there, but I am willing to assume the temporary authority, of my former self and name, in order to sign over all rights to you, if you can arrange for her to arrive very soon."

"Song, I would have to go back across the country to get her. I'm not sure I can do it so quickly—"

"I can give you two days. You've already upset our arrangement by coming, and I can't guarantee my answer will be the same beyond that. We will welcome Edith, and you will deal with the building however you see fit. She will be cared for here. We'll build a bed for her near mine."

Jenny's sons—Edith's grandchildren, Thomas reminded himself—nodded in echo of her earnestness. He let himself imagine it: Edith waking and breathing in the elevation, the clean air like none she'd had in sixty-odd years. Edith sitting in a little wooden chair by the vegetable garden while someone picked jewel-dark roots and rain-polished greens for her dinner. Edith on the porch at dusk, babbling out the fragments of her life as they surfaced in her mind to an audience of passing chickens, then growing quiet again. And just as he had in the days after his body betrayed him, he tried to cajole acceptance with outward expressions of agreement he hoped would move inward. "Okay," he said. "Okay." His chin wagged up and down wildly, like a simple toy sent into motion by an eager hand.

THEY ARRIVED in the late afternoon, after a stretch of silence punctuated only by the occasional sound of the turn signal or a sigh from Edward. The fireflies wouldn't appear for another few days, and much of the campground radiated absence, stretches of empty sites, wooden tables free of human clutter, squat and blackened grills.

They circled the campsites carefully, commenting on the dramatic slant of number sixty-four, pausing to investigate the well-shaded opportunity afforded by seventy-two. Edward, who had not camped once in his life, kept proximity to a bathroom a priority, and narrowed his eyes as they traveled farther from the friendly wooden stalls of the showers. Claudia, though weary, held her initial vision of perfection close, and quickly found flaws in each of the most promising sites.

They had nearly completed the double-loop, an infinity shape paved in concrete, when they saw it. Claudia braked, and Paulie exclaimed. Each opened their door carefully and moved slowly closer, evaluating the patch of dark land that would be theirs for the next eight evenings. The heart of it was situated in a slight valley, and they had to hike down in small steps, Claudia holding up Paulie's hips while Edward struggled with the chafing confines of the cutoffs. Two trees stood on the north and south borders of number eighty, their trunks covered in a mantle of kudzu vines, an impenetrable green. The branches of each strained towards the other in the sky, not quite meeting, admitting an avenue for the sun to flood the rust-colored picnic table. Farther back leaned two smaller trees, echoes of the first, spaced as though destined to receive the blue-and-white hammock that Claudia had impulsively purchased at a roadside store. But this tug of serendipity did not bear comment: at the rear of the site cantered a confident stream, which took its rhythm from the modest but fierce waterfall where it began, and the sight of the fresh rush was immediately soul mending.

"Fuck," said Edward.

"*Fuck* is *right*, Eddy," said Paulie, reaching for his hand. They strode towards the water together, leaving Claudia where she had plunked, cross-legged, in the dirt, finally excused from obligation. At first they stood in the center, where the deepest water played above their knees, and looked around with a kind of guilt, as if waiting to be caught. Paulie was the first to sit, disappearing briefly beneath the surface to dunk his curls, then Edward, whose balding pink crown shone wet and bright in a patch of sun. From Claudia's vantage, it was difficult to imagine that the two heads peeking out of the water, lolling wildly, maintained ties with any bodies.

Eventually she rose, retrieved white towels from the trunk of the car and carefully set them on the table to warm. She began unpacking the supplies they'd brought, stackable rubber dishes and nectarines bundled in starchy linens and a heavy, ovular cooler of water that thudded when shifted. When Paulie and Edward approached, twenty minutes later, shaking the moisture off with the subtlety of feral dogs, she wrapped each of them in the stiff new cotton, and then they ate, surveying the landscape and discussing the very best position for sleep.

A FTER DRIVING twenty miles south to the nearest town, the last place his phone had picked up reception, Thomas cruised the main drag of square wooden buildings, seeking a parking place where he might gather the confidence to make the call.

In the lot of an abandoned drive-in diner, he got out and sat at one of the metal tables, the type covered in waffled plastic and bolted to the earth. The figure of a giant wooden boy biting into a hamburger cast a horrific shadow over the lot; when the hot wind blew, it quivered at its tenuous point of attachment atop the boarded-up kiosk.

Thomas looked at the phone and willed enthusiasm. Though it had been less than a month, he found he could no longer envision Adeleine's shape. He saw the nape of her neck and the arch of her back, as from behind her in the afternoon, and remembered her hand as it held a fork, her hair as it grabbed light, but he could not force the fragments into concert. He considered the possibility that he no longer produced the hectic energy that he had transferred so effectively into loving her. His brain fed him images of cartoon firemen, holding out a trampoline, looking up at a curling orange window, dancing into different positions, bracing to catch something impossibly large.

Thomas prepared for, even anticipated, the number of rings—

it generally took Adeleine at least four to tear herself away from the fabric of her thoughts and answer—but then she was on the phone almost instantly.

"It's me," he said.

He could tell, solely by the way she paused before she spoke, and then by the dull theater of her questions—*Where are you? How are you?*—that their language, one that had taken so long to grow, was lost. Until he began to ask her the same, he didn't consider the alternative: that their dynamic had not been relinquished, but plundered, thieved of the little optimism that had made it possible.

"Her son was here again."

"Did he put up some new eviction notices? Adeleine, I can't really believe it, but Edith's daughter is giving me—"

"He knew I wouldn't leave the house, and he took advantage of that."

It was here that Thomas faltered, and did not pose the inquiries that he surely would have, had he somehow divined the cramped shape of her posture, seen the ragged chew of her fingernails. Across the country, Adeleine sat on the floor with her body coiled as tightly as she could manage, her knees pressed up against her chin, her arms around her shins, the telephone held against her cheek by her left shoulder. Edith, on the couch behind, occasionally placed a hand on the top of her blond-red head and sighed.

"What happened?" he said. "Are you all right? Did he try to inspect your apartment?"

When she brushed away his questions and assumed a

hardened, mostly monosyllabic conversational position, he found he didn't have the focus to chip at it, find his way inside.

"Adeleine. I'm going to ask you—I need you to agree to something. It's not what I expected. Jenny won't come. She's going to sign over the property, but we have to bring Edith here. I don't know how to ask any other way—you need to walk out of there, and you need to bring her with you. Time doesn't give us any alternatives."

"Talk to Edith," Adeleine said. The voice he heard was scrubbed of her, as though she were hours into reading a manual aloud. "Tell her you found her daughter. Tell her Jenny still exists."

"Well—" The phone was already in transit.

"Good day?" lilted Edith.

"Edith," he said. "It's Thomas."

". . ."

"From upstairs?"

"Mm," she said, without much commitment. "We could certainly use your help around here, then!"

"Edith. Your daughter. Jenny? I'm here with Jenny."

"You *are*?" said Edith. A grin moved across her face, touching all parts of it. "How are her grades? Jenny," she continued, "is such a storyteller. I always say, you could hand her a tissue and an orange and she'd give you back a whole world built around them."

"She's—she's certainly built a whole world here."

Adeleine moved to the couch and laid her head in Edith's lap, tried to isolate all the tiny sounds of the body moving breath outward and taking it in.

Thomas looked up at the peeling colors of the hamburger boy, at the blue shirt that had faded unevenly over the uncooked pink color beneath, so that it appeared something was eating away at his clothing.

"Jenny is doing well," he said, too quickly. "She wants you to come visit. She wants to show you her life. Jenny missed you, Edith." To assuage a wave of guilt—the mention of her mother had not exactly filled Song with longing—he tried to convince himself of its truth, recalled how it had been Song's idea and not his. He wished desperately that Edith were there with him so that he could take her warm hand and assure her, see the flicker of recognition as it came, even as it went.

"Will you come, Edith? Will you come visit?" Thomas heard a muffled clatter, then a distorted car horn. He had not broken through her fog, all of its shape-shifting, its short-sighted convictions, and she had put the phone down. He repeated Adeleine's name with increasing volume, begging her to remember him from wherever she'd retreated to.

Edith had gingerly placed the phone at the base of a plant, so that his voice lost itself in the waxy yellow-green leaves, and Adeleine didn't realize the sound as coming from outside of her head for a full three minutes.

"The strangest thing," she said. "You were obscured in my arrowhead plant. I thought for a moment it was finally talking back. You know, you're supposed to talk to them."

"Okay. Sweetheart? This is it. This is the last thing you have to do. I'll make all the arrangements for you. After that—"

"All right," she said, her agreement stopping his voice dead-on.

"How long do I have to pack?" It was moments like this, when questions of poor odds dissolved and an improbable outcome came into fruition, that he could nearly sense the lost parts of his body tingling, preparing to wake up from their long sleep and feel again.

DOWNSTAIRS IN EDITH'S APARTMENT, the two women surveyed the clothing laid out on the bed, some of it removed from the cherrywood wardrobe for the first time in decades: a buttermilk angora cardigan beaded at the collar, a silk dress of peachy violet with a sash at the waist, camel linen slacks dotted with greens and grays, high-waisted denim shorts with a golden five-button fly, a brick plaid shirt with pearled snap enclosures. Edith sat near the foot and moved her hands over the pieces as though caressing a sleeping child awake, touching the grain of her former lives.

Standing with her arms crossed and lips pursed, imagining coordinated pairings, Adeleine envisioned Edith embracing her daughter in these clothes, linking an arm with hers and beginning a long walk. That her own life was missing from these fantasies, hardly considered by the plans at hand, felt like a generous gift from someone who knew her well.

"They're stunning," Adeleine said, holding her left hand with her right. "They're perfect." She opened the two metal latches of the powder-blue vinyl suitcase, which she had also retrieved from the deep corners of the stale-smelling armoire, and began folding the items with care, smoothing creases, fastening clasps. She found some peace in doing so, and answered Edith's mumbled concerns without hesitation, as though contending with matters of geography. Edith looked out the window as Adeleine talked, then stood to grip its cracked, whitewashed frame with her knuckles.

"Fall forward?" Edith asked, groping for any adage that explained time.

"Almost. Back. Spring forward, fall back."

"Are we going on a vacation?"

"We're going to see your daughter. We're going to see Jenny."

"Will Declan meet us there?"

"No, he won't, Edith. I'm sorry."

"They found Jenny? Did she get my letter?"

"She's doing fine, Edith. She's looking forward to your visit. She wants you to stay as long as you like."

"Imagine," Edith said. She was breathless and bright-eyed in a way that belonged exclusively to adolescent girls as they imagined the rest of their lives, the porches of houses where they might live, the gleaming offices where they might work, the forbearing men they might love. "Imagine. *My* daughter." The possibility felled her, and she settled again on the bed.

"Edith," said Adeleine, now behind her in the light, running a hand down her back, then kneeling before her, scouring the ruined face for an answer. "Is there anything else you'd like to bring with you? From home?"

Adeleine cupped Edith's knees and held her gaze. After a brief quiet of consideration, Edith shook her head.

"Oh, no. No need to bring home with me, dear. I know what it feels like."

An hour remained until the car Adeleine had called would

come and take them to the airport, and at the thought of its horn inevitably sounding, even her teeth began to itch.

"What if I did your nails?"

"That would be *nice*," Edith said.

Adeleine returned with a small suede box of her own colors, metallic golds and creamy yellows and sheer whites, and asked Edith to choose one. As though choosing a color to paint her new home, she ran her hands over the bottles with concentration, finally settling on a robin's egg blue. For the next twenty minutes, Adeleine kneeled, first filing, then daubing the tiny brush across tobacco-yellow ridges age had left, pausing to wipe any stray lacquer from the cuticles. She kept her head low, offering frequent praise, ushering Edith back to the moment. "It's a perfect color," she said. "It'll match the sky out the window of the airplane."

Adeleine's body, in anticipation of their leaving, produced a trembling cover of sweat. She held up each individual nail and blew through her puckered mouth; she asked Edith to please stay still; she went to the neatly made bed and sat, imagining statues, stone hands folded. In her mind she counted back from one hundred, the digits pulsating black on white in rhythm with her pulse.

When the two complaints of the horn sounded outside, it was Edith who rose first, who placed a hat on her white head and reminded Adeleine it was time to go. Edith who allowed Adeleine to bury her head in her arm, who guided them down the stoop as though it were a wedding aisle, her shoulders thrown back for the loving audience. They watched as the driver lifted their suitcases and deposited them in the shadowed maw of the trunk. On the top floor, a curtain licked at the arid day through a window left open.

"It was a wonderful party, anyway," Edith said.

THE EXPECTED ARRIVAL of the fireflies still long days away, they had little to contend with, save the fixing of simple meals, the constant presence of insects, the application of sunscreen to necks and backs. By dusk of the second day, Paulie showed more mosquito bites than regular skin, and followed Claudia and Edward around with a bottle of calamine lotion, asking they rub it on new itches. Claudia, clad in khaki shorts and a gray T-shirt that she had bought for the occasion and which clung to her body in stiff folds, began three books before finally settling into one. Edward took jogs that quickly turned into walks around the campground loop, and showered frequently in the forever-damp wooden stalls with concrete floors and bright acoustics. Paulie read a fantasy novel in the hammock for fifteen-minute stretches and sang along to music on his headphones and took naps in the tent, where he admired the diffusion of sunlight through the stretched green nylon and the way the sleeping bags looked lying together, like clouds flying low.

Their fourth morning there, his knees moving high in inverted V's as he ran, Paulie made the mistake of following Edward on his jog.

"Hi, Eddy."

"Hey, Paulie."

"Where you running?"

"Nowhere. Just running. A pointless pastime I have bought into for reasons unknown to me."

"Having fun?

"Eddy, are you having fun?"

"Medium."

"Medium fun, huh?

"How you doing, Eddy?"

Edward stopped moving and bent over, put his hands on his knees and tried to breathe without sputtering. The humidity felt like some windowless waiting room, and the cardiovascular exertion seemed to have run him up some cliff rather than talking him down.

"Are you okay?"

"Paulie." Edward snapped up from his curved position. "I need to be alone. I have thoughts to think, and they're not perky or sparkly or good. I need you to not be here. Okay?"

Without gauging his effect, Edward turned and headed in the opposite direction, past a campsite where a large group of men, all clad in baseball hats, were eating hot dogs under an awning attached to their RV. They had looked up at the sound of his voice breaking, and they watched him pass as they chewed, at the patches of sweat that looked parenthetical on his shoulder blades, at his palms daubing at his eyes in jerky movements as he gained speed. There was nothing, he thought, more humiliating than weeping before an RV barbecue party.

Left behind, Paulie let the numb weight of his body carry him back to their site, and it may have appeared, to the few people sitting out in mesh chairs, that he was carried, the load of his head held by some invisible rope. When he reached his sister where she lay in her hammock, he clambered in, set it swinging. Claudia wrapped her arms around him, then wove her fingers through the cotton grid, securing the embrace, soothing him still, and they felt the diminishing rocking together.

"What is it, Paul?"

"Eddy didn't want me around because he had thoughts he wanted to be with and he ran away crying."

"Sweetie. Edward is, besides being entertaining and generous, an emotionally fucked-up individual. Imagine a broken radio that only plays one station, which is an asshole DJ who makes a greatest-hits playlist of your black days and worst mistakes."

Paulie smiled slightly at this, as profanity had always felt to him like a seal of understanding, a shortcut to extreme feeling that people used when they needed it most.

"You know how his job used to be to make people laugh? That was because he wanted to make them laugh, but also, mostly, because he needed to make himself laugh, because it's pretty dark and nasty inside his brain."

"Dark like a tunnel or dark like the sky in the country?"

"Tunnel. Definitely, tunnel. As a for-instance, when he was a little boy, his parents used to keep him inside for days. And so he was sort of bad at being with other people. There was someone he loved very much, and he wasn't able to hang on to her. And he is mostly good at keeping that to himself but sometimes not. It's real quiet here, and there aren't a bunch of competing noises to distract him. Have you noticed how quiet it is?"

"You could hear a bug cough."

"Exactly. So maybe it is our job as friends to be extra nice to Edward, even when he is acting slightly like a monster."

"Like a fucky monster made of gangrene who is rotting all over everyone."

Laughing into her brother's hair, Claudia brought one leg to touch the ground, guiding the hammock into a sway that was slow and even, and soon they found a sleep that seemed to promise something as they fell into it, a cleaning of the body or an adjusting of the mind.

I N THE TAXI Edith dismissed the congestion of cars with a
fluttery hand.

"It's always like this Christmas weekend." The man behind
the wheel narrowed his eyes in the rearview mirror, poised to
correct her mistake, but saw something in the impotent way she
poured her sight out the window, and stopped.

Adeleine kept her eyes closed and her right hand fixed on the
door handle. The driver spoke in a sonorous voice into a Blue-
tooth earpiece, his syllables so attenuated they seemed coded.
Outside the speeding taxi one borough rushed into another,
Brooklyn finally replaced by the low plastic-sided houses and
dim restaurants and suspect quiet of Queens.

"Declan says it's important to dress to the nines when you're
flying. He says, if you can't show your best self when defying
man's God-given abilities, then when? It's a crime to cruise the
heavens in anything but your finest suit, because what would St.
Peter say about blue jeans? He might send you to hell to change!"

Adeleine's body sank lower and lower, like litter discarded in
a bay searching for its resting point. Eventually her knees on the
back of the seat were set higher than her cheeks, and pieces of
hair moved above her on the upholstery, held hostage by static.

"You know, we took Jenny on a plane. Seven months she was.
And some friends of mine, they said, what are you thinking,

babies should stay safe at home where they belong. And Declan said, nope, our girl's a flyer, I know it. I dressed her in a little corduroy jumper and she stood on my lap, tensing and untensing her toes. We were by the window and Declan said, better keep the shade down, she'll be calmer that way. But she kept reaching for it. She wanted that thing open! She wanted to see where we were! Once I pulled it up she was glued to that patch of blue, would not look away for anything. There was another baby on the flight and it cried like it was starved, and when it would start up wailing, Jenny would stiffen and blink, like she recognized the sound but couldn't remember from where, and then turn back to the business of cloud watching. She'd forgotten everything else, didn't care if we never landed, couldn't imagine any other place."

Adeleine's fingers darted and groped for the window button. She turned her face into the rushing air and arched her shoulders, but her vomit only made it as far as the back windshield, and Edith began to shriek.

"Sir! A young lady has just become ill in the back of your cab! Do something at once!" For the duration of the ride, the driver muttered hard consonants in Gujarati, then some of the profane variety in English. As they careened into the airport under the brash white signs of different airlines, their suitcases shifted audibly in the trunk, and the crepuscular sky fought viciously to keep its color, the violets and blues now thin and strained.

RELIEVED OF THE QUESTIONS that had propelled him, Thomas tried to restore his lost sense of purpose by familiarizing himself with the mechanics of Edith's final home. He followed one of Song's sons, Wallace, a tall man with a lopsided smile and prominent canines, on his rounds. He watched as Wallace affectionately chucked the red throat of a hen, then lifted the bird to retrieve her eggs; as he culled worn sheets from various beds and placed them inside a frail washing machine that sat on the outskirts of the main circle of buildings, alone and painted blue; as he scooped out cat food into a series of wooden bowls with the patience of a priest, and tugged the tips of tails as the felines appeared, one by one, to circle his feet.

Thomas had intended to sit with Wallace during the evening hour in which people spoke, to ask him plainly whether these routines, this place, gave him happiness, but it was evident even in the way the man walked, turning his head frequently to survey the bounty: the familiar faces napping in hanging chairs, the untamed sun-washed herb garden, the one-room homes built for simple lives, the well-worn paths that led to water.

Wallace, tasked with building a bed for Edith, set up on the porch of Song's little house, and Thomas helped as best as he could. For two consecutive afternoons, he handed Wallace the lengths of wood and tools at which he pointed, offered encouraging grunts, fetched pitchers of water and plates of steaming polenta from the communal kitchen. When the work was done, Wallace led Thomas to a squat tin-roofed shed, pointed to a row of dusty paint cans, and opened his arms wide in invitation. Pleased to be handed this small authority, Thomas selected a pale yellow, and Wallace squeezed his shoulder and left him to it.

He spent the rest of the sunlight close to the wood, passing the brush repeatedly over bubbles that formed in the color, stepping back into the garden to appraise the thing from a distance as slat by slat, spindle by spindle, it began to glow.

As he passed the edge of the campground, the ranger's hut and the silver-haired woman in her khaki uniform, Edward waved and kept running. He needed to reach the concrete highway, to get out from the cover of trees; he wanted the sun to burn off the shame he felt for snapping at Paulie, and to feel the man-made surface fixed underneath him as he moved.

He had not expected that leaving New York would feel somehow like going without food, that watching Paulie and Claudia day in and day out would primarily serve to prod at old losses, as a reminder of the family he didn't have. He didn't have his mother, who had spent the last years of her life wheezing in the glow of unsolved murder reenactments; he didn't have his father, who had regarded his sons as poor returns on investment and squinted at them, waiting for their value to rise. He certainly didn't have his brother, who had finally buckled under their mother's neurotic legacy: he had begun coming home from his insurance job, locking three deadbolts, ignoring most phone calls, and showering with bleach.

Once, he'd had Helena, but couldn't understand that romantic commitment was, contrary to myth, built on the conditional, a rolling system that noted each person's deficiencies until they congealed into the untenable. He had gone to great lengths to test the limits of her love, and dared her to fail, and then she had.

The details of it came back to walk with him sometimes: how he had turned, on so many nights, towards the wall, and let her sleep alone on a wide expanse of bed; how she had begged him to open and to excavate, and he had snorted at her self-help speak and dismissed her genuine efforts as affect. Even on the morning she'd gathered her last small things—a wooden box of seldom-worn jewelry, a stainless steel pepper shaker—she'd appealed to him. Standing in the doorframe with the items in her hands, she'd said, "You know, I would go on putting your life ahead of mine forever, probably, if you gave the slightest indication that was truly what you wanted." He hadn't even glanced up from where he'd been lying on the couch—he'd known how she would look, her skin impassioned with uneven color, her hair pinned back to mirror the severity of her face—until he saw her shadow move and knew she was finally gone.

In the heat of the road's shoulder, he tried to attach these memories to the cars that passed, visualized a steel-blue sedan towing away the image of his misery growing stale on the couch, saw a Wonder Bread truck whisking Helena away to somewhere effortless and warm. Moved by a boozy spirit of generosity five months before, their mutual friend Martin had given him Helena's new phone number. "You should call her," he'd said. "Maybe it's been long enough. People get older, you know, and they're more willing to forgive. It's almost never easier to forget someone totally." He had reached for Edward's phone and programmed her name into the contact list in capital letters. Since then he had taken to scrolling through furiously until he reached H, then staring at the digitized representation of the life he had missed—a minute, then two—for as long as he could endure it. It had become a day-ruining thrill, an overdose that required concentrated efforts at recovery. And then, on the side of the road in Tennessee, in running shoes the color of dishwater, with sweat dripping from a hairline that crept farther back daily, with no clear plans for middle age, Edward pressed the little green icon of a telephone. As the rings multiplied, he scrambled farther into the brush, looking for some thicket in which to lie and suffer.

What had he expected? That she would answer and speak his name with wind chimes in her voice? Her outgoing message was simply her recorded name spoken cheerfully, like the answer to a riddle. When the tone came, he took a fistful of grass and weeds between his fingers and gathered, with no small shock, that he was speaking.

"Hey, Edward! I mean, Edward, it's hey. Goddamnit—"

He didn't get the chance to resolve his blunder. The protracted beep of a call on the other line sounded, and her name flashed in bold, spectral rhythm.

HELENA
HELENA
HELENA

B ECAUSE WALLACE'S TRUCK, gray like wet gravel, could fit only three, and Thomas's rental had been mysteriously returned on his behalf, he had to stay behind while Song's son drove the two hours to the tiny municipal airport. Thomas sent with him a hand-painted sign, oil on plywood, that featured their names. His right hand, competent now but never assured, had trembled as he added a flourish to the "A" in "Adeleine" and "E" in "Edith." He had kissed two fingers, tapped them on Wallace's side mirror, and watched the truck bump along the untended land until the trees obscured it.

Outside the arrivals terminal, there was no shade, everything cut away for the shimmering parking lot, and the heat rose in abundance from the concrete, uncut by any wind. Wallace leaned on the hood, whistling long notes under his straw cowboy hat, holding up the sign though the plane still sat on the runway, full of passengers.

The people who began filtering out ten minutes later were rumpled and squinting in the white push of heat. Some, met by relatives in shorts who waved halfheartedly before turning back to their cars, crossed the lot at a clip, rolling suitcases at their heels. Others, solitary, navigated the parking lot like those emerging from a long matinee, not yet accustomed to the changed light.

When the last of them had slipped through the sieve of warmth into air-conditioned cars, the slow automatic doors revealed Adeleine and Edith, the younger woman in a broad sun hat that cast checkered shadows on her milky shoulders, the elder in a pinstriped dress that drooped from her body. He pressed his Stetson to his chest and approached.

"You must be Edith."

Their eyes were similar, the blue-green patterned in symmetry, and the lids slightly hooded, folds like loosely made beds.

"I don't know who you are."

"I'm Wallace. I'm here to take you home. See? Sign right here says so."

Edith kept her face up to the sound of his speaking but clutched both hands on her patent-leather purse, as though feeling for some makeshift weapon within it. Wallace's mild voice washed in, becoming emphatic.

"There's a big lunch waiting, Edith. We're roasting all kinds of vegetables and brewing a vat of cider. We built you a bed from cedar and painted it yellow. There's a fireplace and a porch with a chair just for you, and if you want, I'll show you the place in the woods where I keep a hammock. There are cats, and some are sweet and some spend most days exploring on their own. We stay quiet most of the time, so we can always hear the river. Everything you'll need is close by, and the water is clean. Would you like to come see?"

He put his hand out to her, spread it flat and wide, and acknowledged Adeleine—who blushed in the uncertainty of her part in all of it—with a wink. Edith shuffled across the pavement with a certain dignity, her jaw bobbing as she looked left and right, and when they reached the passenger side of Wallace's truck, he pressed down on the silver handle, led the door's opening as if conducting the first note of an opera.

Though Edward had prepared his voice, called on notes of casual competence, he answered as though being held over a fire.

"Um, hello," she said.

"Helena! It's Edward!" His whole body protested the moment, and he tried to compensate for anxiety with enthusiasm.

"Boy howdy and Jesus Christ. I knew I recognized the number. I just didn't know whose it was."

"Well."

"Well? *You* called *me*."

"Right. How are you?"

"As in . . . how have the last ten years treated me? Or, right in this moment, am I good or bad? Have I consumed any above-average fusion cuisine recently? Is the weather decent?"

"Okay—I'm sorry. Maybe I shouldn't have called. But listen, I'm actually calling about an extremely important issue, one that's keeping me up nights, and that's—joint health."

"What?"

"Are you taking care of your joints? Enough omega-threes in your life?"

"I'm not going to laugh. You're very funny, but I'm not going to."

"I'm not laughing. Do you hear me laughing? I cannot stress

enough the crucial nature of knee bends. How would you like to spend your middle age? The choice is yours."

"Where are you, Edward? What are you doing? Anything? Why are you calling?"

"I'm, uh—"

"Are you right where I left you?"

"Actually, I'm in Tennessee."

"What?" The genuine surprise in her voice exposed a warmth previously hidden, and he was hit by the ghost of their dynamic, arriving at punch lines together at the dinner table, clutching at each other's elbows in glee.

"Yeah. The Smoky Mountains. But specifically, the side of some road, knee-deep in all kinds of weird grass I've never seen before. I'm here to see—they're called synchronous fireflies, and they only do this once a year, only here and somewhere in the Philippines, and they light up all at once, rhythmically, in a dance. It's like *the* destination rave for bugs."

"Are you fucking with me?"

"No."

"Why are you there?"

"Um, I'm here with my neighbor. Well, he's my friend. He's also a disabled thirty-three-year-old who plays the electronic keyboard pretty well and owns several plastic swords. He's very generous and wants to talk to everyone, always, and has barely left my apartment in the last six months. But we're getting evicted. Edith—you remember her?"

"She was amazing. She used to make me tea when you and I fought."

"Really?"

"Really. I farted while crying once and she *winked* at me."

"Wow. Well, she's essentially lost it—she went from forgetful to paranoid overnight—and her son's kicking us all out, so me and my neighbor and his sister decided to take this trip."

"I remain amazed."

"He wanted to come here more than I want . . . I don't know. I guess more than I've ever wanted anything. Except you."

She grunted with an immediate remorse, as though seeing herself lock the keys in the car. "This isn't *fair*. You can't call after years and say that, like we're twenty-six and imagining the rest of our lives on someone else's fire escape. I've *built* things, Edward. I have a—"

As though on cue, the sound of a child, its urgent question. It wanted her, belonged to her. He waited as she murmured sweet instruction in a voice he had never heard, her hand over the phone, and the fact of it banished anything he might have said. He thought he heard her say, "Can you show me what you did with the blue paper?" And then, "No, that's not for eating.

"Look, Edward. It sounds like—it seems that you've built something pretty good yourself. Enjoy that. I can't believe I'm saying this, but I'm proud of you. And also, truly, I have to go. Okay?"

"All right," he said, finally, though the electronic light that signified her had faded.

THOMAS AND SONG and all her sons had gathered to watch Wallace open the passenger side of his mottled truck. The rusted door eked forward and revealed Edith, who remained facing straight ahead, as though enjoying some film playing just beyond the windshield. Beside her in the slim middle seat, barely visible, Adeleine's hair gave a flaxen glow. Wallace bowed and waved for Thomas to come forward, and Thomas felt his toes spread, slightly, to steady his position.

Stepping away from the others, glad to separate from the throng, he approached the cab, where he laid a hand on Edith's knee and squeezed. Adeleine's eyes were closed. He couldn't reach her.

"Edith, I'm so glad you came. I've missed you. I'm so sorry it's taken so long. It was so hard to find the right place, and then so difficult to recognize it once I'd gotten there."

He placed his hand along her chin, waiting until her watery vision focused on him before he continued.

"Jenny and I have arranged everything for you: a quiet place where you can nap, and another where you can just sit and think. Everyone here knows all about you, Edith—I've told them who you are, how much I like you. I know it's not the home you made but you can trust me that it's safe, that the air is clean and the people are good. Will you—please—let me show you?"

Edith blinked and changed, as if she were waking from an introspective lull in a grim lobby, having heard her number called.

"Declan," she said. "You've always been softhearted. I knew that about you from the beginning."

"Edith, it's me. It's Thomas. Jenny's here, Edith—your *daughter* is here and she can't wait to see you."

"Declan! Why didn't you say so, you old goon!" Edith moved her face into a smile and put out her hand with a flourish, each finger proudly flexed. Thomas aligned his forearm with hers, felt them strain together as she descended the cab and began to search the crowd for the face of her child. She scrutinized each with resolve, considering faces and hairlines and postures; it was here, finally, the event she had trained for in so many dreaming hours.

When Song stepped forward, Edith's arm left his, and Thomas noticed that everyone had grown more quiet, if possible: he could hear no one breathing or shifting, only the unseen water moving over rocks and moss, the irregular steps of Edith as she shambled towards her daughter. It had been forty-six years, Thomas knew, since Jenny had posed for that photo on the steps, had parted her painted lips and placed one light hand on her pink leather suitcase. Edith continued shuffling, stirring up sheets of red dirt, until she was close enough to reach out and tug the cloud of hair that floated down Song's chest. Sent wild with want, delivered back to the moment she was handed the tiny life and pressed it to her paper gown, her eyes resisted blinking, and her hands grabbed at the features before her, the lobes of her daughter's ears and the rangy length of her neck.

She let out the sound of many small pieces halting at once, a train's final chuff.

"Her," she said.

Deepening light fell in layers of color, rusty golds and lilacs through the veil of branches, studying the maps of their faces.

The child's only answer was a palm to her mother's temple, slight but insistent.

The mother seemed to know what she meant, and nodded.

THE PATH BACK to their campsite skirted a row of half-decayed logging buildings, multistory wooden structures whose staircases ceased halfway up to the rotted ceiling, where the extant beams hung close and crooked. Edward swept a hand over his sweat-pearled face, felt the spiked hair of his eyebrows and the trenches worry had driven across his forehead. He hoped to present the expression to Paulie and Claudia that would best indicate his remorse, that would immediately earn his redemption. When he reached them, they looked up briefly from their blue nylon chairs and smiled with full lips, their subdued happiness like that of an old couple waiting blithely for a bus.

"Um, guys?"

"Yes, Eddy? Yes, Chiefo?" Paulie held a stick of red licorice in the leftmost corner of his mouth and chewed it slowly, like some dusty movie-cowboy. Claudia, whose hair the humidity had translated into wild curls, winked.

"A wink? You're winking? Aren't you mad?" Edward's body, still posed for apology, held the stiffness of guilt and panic; his knees locked. "Aren't you going to say something?"

Paulie gave an authoritative wave of the sugary wand.

"Like what? Like should I go crazy and yell that you're a monster? Should I throw your things in the river and let them rush away? It's okay, Eddy. We've got so much to do. We don't need to do that. And we love you. Right, Claude?"

"For *some* reason." She lifted her dirty feet from the cooler and leaned forward. A can of Miller High Life flew from her hand; Edward watched as his own shot up to receive it. Paulie observed the exchange with curiosity, as he might a documentary about rainforest wildlife, and chuckled brightly.

"Eddy," he said. "Only two hours till the fireflies!"

THE CAMPGROUND, littered now with sound systems and fans and wide vehicles and red-faced regional families, began to hum in the hour after dusk with small, fitful movements: the zipping of mesh tent doors and fanny packs, the on-off, on-off tests of headlamps. The clusters of people, many of them in tight, synthetic clothing that molded their flesh into unnatural lumps, looked generally cagey, as though they had spent the last of their dwindling energy on a shot at wonder and would take any measure to obtain it. The sky accepted night and the campers began their migration to the riverside grove recommended for observation, huffing as they shifted their long-sedentary bodies. Sunburned and drunk, Edward felt both repelled by their needy anticipation and at risk of catching it.

The three of them set out with the rest of the campground, joined the army of flashlights covered in red Saran wrap so as to not spook the bugs, and moved towards an area where a group of rangers spoke to the gathering crowd. Paulie—whose knees almost cleared his navel as he marched, whose taut fingers at his sides seemed liable to snap off—had fallen into a manic feedback loop.

"Eddy *do you think we'll see them? Claude I hope we see them. Claude do you think we'll see the fireflies? Eddy I hope we see* them!"

As they approached the bend in the river that held the desperate hordes, Edward imagined the ineluctable pushing and sweating and yelling once the spectacle actualized—if it actualized at all—and knew he couldn't be there for it.

"Paulie," he said. "I've heard it's better firefly watching up the river a mile or so. Let's go that way."

Claudia screwed up her face to protest, but Paulie had already begun to follow the confidence in Edward's voice, and so she fell in behind them, listening only to the sounds of the violent mountain stream, looking towards the winks of light up ahead, single fireflies pulsing, oblivious to expectations of awe.

CALIFORNIA DUSK came and went, and they stayed by the fire, the smoke of it shifting like a bored child's attention. No one moved, except to feed the flame with gusts of breath, to rearrange the kindling's structure. All perched on oddly tumbled logs save mother and daughter, who sat several feet higher on a chair designed for two, the community's decades-old gift to Song and Root. Thomas, leaning on a boulder just below them, watched and listened closely, resisting the mollification of the flames. Whether Edith realized the person next to her was one she'd raised and lost, or Song gave any real thought to the convergence of her two lives, was a question whose import seemed to have passed with the light. They stroked each other's knees and hands occasionally, sometimes sighing in synchronicity.

Settled on the ground beside him, her back against the warmed rock, Adeleine remained quiet. She absorbed Thomas's affection without returning it: for most of the night he kept his hand over hers, where the fingers lay flat and never reacted to touch. As it grew darker and more retreated to their homes, his breath caught at the very real possibility that she would decline to retire with him to his modest bed. She didn't flinch when the wind pushed the smoke in their direction, or a stray ember leapt from the pit towards her.

Finally in the company of family, Edith had fallen asleep.

With a loose motion that swept from nose to toe, Song had beckoned the delivery of a blanket, and Thomas observed how carefully she wrapped it around the person who had once been her mother, how she stroked a thumb down the frail cup of Edith's ear. The roughly hewn greens and browns of the wool, as illuminated by the firelight, looked like land sliding and eroding.

ADELEINE HAD, ultimately, fallen limply into sleep with him, but when Thomas awoke from clutching her all night, his arms felt as though they had carried something unwieldy for miles. Her body had left a scent on the linens, sweat that was by turns sweet and putrid, and he found her on the porch, where the midmorning light wheeled through the uneven planks overhead and fell on her face like a complicated question. Her feet were bare, and a polyester slip of a murky yellow fell halfway down her legs. She had not spoken in any significant way before she fell asleep, had hardly moved to find the right position.

"Good morning. How did you sleep? Where are Edith and Song?"

"Went to the lawyer's. In town. Edith was mumbling about watching the tightwire walker and Song was just nodding like a secretary. In some ways they're perfect together."

"Are you feeling better?"

"Well—"

"Adeleine—I want you to talk to me about what happened. It's better if you give it to someone else. Let me take it, sweetheart."

She shrunk at the term of endearment, brought her knees up into the tent of fabric. A silken bow, perilously attached halfway across the chest, seemed as though it would give way any moment.

"You know how badly I wish I had been there. Don't you see all this was for you, as much as for Edith or anyone else?"

"He was—devious. He did the worst things you can do to a person who can't leave the only place she has."

For what was possibly the first time since she had arrived, she looked at his face, watched his thoughts toss on it.

"No, he didn't do that. He demolished the apartment. He destroyed my music and drowned my books. He took what I loved away. Is that enough, Thomas? Or should I tell you about how I tried not to smell or hear him, in order to remember some life of mine that was understandable—should I tell you about how far back I had to go, to find that? Should I tell you that? Would you want me then?"

Thomas knelt beside her, placed a warm hand around her curled toes and gripped them, but she had become silent, unmoved, and would stay that way for the rest of the morning. "I'm just so sorry," he said, but the apology, blocked by the taut line of her stare and her calcifying posture, wouldn't reach her, and so he took it, with regret shadowed by relief, for himself.

FOR HOURS THOMAS remained two feet behind her, as if he were leashed, while she walked: through the outcropping of slip-shod communal buildings, down the crumbling limestone angles that led to the river rumbling, up again and through the vestigial foundations of miner's houses. She shot him looks from time to time, remorseful winces, and he attempted to mirror them. It felt as though infirm parts of his body were eating away at necessary organs, that soon some internal chasm would open and stop him completely.

In the death of what had seemed a bottomless afternoon, under a sun low and terminal, moving among centuries-old trees, they stumbled upon a view of Edith: dressed in a linen shift the color of milked tea, a quarter of her body already soaked by a bend in the river. Her right hand rested on Song's shoulder, and both held soft smiles that abraded the age of their faces. The water, considerate of their position, parted gently around the backs of their knees before rejoining the rush.

Later that evening, Adeleine would offer her declaration, present her resignation from whatever it was the two of them had been. "I'm not coming back with you," she would say, on the porch, the first night that the heat was indomitable, never even interrupted by breeze. But at that moment, from a point fifteen feet above the river, across from the muddled, inverted version of mother and child, she only gave Thomas a hawkish nod and began her descent.

He had never seen her move with such confidence, angling across the rough tops of boulders, her arms spread for balance or flight, her cheeks ripe with that day's exertion, her body unflinching when it met the hurried green chill, and it was how, for the rest of his quiet life, he would remember her.

PAULIE FELT as if his body was a zoo barely containing its wild holdings and they hadn't seen anything yet and maybe it was the earth getting too hot like Claude and Eddy whispered about. The whole globe getting warmer sounded like a good thing, he thought, like something that could help everybody relax and start listening. But the fireflies weren't here and they had come all this way and he had even become so worried and upside down that they'd gone to the emergency room where he'd ridden on a stretcher under a flock of hands flying like startled birds.

But now here they were and running with them was the river and watching over them was the covering of sky. It was black so he stayed in between Claude and Eddy and held their hands and kept their lives connected. They had seen only little flashes like the beginnings of lonely ideas but not the crowd of busy angels he had come for. The water was so strong and fast that it stole the sounds of their steps but still Paulie knew and could feel very carefully how they were moving. He gave the hands he held a squeeze each time he saw the flash of a lone firefly and sent what he called mind mentions out into the night: he thought about the Great Smoky Mountains and all the people who had come to see the fireflies light up at once and about Claudia's way of walking and Eddy's hair sticking up and silently repeated *I love you and I appreciate you, I love you and I appreciate you, I love you and I appreciate you.* He thought it until the bugs caught fire hundreds revealing themselves on every side and he couldn't squeeze their hands fast enough and the whole forest exploded transformed by light.

CLAUDIA AND EDWARD had both secretly nurtured such cynicism about the rare firefly display that the actual event left them giggling hungrily, their glee waning only to pick up another wave. The three of them stood on the path that bisected river and forest and watched as tens of thousands of seed-sized lives enjoyed intricate, urgent communication: flashing in sync or in a wave of great scale, their collected bodies casting a violent and vital green that brought all growth around it detail, then fell dark for a slow count of three, obscuring the mountainous arbor again. Each time they sparked anew it felt like the first leg of a dramatic ascent, the roaring of a spectacular motor.

When their laughter had finally settled in their bodies, they sat on the moist earth and continued to watch an algorithm so expertly designed, so decisively executed, that they never felt the nibble of mosquitoes or the swift hints of a rain. Paulie said something about this being like the beginning of the world, and Edward couldn't even bring his eyes to roll, they were so full, and wet, and open.

I T WAS TWO DAYS LATER, as he sat on the concrete and stucco balcony of a nondescript motel in Virginia, overlooking four lanes of highway traffic, during the afternoon of a heat wave they'd decided to wait out, dressed in nothing but a pair of boxers that read *Wednesday!*, that Paulie's heart failed. Edward and Claudia, enraptured by a talk show—a muscular transvestite and her luminous python—heard only the slight resettling of the plastic legs of the chair as he moved.

When it came, Paulie was considering almost nothing, struck quiet by the weather's weight on his face, still fed by what they'd seen in the mountains. In the absence of his long-kept wish to see the Smokies alight, he was carved out, weeded of ardor. He stared at a penny dropped on a balcony below, watched the traffic as though it were a complex ballet. He let the sweat from his face find its way down his body. He thought of Claudia and Edward, just behind him through the glass, how they talked to each other like children, making small promises about the next day and the next, what would happen, when, why.

The pressure seemed to knock all at once, a prickling in his fingers, a dullness in his jaw, a force on his sternum, and he felt he could answer it.

This is completely safe, he thought.

In Edith's empty apartment, the smell of long-swollen, rotting tea bags pushed against the walls. Shadowed by the mugs left out on the table, partially hidden by a months-old newspaper, an envelope lay slightly curled, Adeleine's writing on its backside blotted by sweat. She had made her letters tiny, unsure how long Edith's voice would continue, and blacked out the mistakes in her transcription thoroughly, in solid boxes of ink.

He surprised me with it and I didn't mind. I wouldn't have known how to go about judging one building from the next, how to test the windows or floors. He walked a few feet ahead of me most of the blocks from the subway, and then when we turned onto our street he put his hands over my eyes. His fingers always smelled like tobacco and . . . butter, maybe, oil . . . and he jingled the keys and told me to look. And I was—scared. We toured every room, opened every door, turned on all the faucets. He ran around pissing a little in every toilet. We got to the top and Declan said, "Well? Well, what do you think?" And I started to cry because, honest to God, I had never had stairs before, I mean never gone up any that belonged to me, never been in a place with another person and not known exactly where they were. I grew up with June's voice right on top of mine, her wheedly elbows everywhere I was, my mother's face behind me in the bathroom mirror. He laughed at me a little and held my chin and he said, "Don't worry, dove. Soon we'll be renting it out, and you and me will be breathing all over each other again." But I had never been alone in that way, able to sit someplace for hours knowing no one would come in. The first nights there I had to beg for sleep. I thought I could feel all the space trying to rush in, all those rooms with no living in them yet, begging for light and the tread of people, this infinite home.

WHEN IT WAS DONE, when he was transformed and handed back to her as something else, in an overly air-conditioned lobby under poorly hung photos of sunsets, the first thing Claudia wanted was a bigger purse: she couldn't fit him into her bag. She whispered this to Edward, and Edward turned immediately to ask the man behind the counter about the closest mall. When they got in the car, they kept the windows down.

Under the fluorescence, past the garish fountains and the smell of chlorine that settled on their tongues, around diamond-shaped planters of waxy green plants, they shuffled, Claudia glancing in the windows of stores as though reviewing bills she had forgotten to pay. At a kiosk meant for teenage girls, Edward bought a shirt, then removed the polo he'd been wearing for three days and pulled the stiff T on. *I love my attitude problem*, it said. He held Claudia's hand. They walked. When she finally pointed at a black shape behind glass, a sagging behemoth of leather and zipper, he placed her on the tiled ledge of a Windex-blue pool and retrieved it for her. She transferred her things into it, wallet and sunscreen and car keys, leaving the jar for last, padding the space with a sweater before placing her brother inside, and brought the metal tag along its track of teeth until the gap was closed. Her mind changed visibly on her face, as though receiving some new and crucial piece of information, and she moved the zipper back a few inches to create an opening.

IN THE MOTEL ROOM, Edward slept, finally, above the covers of the still-made bed, while Claudia moved through the room, the limited visibility of the near-evening, touching the detritus of her brother. From the plastic sack the crematorium had handed her, she removed his signature pink Keds and arranged them on the floor. Inside them, her feet felt for the places where his toes had made impressions, the grooves they had left much larger than the reality of hers, the indentations still slick with sweat. Almost as soon as it arrived, the small comfort of the act was gone, replaced by the tight fear that she might change something essential about the shoes' interior. She kicked them off with a yelp, fell into a clotted weeping that kept her, blind and hot, for ten minutes. When she had quieted, the room reappeared, the wall-mounted television and the bleached floral pattern of the duvet, but amid the tawdry pastels something else found her.

That she had missed Paulie's wallet, its slim worn shape mostly concealed by some jeans of hers on the cheap wood bureau, seemed like a gift, like his hand on the back of her neck.

Their father had given it to Paulie when he turned thirty, the last age Seymour would watch him become, and had spent too much on it, as though he had known. It was a fine brushed leather, the color of a roasted hazelnut just rubbed of its skin, and over the years Paulie had relished the responsibility it conferred:

patted it in his back pocket and lingered while he paid for things at the corner store—cartons of orange juice, travel magazines, holographic key chains. As she stood to reach for it, she realized she had never seen the contents, that this had been one of few private corners of his life.

For reasons she couldn't name, she looked first at the money, twenty-seven dollars, the bills arranged by denomination, a fact that hit her like the sprain of a muscle, knowing what slow, hard work it must have been for him. In his ID card picture he had tried to appear solemn, pained by bureaucratic process, and the image looked little like her brother. In the other pockets, she found a photo of their parents waving on a dock; a scientific drawing of a Japanese flying squid torn, perhaps illicitly, from a library book; a note from Edward, which read, *Dear Mr. Mayor, swing by when you can. I have an adventure planned*; a glossy magazine clipping of a baby's bottom; a snapshot of him and Claudia at a wedding, each pointing at the other with a mouth in an O; and one of them as children, asleep under the kitchen table, their tiny features dwarfed by adult feet.

The sounds were few, the highway and the faucet in the next room and the heavy steps of someone going to fetch ice or a candy bar, but she found comfort in them, that they were similar to what he had heard as he left. She would not vocalize the thought, but Edward had known, when she'd paid for a week in advance, that she needed to stay where Paulie knew to find them. She owed him that, had spent her life on that promise.

In the dark hours of early morning she was awakened by nothing, her body distrustful of the stillness itself. Her hand shot to the lamp like a reptilian tongue. Edward's eyes opened as though they'd only just closed, and he turned to see her.

"It would have happened no matter what," he said.

She looked like a beggar, no aspect of her life uncharted on her face.

THEY SPENT A STRING OF HOURS that felt interminable there, moving from the bed to the toilet, the toilet to the bed, the bed to the doors of the balcony, but they didn't step outside. The chair remained where it had fallen when they had wrested him from it. They used the bulky telephone to order food, ate little of what arrived, let the plastic and cardboard pile up in the heat with the turning smell of leftovers. Housekeeping knocked twice, three times a day, and each time they bellowed, "No, no—not now," their conviction about this their only real expenditure of power. As they fell asleep, Edward knocked his knuckles on the nightstand between them, where Paulie sat in his jar, quiet, unrecognizable.

ON THE FOURTH DAY he asked her. She was sitting up in bed, the top sheet around her hips, the remote lying across her slack hand. The television was dark, the only noise a fly caught in the bathroom.

"I thought it might be too much," he said.

"Not too much. Never enough."

"Okay."

And he crawled into bed with her, the laptop under his arm, and opened the screen.

As he scrolled through the list of files, struggling to remember the contents of each, Claudia beheld the electronic glow as though it were an archaeological wonder.

"What's 'Alphabet'?"

"Oh, that one, no, I don't think it's—"

"What? You don't think it's what?"

"Okay, Claudia, Jesus. Okay."

At first there's just the keyboard, set up in a corner of Edward's apartment. A red silk curtain blows into the frame, then Paulie, in a tuxedo shirt and a pair of swim trunks, on the right leg of which is a neon gecko.

"Okay, Paul, what is it? You said this was very important."

"It is. Important and educational."

"Educational in which regard, Paul?"

"Well, Eddy, you know, when two people spend a lot of time together they sort of build a language together. Each person picks up a bit of the other. And in our case, I've picked up a lot of you."

"How so?"

Paulie slips behind the keyboard and hammers out the beginning of the alphabet song, teasing a little, then starts again, singing this time.

Cock smith, tool belt, fucknut tree,
These are the words you've given to me.
Jizz doctor, fecal cream,
You are just an enema fiend.

Now you know your dick has fleas,
Rectum's got a bad disease.

The frame shakes until it loses Paulie entirely and settles on the open window. Edward's laughter rises and wheezes.

Edward searched her face in his periphery without turning towards it. "I swear, he just comes up with this. Came up with it."

Propped up by the roughly starched pillows, Claudia gaped.

"How much of this do you *have*," she asked.

"I think there's maybe thirty-seven, thirty-eight hours. But most of it is like, Paulie discusses soup. Paulie inspects a dead bug. Paul ruins several commuters' subway rides, armed with only a mood ring."

Claudia nodded, the joy gone from her face as she calculated how few days she could fill with what was left. In the breezeway outside their room, two men bickered with low energy about routes, bleating the numbers of interstates, calling out the names of towns like they were items for sale at auction. Her skin itched from not having showered, her muscles felt fatigued from not having used them.

For the first moment in her life, time multiplied in front of her, unimagined, unimaginable.

THE RESTING PLACE YELLOW. Just wide and long enough. Near it another where the quiet woman slept. At the beginning chickens. The nothing of forest. Men with blue eyes came with things to put in her mouth. Soft and warm as what she had given her baby. They all walked to where the land stopped and they moved into the cold green and they kept her hand while everything watered around them. Back in the room the woman shaking down her silver head nest. She brought in the arms of some trees and lit them. Through the glass hole birds. Cheep cheep cheep then dark. Staying near the heat until the wet was gone. The men again with things to swallow. Fingers on her neck. They changed her hair and the woman's hair until they were ropes. Different shapes for wearing. Big forms of white for sleeping in. One more time outside. All their faces up to see the big sky fruit. Then the woman's eyes on her and a long look. A hand low to guide her. Was there a missing. Something gone. A man with her in the mornings. Black circles that played music. Boxes full of bodies that zipped under the earth. A building at night golding onto the street. Had this always been her life. Had she always known the woman. No. Yes. Always.

THE NEIGHBORS HAD WATCHED with some curiosity as he rehabilitated the house, floor by floor, room by room, over the course of the year, and sometimes waved when they saw him, through an exposed frame, working in his uneven way. He hadn't hired any help, and often continued after midnight with his work, lit by bare bulbs clamped to paint-splattered ladders and fed by dried apricots and cashews he kept in his corduroy pocket. A careful preservationist, he matched the original colors of the doors precisely, fingering each swatch on a great fan of color samples, and restored the gilded leaves of the stairway wallpaper himself.

Vestiges of the other tenants, diligently dusted and bubble-wrapped, stood in man-sized towers in the foyer. Edward had called to say they'd be arriving in a day or so, and Thomas had busied himself with the last of the cleaning. He got down under the tubs and scrubbed the claw-foot detail, pushed cloth across window glass in even lines, braced himself on the mop as he moved it through the bright spaces.

They had driven for ten months, Edward and Claudia, stopping every few days to sleep off their grief in some nameless small town. On the top floor Thomas dozed in an armchair, both his arms slack, a book tented on his chest. All the rooms were empty, all the windows open. After the car pulled up, battered but polished, it idled a while.

ACKNOWLEDGMENTS

Writing about a syndrome so unique as Williams was a challenge that kept me up nights, and I will forever be grateful to Jessica Vecchia of the Williams Syndrome Association, who answered my questions and connected me with a family brave enough to tell me their story: Frank, Josephine, and Sara Catalonatto. The insight and anecdotes they shared, and the frankness with which Sara spoke about her condition, were truly invaluable in my creation and understanding of Paulie.

I drew inspiration for the paintings described as Thomas's from the art of Casey Cripe, whose enormous talent astounds.

Jonathon Atkinson, Victoria Marini, and Eli Horowitz were early readers of what became this novel, and their honesty at that stage was crucial in my perception of the project.

J.B. lent me an important piece, and for that I'm deeply appreciative.

Alexandra Kleeman, skilled writer and reader, provided soul-mending encouragement.

Jin Auh, Megan Lynch, and Laura Perciasepe all served as mothers of this book at different stages in its path away from my anxious grip, and they deserve many thanks for helping it to walk.

John Wray, who is sometimes called John Henderson, put on an impressive series of hats in the service of this novel and its author. For his tireless line notes, afternoon serenades, long dinners, alacrity as hospice nurse, infectious curiosity, willingness to drive five hundred miles last minute to see some fireflies, and perhaps most importantly for giving me a room of my own, I am beholden (and more than a little blessed).